*For my family, friends
and my amazing NHS Cystic Fibrosis Team*

CONTENTS

HAZEL MEREDITH-LLOYD

Baby Steps

CHAPTER ONE – JENNY

'Kyle,' I say, staring at a mark on our living room floor as if it holds the answer to the question I hardly dare ask out loud, 'you know what we said about adopting?'

'Yes,' he says, also suddenly fascinated by the laminate flooring, 'we kind of said we'd wait for a calm time before looking into it properly.'

'Yes,' I continue, eyes still fixed on the knot in the fake wood that is now bizarrely starting to resemble a baby's dummy, 'Well, two things really. One, that was quite a while ago now, and two, I'm not sure there's ever really going to *be* a calm time.'

There's silence for a moment as he takes a noisy slurp of his tea. I glance at him for a second then return my gaze to the dummy shape. Out of the corner of my eye, I glimpse him turning to look at me. Oh god, does he think I'm mad to suggest this?

'So, what are you saying?' he asks, in his calm, measured way. His calm, measured way that inexplicably makes me mad with fury when I'm wound up, like I am now.

'Well, it's quite clear really, isn't it?' I say, turning finally to look at him properly.

'You want to start looking into adopting?' he says, 'Like, now?'

I nod. Words won't come out because I'm afraid if they do, that tears will follow them. What if he says no? He takes another sip of his tea. Another noisy sip. I love this man with all my heart but right now, I could pour the tea over his head. He hasn't done anything wrong, but I just don't feel rational at the moment. I mean I'm suggesting something quite outrageous really when you think about it. Until meeting me, I expect Kyle just assumed he'd have his own biological kids one day who would have his lovely smile, kind eyes and be saddled with his family's traditional middle name of 'Digby'.

I, on the other hand, have very good reasons for wanting to adopt rather than try to get pregnant. I don't want to risk passing on my cystic fibrosis gene, I've got a side order of diabetes to contend with and besides, my years as a youth worker have taught me there are a ton of children in care already in this mad, overcrowded world. Why, therefore would we go to the trouble and risk of producing more when we could put our skills to good use and be a family for those who already need it? I could use my youth work training and Kyle would look after them in the warm wonderful way he always has me. Added to that, he could teach them the skill of being infuriatingly calm in times of stress and how to slurp tea at a thousand decibels.

Kyle lowers his cup of tea and breaks into a smile. 'Okay then,' he says with a shrug, as if he's just agreed to pop to the pub tomorrow lunchtime, 'let's give it a go.'

I run over to him and squeeze him tight, burying my head in his shoulder. He tries to look into my eyes, but I hold him tighter and push my head so far into his warm body, I'm sure I hear him give a slight gasp of pain. When I finally pull away, we're both wearing similar expressions. Expressions that are part excitement, and part shock at the monumental step we've just agreed to take.

CHAPTER
TWO – KYLE

When Jenny finally lets me go, I pace about the room a bit, whilst she sits perched on the end of the sofa, clutching a notebook that she seems to have produced from behind a cushion.

'So,' I say, clapping my hands together like I've seen sports coaches do in films when they're trying to get the underachieving team of mismatched kids to produce a win in time for the closing credits. 'So,' I say again.

'So?' says Jenny. She's now produced a pen along with the notebook and is flicking through the post-it-note marked pages.

'So,' I say again, with another hand clap for good measure, 'let's do this!' I pace a bit more. 'Jen?'

'Yes Kyle?' she says, a hint of a smile playing around the corners of her lips.

'What is it that we… er… do, exactly? Like first, I mean. Is there someone we should phone or something? Or is it all online these days? Or an app? Is there an app? Like a sort of adopting version of Tinder? Maybe "Kinder" or something like that. God, no, that sounds wrong – not Tinder, no, I'm not suggesting we swipe right... or is it left... I'm not suggesting we swipe anybody!' I stop pacing and look at Jenny, who is trying not to laugh. 'God, when we speak to the Social Workers, you will do all of the talking, won't you?' I say.

Jenny stands up, takes my hand, leads me to the sofa and pulls me down to sit next to her. She opens her notebook, which I now notice has pictures of little stick people holding hands all over it and shows me a page full of names and numbers. But this isn't a little black book of potential dates. This is a list of phone numbers next to words like 'Action for Children', 'Adoption Matters', 'Adoption Focus', and 'Jigsaw Adoption'.

'Are they adoption agencies or zones in the Crystal Maze?' I say to her. She laughs.

'I've been doing a bit of research and made a few calls,' she says, looking a bit bashful. 'Nothing serious, I haven't gone behind your back or anything, I just wanted to be aware of what was out there, you know, get one step ahead what with my dodgy genes and everything.' I nod and put my arm round her, moving closer to look at the list. She has highlighted the different agencies in various colours and down the bottom of the page she's drawn a key with blocks of each of the colours and words such as 'seems good', 'lovely lady on phone', 'distracted sounding man', 'bad phone line', and most surprisingly, 'retired racing greyhound adoption'. Jenny points to one of the agencies next to which she's drawn a selection of little hearts. 'This one looks good and has an open meeting this Saturday afternoon. Are you doing anything this Saturday afternoon, Kyle?'

She's used my actual name, rather than call me Ky or one of her pet names for me, which makes me realise that my initial response of 'Yes, I'm going to the match with Jake' is not the right thing to say in this instance. 'Yes,' I say, pulling her close and kissing the top of her head as she leans into me, 'I'm going to the 'Nurturing Families' information event with my wonderful wife and mother of our future children.'

CHAPTER THREE
– HELEN

I can hardly believe my eyes. I'm looking at a giant baby. Rosy cheeks, dummy, bib with little yellow ducks on it and it's saying my name. But it really is a giant baby. It must be at least six feet tall. I blink hard.

'You alright, Helen?' the baby says, 'you look a bit peaky.' Then it removes its giant baby head and tucks it under its arm. Glen from the panto team smiles at me, his head poking out of the brightly coloured babygros. The costume suits him, in a bizarre way, but how he manages to tap dance in it is beyond me.

I've been working at 'All the World's a Stage' theatre company for a while now but my days are far from dull. You never know when someone will walk in and ask you to zip them into their fajita costume or reattach their tail. It definitely beats working at Bazza's, my old job where I worked in customer services of a novelty gift business. Bazza, the owner and ringmaster of the five-ringed circus that it was, acted like he was the bounteous leader of an empire rather than the kind-hearted but decidedly OTT owner of a dodgy discount gift business. I once spent a memorable afternoon there refunding angry customers who had received more than they'd bargained for when ordering the 'Baby Blue' doll. Bazza hadn't read the details properly of what he was bulk buying. Modesty prevents me going into details, but let's just say, they certainly shouldn't have been placed in the toy department.

I expect, as much as Glen's loved the panto, he'll be relieved when it finishes. I've never known a panto go on so long, but Carrie and Lacey, the married couple who own the theatre company, say everyone needs cheering up after Christmas, so ours runs a couple of weeks into the new year. The grand finale happens on 'Blue Monday', which is supposed to be the most miserable day of the year, when people are penniless and down in the dumps after Christmas and payday and Spring seem a distant dream. The show aims to turn this day around and the house is apparently always packed to the rafters for it.

I help Glen with his expenses form – he's had to buy a mega pack of plasters because the big plastic bib is chafing his neck and before I know it, it's time to go home. I'm keen to get away on time today as Jake is taking me to a new restaurant he's found. We're still celebrating the fact we got engaged at Christmas. I smile at my beautiful ring. The stone is the same colour as Jake's ocean-blue eyes. I grab my bag, pop my head round the door to say goodbye to Carrie and Lacey and drive home singing to the radio. I let myself in, throw my keys on the side and run upstairs to jump in the shower. I grab my shower puff which is hanging next to Jake's Minions sponge – our toiletries look as happy to be living together as we are. I was over the moon when he accepted my invitation for him to move into my place after he proposed, turning that usually dull week between Christmas and new year into one of the best of my life.

He'll be standing at the bar when I get to the restaurant and we'll do that thing where we pretend not to know each other and chat each other up as if it's the first time we've met. We do this once a month and it's always so much fun. Each month, I try to think of something new to say about myself that he doesn't already know. It's getting harder each time but it's worth the effort. It definitely keeps things fresh.

CHAPTER FOUR – JAKE

I'm going to be late but I can't leave yet. Every penny I have is riding on this, as well as my home. And the last thing I want is to end up back in jail. I look at Helen's Dad, my eyes pleading with him to have mercy on me. If he could just let me off the rent this one time, I think I can survive. I know I should have walked away ages ago, but I just kept losing more and more money and then I sold most of what I owned, clinging to the thought that my fiancée's father would help me out of this mess. He knows I'm just down on my luck at the moment and that I'm a good bet if he can just go easy on me for a little bit longer.

My phone beeps. A message from Helen. She's looking forward to tonight. Oh god, I'm running out of time to change. Luckily, I've got a clean shirt in my bag, if Helen's Dad doesn't take that too of course, along with the one on my back and a pound of flesh if the look in his eyes is anything to go by. A roll of the dice. Double six. I know what that means before I've even looked.

My poor little dog. How could Helen's Dad let this happen to my poor little dog?

But walk to Park Lane he does. With Helen's Dad's hotel on it. I'm wiped out. I pay him my money and slide him over the millionaire's shortbread I promised him if he beat me. I never lost at monopoly until I met my fiancée's father.

'Nice one,' I say, trying to smile in the face of defeat. 'Sorry, I've got to dash, can't keep Helen waiting!' He waves at me, a glint in his eye and a mouth full of shortbread and I dive into the back room of the board games cafe where I work to change my shirt. If the traffic lights are on my side, I can still make it on time to the restaurant. I've got to be at the bar before Helen walks in and settle into my handsome stranger role.

The lights are kind to me and I get there before Helen. I pull out my wallet to buy a drink and find a couple of monopoly notes in there. They're ones I keep in there to remind me of when I won twelve games in a week. I just wish the money was real. I'm never going to make a fortune working in a board games café, even if it does have every monopoly set going, including one of my personal favourites, the minions one.

CHAPTER FIVE – JENNY

Saturday comes around eventually, but I have to go to work in the morning. I suppose this is a good thing, not least because I love my youth work job, but also because it stops me fretting too much about the information event this afternoon at the 'Nurturing Families' adoption agency. This morning I'm working with a group of very motivated young people who are part of youth forums and committees. My work gives me the opportunity to mix with a wide variety of young people, from ones like these who I could see doing a much better job of running the country than our current government (not that that's saying much!) to ones who have been excluded from school and feel that being asked to pick up their litter is an infringement of their civil liberties.

But I love all the groups equally. I'm just as fulfilled persuading a group not to let off the fire extinguisher in the accessible toilet as I am running a trip to visit the council chambers. I can see the kids I work with ending up on very different sides of the justice system, but I'm determined to do my absolute best for them all. I just wish I could also have some kids of my own to give my all to, but that situation has been complicated by my dodgy DNA.

I can cope with my cystic fibrosis, or CF, challenging as it is, but that doesn't mean that I want to pass that challenge onto my children. Kyle is an amazing husband and I know he will be an amazing dad, but unfortunately, he carries the cystic fibrosis gene which means if we had a baby, there would be a fifty-fifty chance of the child having CF. And as positive as I am about my life and the validity of everyone, regardless of their health issues, I have made the personal choice not to take the risk of passing this challenge onto my children. Besides, in my career as a youth worker, I've seen so many examples of children in care who desperately need a new family and a new chance at a safe and fulfilling life and I would love to parent those children.

When I'd been dating Kyle long enough for the subject of having children to come up, I told him all about what me having CF meant for any family plans he might have if he stayed with me. And with me having the attitude that if things were going well with a boyfriend, then I needed to prepare them, the subject came up quite quickly. So, whilst most couples would be gazing into each other's eyes and trying out new restaurants, I was giving Kyle a lesson in genetics which contained more statistics knowledge than Rachel Riley at a maths convention.

'So,' I said to him, halfway through a game of ten pin bowling, about three months into our relationship, 'if we stay together, do you want children?'

'I can't say I've given it that much thought, but I suppose I've always assumed I will have kids one day,' he replied, throwing his bowling ball into the gutter.

I searched for a light enough ball for my go and stood in front of him, cradling it in both hands. I was holding it that way because it was quite heavy, but I realised afterwards it looked like I was about to start rocking it to sleep and singing it lullabies.

'Is the ball a bit heavy for you, Jen?' he asked, a slight look of concern on his face. 'Nope, it's absolutely fine,' I said, 'it's just, as I've mentioned, CF is genetic. About one in twenty-five people do carry the gene, usually without knowing it, as carriers don't have any symptoms of CF or suffer ill-health because of it.'

'Okay Professor,' Kyle said, smiling, 'Are you sure you wouldn't like me to find you a lighter ball from one of the other lanes?'

'Nope,' I said, turning swiftly round, chucking the ball randomly down the lane and somehow getting a strike, 'but it's only when two carriers get together that it's possible to have a baby with cystic fibrosis, and then there's only a one in four chance of that happening.'

Kyle nodded at me then looked up to where an animation of a penguin in a tutu was dancing on the screen above our heads, striking a match to celebrate my score. I moved a step closer to him and his gaze returned to me. He smiled.

'Would you like another drink, Jen?' he said.

'No thanks,' I said, continuing my genetics lecture, 'however, if one of the people has cystic fibrosis, like me and gets pregnant by someone who carries the gene then there's a fifty percent chance the baby would have CF. Have you taken all this in or is the penguin distracting you?'

'No, that's all good,' said Kyle, 'I read about it on the CF Trust website a little while after we met.'

'Oh,' I said, 'Anything you want to say?'

'Well done on your strike, Jen,' he said, 'you've made the penguin really happy.'

He took it all in his giant six-foot-six stride, as he always does. Both me beating him at bowling and the lesson in CF statistics. He immediately offered to have a carrier test so we knew where we stood and when it came back that he was a carrier, he offered to let me find someone else and blamed himself for adding to my CF genes. I then offered to step away from him and let him find someone else too. It was a kind of reverse dumping, where we both tried to leave the other one but neither of us wanted to.

'But I love you and I don't want anyone if I can't have you!' I yelled at him, tears running down my cheeks.

'Me being with anyone else is out of the question!' he replied, blinking hard.

'What about my genes?' I said.

'I prefer you in skirts,' he grinned, 'but whatever makes you comfy…'

'You're an idiot!' I laughed, wiping my nose.

'Right then,' he said, 'we might as well get married!'

'No point in waiting!' I replied.

We were in a beer garden in the town centre at the time. Goodness knows what the other people there thought of us. Kyle stood up, grabbed me by the hand and led me straight out of the pub garden and into a nearby jewellery shop. We chose matching engagement rings and messaged all our friends to come celebrate. They were rather surprised as we'd only been together five months, but when you know, you know. I think having to think about all the CF and family implications early, far from breaking the relationship this time, had glued us together. We'd talked about the potential difficulties, but despite it all, life just seemed to make sense now we had found each other. Being with Kyle after some of the lousy boyfriends I'd had was like skipping in the sunshine after traipsing through the rain.

Looking back, maybe I'd been a bit harsh on some of my boyfriends. I think I wanted to test them to see if they would stick by me if the chips were down - if things got difficult because of my CF. Sometimes I'd test them too much, too soon. I mean, it's a bit much to expect someone to have all the right answers about adoption and how many times they'd visit you if you were in hospital when you're only half-way through your second date. One minute they're trying to decide whether to have sweet or salty popcorn and the next minute I'm asking them if they would rather adopt one child or two. By the time I got to dating Kyle, I'd decided to slow down a bit. After all, we waited nearly half a year before getting engaged and only got married within the month!

I realise I've been daydreaming and the young people I'm working with are calling my name.

'Jenny! Can we stay late today?' asks Michael, one of the group.

'Not today, guys, sorry, I've got to go somewhere. Maybe next week,' I reply.

'Ooh, where you going?' Sally, one of the girls asks. 'Is Kyle taking you on a date?'

I know I shouldn't say anything yet, it's such early days in my adoption journey and there are so many reasons why it might not work out, but I'm bursting to talk about it and it just sort of slips out that I'm going to an adoption information event. Some of the group just nod and carry on playing pool but a few of them, the ones who I've worked with the longest, get really excited.

'Ooh, it's like you've just told us you're pregnant!' says Ellie. I can't help but smile.

'Will you bring the baby back with you today?' asks Cara.

'Can you bring them to the youth club next week and we'll look after it?' says Jack.

'Hold on guys,' I say, 'I really appreciate your support, but it all takes rather a long time and nothing is definite yet, we might not get approved to adopt!'

'Of course you will!' says Anya.

'Wouldn't it be lovely to be adopted by Jenny!' says Pippa, one of the younger members of the group. As the others agree, I think my heart is going to burst and my eyes fill with tears.

'Thanks guys,' I say, 'but as I say, it's really early days, I have to pass a medical and all the assessments first, then you have to go to an adoption panel and then you have to be matched with the right children, who are likely to be children rather than babies…'

'Well, I can speed things up,' says Danielle with a chuckle, 'Adopt us! That way we could play pool all night and eat anything we want from the tuck shop!'

***

When we arrive at the adoption information event, there's so much to take in that I don't know where to begin. Kyle, however, doesn't seem to be having this problem. He's found a focus and is sticking to it.

'God, Jen, look at all the cars,' he says.

'What?' I say, looking at all the other people arriving whilst trying not to seem as if I'm staring at anyone.

'They're all so much newer, bigger and generally better than mine,' he says, 'I already feel inadequate and we haven't got through the door yet.'

'Really?' I say, a grin twitching at the edges of my mouth, 'You're worried about the size of the other men's *cars?*'

I raise my eyebrows at him suggestively and we both give a little laugh. Then we resume our visual assessments, me of the other potential adopters, Kyle of their vehicles. He takes hold of my hand, smiles at me in what I think he believes is a reassuring manner and we take our first step into the building.

'Right!' he says, 'let's do this! Let's show them we are the mature, child-ready people we need to be!'

'Hello,' says a smiley woman on reception, looking at the car keys in Kyle's hand. 'What type of vehicle do you have?'

'Only an old rubbish Corsa,' he says, his face falling. I give him a look. 'But I'm hoping to get a pay rise soon and swap it for something more people carrier-y. You know, to er... carry little people.' The receptionist's eyes widen. 'Not just random little people...' he adds hastily in case she thinks we're some kind of kidnappers, 'our own... well, you know... if...'

'It's okay,' smiles the lady on reception, 'I just need to issue you a parking permit so you don't get clamped. It's not a test.' She's obviously used to jumpy prospective parents. We exchange looks as Kyle fills out the parking slip. I expect she's used to men worrying they have something to make up for and unnecessarily overcompensating by boasting about the size of their engines.

'Just through there,' says the receptionist, pointing to some double doors with a laminated sign saying 'Nurturing Families Adoption Information – Introduction Session' on it.

I stride forward and open the door. Heaven knows what Kyle will do if I let him go in first. Maybe suggest we all throw our car keys in the middle and have an arm-wrestling competition to decide who takes home the best vehicle at the end of the day.

A woman with a clipboard ticks our name off a list and shows us to some spare seats. She has a bright yellow sticker with the word 'Bridget' written on it stuck to her lapel.

'Look Jen,' grins Kyle, 'she's named her jacket after your favourite rom com character.'

Smiling at my husband's attempt to ease our nerves, I whip out my notebook and pen. I feel like a journalist ready for an important press conference and have to physically stop myself from sitting literally on the edge of my seat. I look round at the other couples. Some of them are already in deep conversation with the people sat near them, whilst others are staring straight ahead at the PowerPoint slide displaying the same words as the laminated sign on the door. A lot of people look like they're too nervous to speak in case they say the wrong thing. Several of the couples are holding hands and Kyle takes hold of mine again.

'Ky,' I say, placing his hand back on his own leg, 'I love you, but I need to be able to take notes.'

'Do you think there's going to be a test?' asks the lady sitting next to me.

'No,' Kyle says, reassuringly, then looks at me, his eyes widening, 'Is there?'

I shake my head. 'I shouldn't think so,' I say, smiling at the lady, 'I think that sort of thing comes when your social worker does the home visits.'

Kyle shifts in his seat. If he's this concerned about the state of his car, he's sure to be binge watching *How clean is your house* before the social worker comes round.

The lady next to us introduces herself as Sandy and we strike up a conversation. Out of the corner of my eye, I see Kyle looking round awkwardly, giving little nods to other potential Dads present. By the expression on his face, he's willing the organisers to get going so at least he knows what to focus on. Luckily it seems that the Nurturing Families fairy godmother has heard his silent pleas and the lady who showed us to our seats puts down her clipboard and claps her hands together. Kyle looks as if he's been taken back to primary school and is about to be told off for talking in assembly. I'm pretty sure my mouth has dried up and I'm incapable of speech.

'Welcome, everyone,' she says, 'to the Nurturing Families adoption information introduction session. Thank you for coming. The plan for the afternoon is that we do a short presentation which will hopefully answer a lot of your questions and then we'll break for some tea and biscuits – always what people come here for …'

'Apart from the babies,' whispers Sandy, just as Kyle says 'Ooh, biscuits!' I nudge him gently with my foot.

'Then after we've had a break and a chance to chat to each other,' continues Bridget, 'we'll have a Q and A session then hopefully send you home feeling a bit more confident about what the next step is that you'd like to take.'

Some of the people listening look actively disappointed at this plan for the day. Perhaps they thought there would be a big red theatre curtain that the social workers would pull back to reveal a nursery full of babies and toddlers, just waiting to be taken home in a party bag. Wanting to feel like I'm doing something useful, I jot down 'Q and A' 'next steps' and 'biscuits' in my notepad.

But despite the fact I've longed to be here, my mind starts to wonder. The thing that I can't help but keep going over from the information I've read is that the agencies advise that you wait at least six months after a miscarriage or your last failed round of IVF before starting the adoption process. They say you need time to come to terms with not having a biological child before you turn your focus to adoption. I get that you need time to grieve and think. But for me, and I'd have thought for many, many people considering adoption, you are on a long and difficult journey where your destination is to have a child. You cannot step off this rocky path until you either become a parent or decide to try to come to terms with not doing so.

I fully appreciate that adopting is different to giving birth – for a start, the children you adopt already have names, personalities, opinions and preferences, as well as experiences, a lot of which are negative and traumatic. They say it is more accurately called 're-parenting' rather than parenting. You won't be pouring over baby-naming books or choosing which relative not to offend as you won't be deciding what to call them. You might not be decorating their rooms in things that you have chosen – it doesn't matter if you've always loved Peter Rabbit, if the child you're adopting is four years old and a spider-man fanatic, that's what you need to put on their walls. But although I admit there's a little bit of me that lingers by the Winnie the Pooh wallpaper, none of that matters in the grand scheme of things. I want to nurture a human. The fact that the human didn't come from my body doesn't matter to me. Even if I did give birth, my child would still be an individual, and I would respect that and not try to make them a miniature version of my Winnie-the-Pooh-loving self. So, no, you won't be naming them but you will be giving them love and a new chance at life. I think that more than makes up for having to decorate their room in their favourite colours rather than yours.

But as for doing your grieving before you even start the adoption process – that's just not possible in my opinion. Because we're not just grieving for the child we miscarried, we are grieving the children we fear we will never have. The emptiness of longing for a child but not knowing if you will ever be able to have one, cannot be filled in a number of months. In order to even begin to move on from this exhausting sadness, I need to find out whether I can ever have children and the method I choose to explore is adoption.

It's been two decades since a Cystic Fibrosis specialist stamped on my heart by answering my complicated 'Will I be allowed to adopt?' question with a simple 'No'. Luckily, their casually devastating one word answer turned out not to be correct, well, not these days anyway. Things have progressed greatly in the cystic fibrosis community and most things are now possible.

A few years back, when the question of having children was pushed to the forefront of our minds by a pregnancy which we only knew was happening at the point at which it was dramatically and tragically no longer happening, we received some 'Genetic Counselling'. I can't imagine the thought processes which led to this mislabelled lesson in statistics taking place in the midst of the local hospital's maternity unit. The maternity unit that one of my mystified first-time father friends was walking out of as we arrived.

It sounds like a cliché, but when we lost the baby we didn't know we were having, I literally didn't know what to do with myself. It was as if my brain and emotions crashed like an overloaded computer. Everyday tasks like getting dressed and getting off the sofa felt insurmountable and pointless. We tried to soothe the pain that enveloped us and pay tribute to the little life that was gone before we knew it was there by buying something to remember it by. Whilst walking aimlessly round a little village one endless Sunday afternoon, we chose a glass paperweight with beautiful colours swirling through it, that let in the light. It was a simple ornament, down to earth, not overly expensive but it made concrete the feelings we had no words for. We didn't put it in a prominent place in the home. It would have been too painful for us to do so. But we knew it was there, just out of sight, on a shelf in the corner. It was something physical to show us that we weren't imagining the brief life we had produced. Our emotions had been ripped up and scattered like scraps of paper in a storm and we needed that paperweight to anchor them.

After kyle had gone to work each morning, I could let my false smile drop and attempt to do my chest physio and get dressed. But more often than not, I'd feel so depleted and my body so heavy that I'd drop onto the bed and sob. It was hard enough to fit my morning health routine in at the best of times, let alone when my body felt weighed down by loss. I'd sometimes wrap the smooth round paperweight in a blanket and stroke it as if it was the smooth head of the baby it represented. Bizarrely, this would soothe me and when I was finally empty of tears for the moment, I would feel temporarily lighter and be able to drag myself into the shower to begin to get through another day.

One weekday, when I was unable to face work, I was downstairs and there was a knock on the door. It was a flower delivery company with a huge bouquet. The lady next door had recently had a baby and her workmates had sent these for her. As she wasn't in, the company had come next door and asked me if I could take them in for her until she returned. I agreed with a smile and placed them in our tiny kitchen. Our house at the time was a small terrace and the kitchen and living room were open plan. The flowers seemed to take up most of the ground floor and I spent the day carefully avoiding them, their vibrant colours mocking me, matching the hues of the swirls of my paperweight.

But life continued and over time, bit by bit, I felt less heavy. I put the paperweight a bit further away in a safe place where we could see it if we wanted to, but it would no longer catch us unawares as we walked past the shelf. We discussed adopting and decided that once we'd had six months or so of stress-free time, we would start the process. But you rarely get six weeks of stress-free time, let alone six months, so in the end, we just decided to go for it.

We've subscribed to an adoption magazine which also has a bizarre kind of supplement with children in it. In this strange Argos catalogue of kids, are photos and brief profiles of children who need adopting. These are the 'harder to place' children, sibling groups, older children (by older, they mean anyone past toddler age - a six-year-old is practically a pensioner in adoption terms) and children with special needs.

One thing that stands out is that there are a large proportion of 'fantasy' names among the children waiting. Lots of 'Beloved', 'Cherished' and 'Star's. The names of the children seem to be at odds with the way they've actually been treated by those who've named them. I puzzle over why this might be. All I can think, with my youth worker head on, is that maybe the unusual names given matched the fantasy the birth parents had in their heads of how parenting would be. And when the reality didn't match the dream, they couldn't cope. Who knows – many of the parents have experienced awful childhoods themselves so have perhaps been unable to parent with care and compassion that they themselves have never been shown. That's not to say that everyone who has experienced neglect or abuse will go on to behave in the same way. I have colleagues who grew up with some of the worst parenting you could imagine and they make the most caring and wonderful parents and youth workers you could hope for, giving their children everything they wished they'd had.

I just hope that I will be given the chance to parent and give some children who need it the chance to be part of a loving and nurturing family. With Kyle by my side, it will be a challenging but wonderful experience. He's takes everything in his steady stride and is so balanced and mature.

Suddenly, I'm jolted out of my reverie by Kyle. He leans over to me, takes the pen gently out of my hand and with a smile that never fails to melt my heart, circles the word 'biscuits.'

CHAPTER 6
– JAKE

I love my job and my colleagues and customers at the board game café are generally the nicest people you could want to spend your working days with, but I'm never going to make my fortune working here. I need to have some kind of additional income stream. I've been turning something over in my mind for a while now and I think I might have hit upon a workable idea. I'm going to invent the new Monopoly!

By which I don't mean I'm literally going to invent Monopoly, I think Hasbro would have something to say about that, but I'm determined to produce a new game that is as popular. I've been playing around with a few ideas and mention it to Kyle over a pint or two. He comes up with some good ideas too and we decide to work on it together. It's going to be a game based around running a successful pub. I mean, who doesn't love a pub? As you move around the board, you have to collect items by landing on or bidding for appropriate squares. So, you'll need a licence, bar staff, barrels of beer, tables etc. Then once you've gathered all the things you need, you move onto the next stage, receiving tips or forfeits depending on where you land. By his third pint, Kyle was well into the swing of it.

'And then if you land on 'Fight' you have to act out the best fake fight you can and the winner moves forward and the loser moves back!' he says, enthusiastically raising his pint as he does so and slopping half of it over the table.

'And if you land on 'Pub Quiz' there's a trivia question and bonus squares for those who get it right!' I chip in, being careful not to spill any of my drink.

'And then there can be a timed challenge at the end called last orders!'

'What?' I say, the noise in the actual pub we're in drowning out half of his sentence.

'Last orders!' shouts Kyle at the top of his voice.

'Keep it down, lads,' says the barman, 'It's only half ten, I don't want folk leaving yet!'

We decide to move onto a quieter place so that we can hear each other better. The fresh air on the walk to the next pub sobers Kyle up a bit and I take the opportunity to ask him how the adoption meeting went.

'It was alright,' he says, putting his hands deep into his pockets.

'Just alright?' I ask.

'Well, you know, there was quite a bit to

take in,' he continues, 'I didn't want to let Jenny down, she seemed so prepared. Well, I suppose she would be, she's been thinking about this sort of thing ever since she was young.'

'Yeah, it's amazing the way she handles everything,' I say.

'Exactly,' says Kyle, 'Until I met her, I just kind of assumed I'd have kids but never really gave much thought to it. You know me, I like to take things in my stride as it happens and not get too wound up about it in advance. But this is like the opposite of that. There is so much to go through before we're even told if we're allowed to adopt.'

'Oh, no one could turn you two down, mate,' I say to him, putting my arm round his shoulder and giving him a brief and slightly awkward sideways hug as we walk along.

'I hope not, but Jenny's a bit worried about the medical,' he says. 'We both have to have one but of course, hers is a little more complicated than mine and she needs her specialist's approval and everything.'

I try to work out what to say. I often think about how lucky me and Helen are not having to deal with all Jenny and Kyle do with her health condition. But I know he wouldn't swap her for the world and neither would we, she's solid gold.

'She's strong and resilient and full of understanding,' I say as if I'm practising my adoption reference Helen's told me they want us to write. 'That's got to count for a lot. And she's doing well, health-wise, isn't she?'

'Yes,' says Kyle, 'her specialist is fully in support of her adopting. It's just she can't relax until all the many other people who get to decide whether we have a family officially agree with him.'

'Right,' I say, 'yeah, it must be hard to chill with all that going on. How about we go in here and have a few more pints?'

Kyle nods and we pull open the door to the Old Boot, one of our regular haunts. The noise hits us instantly, as does one of the drinkers inside. It's my mate Phil. He can be a bit of a lad but I do owe him one as he let me stay with him after I broke up with my ex, Joanne. It was the year my mum had been killed in a hit and run accident and I was a bit of a mess. It was also the year I met Helen – quite a year really, you could say. Helen and I met, in fact, literally as Joanne was throwing me out. Phil took me in, with all my baggage, literal and metaphorical.

'Jake, you loser!' slurs Phil, who's obviously been out drinking a bit longer than we have. 'Why haven't you replied to my message!'

'Had a bit on, sorry mate,' I say, rubbing my arm where Phil has given me a 'friendly' punch. 'Remind me what the message was about?'

'Mountain boarding mate!' replies Phil. 'We're all going on Saturday, come on, don't be a loser, you've got to come!' he looks at Kyle, 'and you, Kyle!'

'I've got to work on Saturday, sorry,' I say.

'You said you had the day off!' says Kyle. His face changes when he suddenly realises what he's done. 'Sorry Jake,' he mouths, 'I wasn't thinking...'

'No worries,' I say, 'Go on then, Phil, I'll give it a go, if Kyle does.' I turn to Kyle. 'It might help take your mind of things - what's the worst that can happen?'

'Alright then,' agrees Kyle, accepting a drink from one of Phil's group. 'What harm can it do?'

***

Well, what a ride. Mountain boarding is amazing. The wind in your hair as you speed down the hill, smoothly negotiating the twists and turns to the whoops of your friends. At least that's how we'd imagined it would be when we agreed to it with a pint in our hands. Phil, despite nursing a massive hangover, sped past us as if he'd been born with a mountain board attached to his feet. Kyle, however, completely lost his balance and is currently on the floor, his leg screaming at him for trying to make it go in two different directions at once.

I drive him to the hospital where they take X-rays and give him a pair of crutches and the wonderful news that he's ruptured his anterior cruciate ligament.

'I'm so sorry, mate,' I say, 'I should never

have asked you to come.' I feel terrible putting him in this situation with all he's got going on. 'But hey, at least you've got a cool footballer's injury,' I add, trying to bring a smile to his pained and anxious face.

'But not done in a semi-final match against Arsenal,' he groans, 'no, done by a stupid bloke, who has never been great at activities requiring an element of balancing, who was trying to keep up with his mates and take his mind off things.' He puts his head in his hands, 'What is Jenny going to say?'

'Don't worry, mate,' I say, 'she'll look after you.'

'Yeah, I know,' Kyle says, rubbing his face with his hands, 'but I'm supposed to be looking after her. One of the things that reassures her when she's worrying about her medical assessment is that they can see how good my health is and that I can do a lot of the stuff that she might find a bit trickier. Now I've got to convince the social workers that I can do it all whilst on crutches.'

'Maybe, we don't tell Jenny until we get home then,' I say, 'once she sees you, she's bound to be less likely to get cross.'

Kyle doesn't look so sure, especially as a text arrives from Jenny, asking when we're coming home. I message Helen and tell her what's happened and ask her to go round to Jenny's, giving her strict instruction not to say anything.

'Jenny is a reasonable woman,' I say, 'I'm sure she won't get too angry with you.'

'Yeah,' says Kyle, 'I mean she's usually fairly cool and collected. There was that one time she woke up from a dream where I'd apparently kissed someone else and was angry with me for the rest of the morning, but that was just a blip… just like this knackered knee is just a blip.'

'That's the spirit, mate,' I say. Yep, everything will be absolutely fine.

CHAPTER 7
– HELEN

When Jake rung me and said he was at A & E my heart jumped into my throat. To my relief, he and Kyle are both okay, albeit with one less functioning anterior cruciate ligament between them than they started the day with. Poor Kyle. And poor Jenny. They've asked me to go round to see her but not mention why I'm there or that Kyle has had an accident at the mountain boarding. I have to admit I was surprised that Jen was so cool about Kyle going – she usually worries about him keeping well, yet she was surprisingly calm about all this. I suppose she's got so much on her mind with the adoption things whirling into action that she didn't think too hard about what he was actually going to be doing. I remember her saying it would be good for him to spend some time with Jake and his mates as she felt he was a bit overwhelmed with all the information they'd had thrown at them at the adoption introduction session.

I walk over to her house and ring the

doorbell. She looks slightly shocked that I've arrived out of the blue. I normally give her notice as her health regimes can be a bit complicated with her physio etc, but she invites me in nonetheless and we're soon chatting away about work. She's recently been on a day trip to a theme park with one of her youth groups and tells me all about how one of the kids went missing for half an hour after the meet-up time and they had to search the place for them, eventually finding them asleep in the tunnel of the train in the kids' playground. She gives a laugh and rolls her eyes, taking another sip of her wine.

'At least I'll be ready for anything if we get to adopt!' she says, 'Are you sure you don't want a glass, Helen?' She gestures towards the wine bottle.

'No, I'm great with this, thanks,' I say, sipping at my fruit tea. The packet boasts that it's strawberry and cranberry, but as usual it would be more apt if it was called 'old sock that's been left in a fruit bowl'. 'So, what's the next stage of the adoption thing, then?' I ask.

'Well, they assign us a social worker to do our home assessment over the next few months, during which we discuss just about every aspect of our lives and families ever and then we go to panel who ask us more questions and decide whether we're suitable to adopt,' she says.

'Blimey, it's mad, isn't it?' I say, 'No one

asks people any questions at all before they try for a baby the normal way.' I kick myself mentally. 'Sorry, Jen, I didn't mean to say "normal", I mean the biological way.'

'That's okay, silly,' she says, 'I knew what you meant! And no, it doesn't seem very fair sometimes. I think of some of the kids in our youth clubs and the way their parents treat them and it makes my blood boil. But at least this way, if the panel say yes, we will get to give some kids a new family and a new chance in life.'

'Well, you and Kyle have always been like family to me,' I say. 'Goodness knows what I'd have done when I was all mixed up after Will dumped me. I'd have thrown away everything I have with Jake if you hadn't given me the parent talk.'

'Well, I'm glad that we could help,' says Jenny, 'We love Jake and he's perfect for you. I'm so glad you're going to be our adoption referees. They talked about the importance of having a good support network and you both sprang instantly to mind. There's a friends and family evening coming up soon – will you both come along with us?'

'We'd love to!' I say and give her a big hug.

'Kyle's not enjoying the masses of forms we have to fill in,' Jenny says. 'And of course they come round, assess our house, our background, our jobs, our families, friends and everything and see if we're up to scratch.' She looks down.

'But the worst bit is we have to have medicals. I'm dreading that. Apparently, it's not much, but of course, you know… and I've also got to get my specialist to complete their letters of support.'

'I'm sure you'll pass with flying colours!' I say to her. She smiles bravely, but she doesn't look convinced.

'My specialist is fully behind me adopting, but on paper, it just doesn't sound like I'm the ideal candidate for parenthood, though does, it?' she says, her eyes filling with tears. 'Dodgy genes, dodgy lungs, dodgy pancreas.'

'Dodgy thinking! You're in great health, Jenny, you cope with it all really well,' I say, 'and you are ten times more experienced in looking after kids than the average parent! I mean, not everyone could control a minibus full of rowdy teens the way you do. A baby will be a doddle after that – at least when you put them down, they can't run away and set off the nearest fire extinguisher!'

'That's the thing, though, it's unlikely to be a baby,' she says. 'A lot of the kids needing to be adopted are toddlers or older. And with me being a more, shall we say, 'interesting' candidate, it will help our application if we are willing to take some of the more difficult to place kids.'

'What does that mean?' I ask.

'Sibling groups, children with disabilities or behavioural issues, older children and so on,' she says.

'And is that okay with you, Jen?' I ask gently, 'missing out on the baby stage?'

'Oh yes,' she says and gives a broad beam, 'Picturing me and Kyle with kids, I'm happy to fast forward to toddlers or above. I just wish I knew that we'd be approved. I don't mind if they're older or have additional needs. I mean look at me, I've got additional needs coming out of my ears. I know how to help them deal with being different and tough stuff.' She takes a sip of her drink. 'I suppose I'd like them to be pre-school age if possible, so I've not missed out on all of that kind of thing. Well, one of them, at least.'

'One of them?' I say. Jenny giggles at the look of surprise on my face.

'Yes, we thought we'd say we could adopt a sibling group of two. I mean we'd like more than one child and as they said at the event, sibling groups need adopting and it's often easier to adopt two children and keep them together than have one, then have to go through all the assessments again a few years later when you want another.'

'You'd have to be reassessed for your second one?' I say.

'Yes, and then the second child would have to be a good match to fit well with the first one, who might feel threatened by a new addition to their home,' Jenny says.

Goodness, it's complicated.

'But at least we've got Kyle to convince the adoption panel that he's strong and dependable and more than makes up for my additional health needs,' says Jenny, looking happy again.

'Er, Jen,' I say, 'There's something…'

At that moment I hear a key in the door and I hear the noise of three feet and two crutches negotiating the piles of shoes in the hall. The door to the living room opens.

'Oh my god!' exclaims Jenny, a horrified look on her face. 'What are we going to tell the social workers now!!'

***

But after her initial shock, Jenny takes Kyle's injury quite well. Admittedly she gets quite wound up at first about how this will affect their adoption application, but Kyle is able to reassure her that he's going to be okay and that the crutches are temporary.

'Try not to worry too much, Jen,' I say, 'We've just been talking about how the adoption process takes months, and then you have to wait to be matched with the right children, so Kyle will be back to standing on his own two feet without assistance by the time little ones come into the picture.'

Jenny doesn't look convinced but we get Kyle comfy on the sofa, give him some painkillers and promise them that we can give them lifts anywhere they need whilst he's unable to drive.

'But,' she says, her voice rising to a pitch more suitable for dogs, 'how on earth are we going to convince the social workers that we are a fit, vibrant couple when one of us has defective DNA and the other is on crutches? You hardly look fit to chase after a couple of toddlers, Kyle!' There's a silence as we all try to think of something useful to say. Just then Jenny's mobile rings. She goes into the kitchen to answer it. A few minutes later she returns, a look of relief on her face.

'Who was it?' Kyle asks, shifting uncomfortably to try to reposition his leg.

'The adoption agency,' says Jenny. 'Apparently we can't start the home visit assessment for another fortnight.'

'Oh, no,' I say, 'is everything okay, Jen?'

'They've not heard about my leg, have they?' asks Kyle, 'have they been watching us?' He glances round the room as if he's expecting a social worker to appear from behind the bookcase.

'No, you goose,' says Jenny, 'they're an adoption agency, not MI5!'

'What's happened then?' I ask, sitting down. I can feel the colour draining from my face. I hope there's not more drama, I'm starting to feel a bit wobbly.

'Well, Ky,' says Jenny, a big smile on her face. 'Looks like you don't need to worry quite as much about what impression you having a leg out of action will give them – Our social worker can't visit us for a couple of weeks because he broke both of his in a skiing accident. He's been getting on well with physio but needs another fortnight. So, I suppose that shows an injury isn't the end of the world and you don't look so bad now, with only the one bad leg.'

CHAPTER 8
– JAKE

With Jenny and Kyle looking happier, me and Helen leave them to it and head home, making them promise they'll call us if they need anything. I ask Helen if she's okay, as she's looking a bit looking pale. She asks me to pull up outside Tesco, saying she needs some paracetamol for a headache.

When we get in, she disappears to the bathroom. I start to flick through the tv channels to see if anything good is on. I've just settled into a quiz when she reappears, looking even more pale and holding something behind her back.

'What's up, Helen?' I ask her, getting up and attempting to give her a hug. She steps back and holds out the thing that is in her hand. At first, I can't work out what it is, then I see the word 'pregnant' clearly written across the little window in it.

'Oh!' I say.

'Oh,' says Helen.

I draw her into a hug. 'Are you okay?' I ask, stroking her hair. 'How do you feel about this?' My mind is reeling. All I can think is I need to tell my mum. But I can't, she's no longer with us. My dad's in Australia but may as well be on the moon for all the contact we have since he walked out on us. Yet my mum wore the wedding ring he gave her until the day she died. She said she had no desire to pretend her marriage didn't happen as without it, she wouldn't have had me. Families are complicated. I always keep mum's ring in my pocket and I am suddenly very conscious of it there, as if it has heated up and is burning onto my skin.

'I had a feeling I might be,' Helen says. 'I'm sorry, I should have said something before.'

'Well,' I say, 'it would certainly have made a good reveal for one of our "mysterious stranger" date nights.'

'I thought I was imagining things, so I kept it to myself,' Helen continues, 'I know it's unfair that I've had time to think it over and you haven't.' She holds me tighter and speaks into my shoulder. 'Jake, I know this is a surprise and a bit soon, but I really want to keep it.'

I place my hands gently on her arms and pull back so I can look at her. She's right, it is soon but it's also right. It's Helen. I couldn't imagine not wanting a child we'd created together. I kiss her.

'Is that alright with you, Jake?' she says,

looking up at me hopefully.

'Of course it is!' I say, 'I always imagined us having kids. Not quite this soon, but hey, when did we ever do things slowly?'

We kiss again and then hold each other for the longest time.

'Jake?' says Helen.

'Yes,' I reply, leading us gently to the sofa. I need to sit down, who would have thought that mountain boarding would be in second place in the list of things that have made my legs weak today.

'How on earth are we going to tell Jenny and Kyle?' she says, biting her lip.

'They're our friends,' I say, 'they'll be pleased for us.'

'They will,' says Helen, 'but it seems so unfair. They're jumping through hoops to get children and we didn't even have to try.'

'I know,' I say, taking hold of her hand. 'But look at it this way, we're all going to be parents at the same time, albeit in different ways. What could be better than that?'

Helen nods but she doesn't look sure. I wish I was as sure as I sounded.

CHAPTER 9
– JENNY

I always knew Kyle was really helpful – he thinks nothing of doing the majority of the housework because of my health conditions – I don't always have the same amount of energy as other people, so I choose carefully what to spend it on. For example, when we have children, I'll make sure I'm not working too many hours, so that I devote the best of me to them. Also, with housework, dusting and hoovering aren't my forte due to my lungs and cooking meals becomes tricky at times with diabetes as when my blood sugars are dropping, I end up eating half of it before I've properly made it. So Kyle will pop in to see how I'm doing and instead of a nice pasta dish, there will be some plain pasta half cooked in a pan and I'll be scoffing chunks of cheese and breadsticks, scattering crumbs everywhere so that the kitchen looks like a three year old's birthday party has just rampaged through it. He takes time to do the most beautiful side salads, whilst I feel so rubbish when I'm hungry that it looks like I've prepared his by dumping the contents of the food waste bin onto our plates.

This eating as I cook can make my blood sugars go too high, so by the time I come to eat the meal, I need more insulin than normal. I could be more organised, I'm sure many people with diabetes manage just fine, but I never seem to start thinking about making food until I'm already hungry and with diabetes, that's a recipe (if you'll pardon the pun) for disaster.

As for ironing… I did one of Kyle's shirts for him once and he said I ironed more creases into it than I took out. Strangely, I never perfected the art. That has nothing whatsoever to do with my health conditions though, I just hate ironing, but I somehow haven't mentioned that to Kyle…

I try to play my part in other ways. I tend to be the one who keeps the diaries, organises things and fills out the carefully highlighted calendars. I'm the one who ensures everyone has a thoughtful and affordable Christmas and birthday present. Annoyingly, all the time I spend organising essentials remains quite invisible, unlike the things Kyle does. You can easily see the beautiful meals he prepares, the clean house and all the salary he brings home from his senior position in the customer services department of the council. You only really see the things I do if I don't do them – if the bills don't get paid or the car tax isn't renewed it becomes quite obvious but as long as I'm on top of it all, no one would know I'm even doing anything. Plus, even in this day and age, there is still a lingering sexism about who should do what in the home. The amount of people who exclaim, 'Oh, isn't he good!' every time they see Kyle brandishing a dish cloth is unbelievable. No one would want to give me a medal if I hoovered the house, and yet seeing Kyle do it prompts praise normally reserved for an ultra-marathon runner.

But in fairness, it's only now he's semi out of action that I'm realising just how much he does do. For a start, I'm taking him to work as he can't drive at the moment and we've had rather a lot of takeaways recently. Plus, this is exactly the time I could have done with his strong arms as we're attempting to turn our two 'spare rooms' into two children's rooms. As mad as it seems, I've been told by the adoption agency that they'll want to look at the bedrooms during the home assessments so, despite the fact that we don't even know if we'll be approved to adopt, we have to get them ready. I'm sure all my friends will think I've finally lost it when they come over and see that our bookcases of books we'll never read again and the desk we never use have been replaced by a toy box and a child's chest of drawers. We need to order another single bed (we already have one spare bed in the room I'm in now) and suitable wardrobes etc but first of all, we need to find somewhere to put all our stuff. As I gaze at it, feeling more tired by the minute, I'm starting to think a skip might be a good start.

But then, just as I'm about to load up boxes and bags for the charity shops, I'll find a book that a young person from one of the youth clubs bought me, or something from a Christmas cracker from a brilliant party we went to years ago. As soon as I look at the individual items, I can't imagine throwing anything away. But I'm going to have to - that or move into a TARDIS (bigger on the inside) because there are hopefully two children out there who need this home more than one of those fortune telling fish or a miniature pack of playing cards does.

In between all the sorting and reminiscing over old clothes that no longer fit me, I stop and try to imagine what the rooms will be like with children in them. Not just the furniture and wallpaper – we've decided to leave the walls magnolia as they are and buy some of those transfers you get from B&Q when we know which children we're having. That way, we can personalise the rooms at the last minute with Thomas and friends or Paddington (an adoptee himself, nonetheless) or whatever it is they like. Add a duvet cover and the place will hopefully look appealing to them. I can picture the rooms. But can I picture what it will feel like to have children in them? To have children? Our adopted children? *Our* children?

I pick up an old teddy bear of mine which is wearing a customary bear outfit of jolly T shirt and nothing on his bottom half. He has a sweet face and his little button eyes look at me hopefully. I pop him on the spare bed and tuck him in up to his furry chin so he looks cosy. 'Don't worry,' I say, patting him on the head, 'you'll have someone new to cuddle you soon.'

'I hope...' I continue, crossing my fingers.

Leaving Ted in the bed, I traipse downstairs and add another bag of stuff to the two huge boxes in the hall, full of things for the charity shops and some for the tip. With another trip up and down, I dump a pile of books next to the boxes and head back to sort out another drawer. I'm starting to get tired and the dust is getting on my chest. I'm going to have to rest soon. The last thing I want is to get run down and unwell when the social worker comes to start our assessment.

I pull up a stool and sit next to the drawer. Mustering up some remaining energy, I yank it open. In it are some old clothes of mine that I don't wear any more but don't want to get rid of. Festival T-shirts that no longer fit but hold such memories I can't bear to chuck them out. I start reminiscing as I read the faded line-ups on them and remember the days me and Kyle spent in muddy fields, singing and queuing for portaloos, both of us laden with rucksacks full of my medication, insulin and enough snacks to keep an army going, let alone one person with diabetes. But I always like to be on the safe side, prepared for all eventualities. As I put the T-shirt back in the drawer, I catch sight of something pink and woollen. My heart starts to thud in my chest as I pull at it and a tiny cardigan appears. It's a stripey one with big buttons and according to the label, for a four-year-old. Checking that the door to the bedroom is closed, I reach back inside the draw and feel around at the back. I squeeze my eyes tight, partly because I'm scared to look and partly to keep the tears from coming out. My hand alights on two small woollen items. I open my eyes and sure enough, there, clutched in my now clammy hand is a tiny pair of blue booties. They still have the price label attached. I hold the cardigan and the booties to my chest, breathing in shakily and feeling my heart continue to thud so loudly, I'm sure Kyle will hear it from downstairs.

I bought these clothes a few years ago, on holiday. It was a holiday we had taken a few months after my miscarriage. Kyle had booked it to try to cheer me up but we'd got into a silly argument one day over which kind of cake we wanted in a café. I'd marched out of the café and wandered round the shops on my own for two hours, refusing to answer Kyle's increasingly worried calls. After about forty-five minutes I'd walked into the baby section of Boots. Looking around as if I was being followed, I'd let myself reach out and stroke the soft baby clothes. I'm surprised I didn't get arrested for shoplifting, the amount of time I spent in there. I must have studied every item of clothing, planning my baby's wardrobe in my head, deciding on what they'd sleep in, what t-shirts they'd need for sunny days and what jumpers would keep them warm in winter.

After about half an hour of this agonising inventory, I could see the shop assistants starting to look in my direction, so, feeling foolish, I grabbed the little pair of blue booties and headed for the counter. As I left the baby section, I passed some clothes for older children. I knew even then that sibling groups placed for adoption often had older children in them and that so many people wanted babies that we would increase our chances of parenting if we were happy to welcome an older child into our family as well. I didn't care if they were older, I just wanted them to be mine. I looked at the shelf. There was the prettiest pink cardigan I'd ever seen. I grabbed it before I could change my mind and took it to the till with the booties.

I'd then rung Kyle, apologised for worrying him and we had a tearful reunion. We went to the beach and had ice creams and held hands walking along the prom. I kept the clothes at the bottom of my rucksack, then concealed them in my suitcase. When we got back home after our holiday, I'd hidden them in this draw, taking them out and holding them to my cheek every now and again, willing the little people who they would fit to come into our lives one day.

Here, in a drawer I need to clear to create an achingly empty furnished bedroom, are two items of clothing for children that I may never have. I wipe my eyes and place them back underneath my faded festival t-shirts.

CHAPTER 10
– KYLE

It's so frustrating not being able to do much. I feel guilty watching Jen run around doing all the house stuff and trying to sort the kids' rooms out. 'The kids' rooms' – that sounds weird. Hopefully once our social worker comes and starts doing the home visits and assessing us, I'll have a better idea of what's going on and it will all feel a bit less surreal. Having two rooms decked out for kids that we don't yet know if we'll have is definitely going to be interesting. But Jen is throwing herself into the sorting out, although I'm not sure she's made much space up there as yet - she keeps running down to show me things she's found, like ticket stubs from our first cinema date and empty bubbles containers in the shape of champagne bottles that we had on the tables at our wedding.

I'm working from home some of the time and on the days when I need to go in, Jen is driving me. I hope she doesn't get too run down with all the extra stuff she's doing. I know how keen she is to show the social worker how fit she is for looking after two kids. Two! I tried to take it in my stride when Jen suggested we go for a sibling group of two – it makes total sense of course, but my workmates who have kids had them one at a time, apart from Dev who has twins, and that seemed hard enough. Never mind two running, talking, little people who will arrive one day laden with baggage both literal and emotional.

I look around the living room I'm currently sitting in with my bad leg propped up on the sofa cushions. I'm trying to imagine it with a couple of children in it. Toys on the floor, play dough on the carpet and spaghetti hoops on toast. I take a deep breath in. A lot of change is coming. A lot of adjustment. And not just for me and Jenny. I can hardly begin to imagine what it's going to feel like for two kids to be picked up and plonked with two virtual strangers and told we're their new mummy and daddy.

I decide to distract myself from such things and message Jake. Maybe he'd like to come over and we can talk about that board game idea we've been kicking about. Unusually for him though, I just get a really short reply, saying that he can't at the moment but he'll be in touch soon. Maybe he's wedding planning or something with Helen. I don't think they've set a date yet but I suppose they might be looking at venues and things like that. They've got plenty of time though and no pressure. I get a pang of guilt as I feel a twinge of envy for Jake and Helen's relatively simple life. I mean it's not like they haven't had their fair share of things to deal with – poor Jake lost his mum in a hit and run accident just over a year ago and is only just starting to deal with his loss. His dad, Rick is less than useless, having left them to live in Australia with his bit on the side when Jake was a teenager.

I grab a notebook and decide to have another think about the board game idea. I reckon we might be onto something here and it would certainly help to have another income stream, what with there soon to be two extra mouths to feed around here. I suppose Jake and Helen will have kids in a few years too. It'd be nice to do family stuff together. I'm glad they aren't planning to start a family just yet though. Jenny is a very generous spirit but I've seen how hard it's been for her watching everyone else have babies these last few years. She smiles and accepts baby cuddles and buys thoughtful gifts, but each time it's happening for someone else and not for us, I see it chips away another little piece of her.

I really hope our bloke is a nice social worker and he makes it seem a bit less daunting than all the paperwork we've filled in so far. It's all tick boxes as to what we would and wouldn't accept in a child – behavioural difficulties, different disabilities, experience of different kinds of abuse. I shudder and go back to thinking about the board game.

I start to jot down ideas. We've done a good bit of planning as to how the game will actually work but we also need to think about how we're going to get it made and distribute it – as well as getting people to actually buy it. I start to make a list of people I know who might be able to invest. I've written down the names of some of my colleagues who have a bit of cash put aside – the ones who own caravans they can pop to on a sunny weekend – I work for the council so I'm not exactly surrounded by millionaires. Then one pops into my head. Bazza! He was Helen's boss at the Novelty gift company she used to work at. Bit of a mad bloke but his heart was in the right place and he could sell woolly hats in a heatwave. He once managed to sell a line of musical kitchen utensils which played tinny versions of Motown classics when you used them. We still have an oven timer which plays 'You can't hurry love' and a cereal bowl that plays 'I can't help myself (Sugar pie, honey bunch)'. The only problem is, you can't wash any of the items because the battery compartment isn't sealed properly so our cereal bowl currently contains a couple of buttons that fell off my shirt and the car keys. But nonetheless, I could see Bazza being an asset. I message Helen to see if she minds me contacting him.

Strange. I get an uncharacteristically

short reply from her as well, saying she'll get back to me later. I hope they're okay.

I think about them off and on all week but don't like to pester them. They'll get back to me when they're free and in the meantime I've got my adoption forms to keep me busy. And my leg. Luckily I haven't had to wait that long for my appointment for my hospital appointment and we're soon sitting in the physiotherapy department.

'How long have you been into extreme sports?' asks Keith, my physio, running his hands over parts of my leg I usually reserve for Jenny.

Jenny stifles a giggle. I clear my throat and say in as manly a voice as I can manage, 'Er, I'm not, really.'

'Oh,' says Keith, 'but, the mountain boarding?'

'A one off, I'm afraid,' I reply, giving Jenny a hard stare as her eyes dance with humour. 'A mate's idea, not mine. I just went along for a laugh, really, not that it's turned out to be very funny.'

'No, it's quite serious, really,' says Jenny, having finally composed herself, 'I have health conditions. Kyle is supposed to be the fit one, making up for my restrictions, so it would be kind of handy if he could get match fit again as soon as possible.'

Keith looks slightly concerned.

'Is it bad news?' I say.

'No, not at all,' he replies, looking warily at Jenny. She is quite a force to be reckoned with when she has her mind set on something and I realise poor old Keith thought he was in trouble.

'Will he have to have an operation?' she asks.

'No, not necessarily,' replies Keith, reading my scan results. 'From the look of things, it should be okay for normal use – it's just if you wanted to be taking part regularly in particularly vigorous activities, we might need to strengthen it up a bit for you so an op would be the way forward in that case. What sort of activities are you intending on doing?'

'Running after toddlers, mainly,' I say.

The frown returns to Keith's face.

'Our own, I mean,' I add. Oh good, now my physio thinks I'm some kind of child catcher. Helen said her company were doing Chitty Chitty Bang Bang next year, maybe I should audition.

'How old are your children?' asks Keith.

'We don't know,' I say.

Keith's frown furrows so deeply into his face that I'm worried the wind will change and he'll stay that way. Luckily, before he can alert the police, Jenny chips in.

'We're applying to adopt,' she says, patting me firmly far too close to my injured knee for my liking.

'Oh!' says a relieved looking Keith, 'How

lovely! Well, we'll draw up a physiotherapy plan and we should have you fit for pushing a pram before you know it.'

'It probably won't be a pram,' says Jenny, oversharing as she often does. I think a lifetime of having to explain her health needs to everyone has resulted in her offering up far more information than necessary. I once caught her telling the plumber about my magpie saluting superstition. I shift position with a little groan to indicate that we perhaps should get back to the topic of my knee, but she continues, 'They're likely to be toddlers or infant school aged children, hence the need to be up to running.'

'Children, plural?' asks Keith, 'Ooh, brave! And running ones at that! Well done you!'

Jenny beams. I wish I felt as confident as she did about all this. I'm not sure I can keep up with her at the moment, let alone a couple of toddlers, with or without my anterior cruciate ligament.

When we get home, we carry on filling out some of the forms the adoption agency have given us. Jenny scribbles away at hers as if she's writing a novel, pausing only to look up at me every so often to see how I'm getting on. My form is as blank as my mind.

'How you doing?' she asks, leaning over. I hold the paper close to my chest as if she's a classmate trying to copy my maths test.

'Fine!' I say. She leans over and grabs my

paper.

'Why does it say "Philip Larkin"?' she says.

I shift awkwardly in my seat. 'You know,' I say, 'the poem.'

She shakes her head.

'The one about parents and faults…'

'I think they're after our childcare experiences and skills,' she says, 'not an English essay.'

I cross out my meagre notes.

'And it might be best to steer clear of the F word…'

'What should I write?' I ask her. 'I don't know what to put – how are you writing so much?'

She thinks for a moment and then, to my relief, her face softens. 'Well, I suppose it's similar to all my youth work stuff really,' she says, taking pity and coming to sit next to me. 'We're always having to reflect and talk about our feelings in all the training. I guess after a while it just comes naturally.' I'm glad she's come to help me now rather than sighing at my efforts. I know that with her health issues she has to be strong and she spends a lot of time preparing herself for things, but sometimes she is so determined, she forgets the rest of us have our own way of doing things and might not be up to speed with her. Like poor Keith, for example, who thought he was about to be put on the naughty step for not having fixed my knee already.

'But what should I put here?' I ask her, pointing to a question about what I feel I can give to children who have experienced trauma. 'I've never worked with children, let alone ones who have experienced trauma. I'm going to let you down.'

Jenny puts her pen and paper down and envelops me in a hug.

'You idiot,' she says softly, 'what have you done today?'

'Nothing much,' I say, 'apart from make the physio think twice about treating the leg of a suspected kidnapper.'

'Nonsense,' she says. 'We got up, what did you do then?'

'Made us breakfast,' I shrug.

'And, after you'd made food for both of us?'

'Wash up your nebulisers and put a load of washing on, whilst you got showered and did your physio, you dropped me off at work where I stayed until it was time for my appointment.'

'And what will you do after we've filled these in?'

'Do the shopping – online cos of my stupid leg - and make us tea.' I say, not sure where she's going with this. 'I'll be glad when I can get back to Aldi, it's costing a fortune having to get it delivered.'

'Exactly,' she says.

'I'm not with you?' I reply. 'Surely they don't want to know about my supermarket preferences and how I make spaghetti bolognaise?'

'No, but they will be impressed at how you shape your days to support me and my extra needs and how I've supported you with your leg. We make an excellent team. I might be a whiz at filling in all this emotional stuff, but it's no use me using all my therapeutic skills to calm the kids down if the cupboards are bare and there are no clean clothes.'

I hug Jenny back, feeling better. She's right, we do make a good team. I still don't know what to write on this bloody form though.

CHAPTER 11
- JAKE

It's manic at work today. It seems like everyone has decided that they absolutely have to play board games and eat nachos and they all have to do it today. At one point people were queuing out the door. I've worked through my break and am absolutely ravenous. I'm just about to go on my lunch break when I feel a tug on my apron. It's a little lad, wearing a t-shirt with a dinosaur on it. A dinosaur and a large amount of chocolate milkshake. His bottom lip is quivering.

'Please,' he says, a sob threatening to escape, 'my milkshake has fallen over and it's all over my T-Rex!'

It certainly is, and all over the floor, I see as I glance over to where the little lad's dad is trying to mop up the spillage with a handful of serviettes. He just seems to be wafting it under the table though and getting most of it on his rather expensive looking trainers in the process. I crouch down so I'm level with my little distressed customer.

'Don't worry, matey,' I say, 'we'll get you another milkshake in just a few moments. Let's just take the mop over to daddy first, shall we?' My young customer doesn't look convinced. He looks longingly at the milkshake machine as if he doesn't quite trust me to make good on my promise. His T shirt is soaked with chocolate milk. I grab the mop and head over to his dad, relieved that the lad is following me.

'I'm so sorry!' says his dad, looking flustered. 'Today would be the day I forget to bring a change of clothes with me as well. My wife will kill me if I take him to the dentist looking like this.'

It crosses my mind that the dentist might be a bit more concerned about the effect the chocolate milk is having on his teeth rather than his T-shirt, but I look over at our merch stand. There are some half-price kids' T-shirts on there and I grab one that looks about the right size and hand it to his dad. 'Don't worry,' I say, 'worse things happen at sea!'

'Sorry, mate, I don't get paid til Friday,' he says, looking embarrassed. 'I spent my last money on the milkshake. I've been promising Toby we could come here for weeks now.'

'Not a problem,' I say, 'we've been trying to shift these since Christmas, you'd be doing me a favour if you take it off our hands! Now, I'll just go and get you a new milkshake.' He goes to look in his wallet. I shake my head, 'Replacement drinks on the house,' I say.

Soon my young customer is beaming in his new t-shirt and only has milkshake round his mouth. The dad thanks me again. I smile at them and tell my colleague I'm off on my lunch break at last. I grab a sandwich and some flapjack and head into the back room.

As I eat my lunch, I fire off a quick text to Helen. 'How you feeling? Manic at work today but I just rescued a small child and a drowning T-Rex so I reckon I've got this parenting business sussed.' A few seconds later a reply appears.

'No idea what you're talking about!' she texts, 'but you're my hero!'

'I'll tell you all about my Jeff Goldblum style heroics later,' I message back.

She replies with a heart emoji and I scoff the remains of my flapjack. I'd love to stay out here away from it all a bit longer but I'd best let someone else grab some food. As I remerge into the café, I glance over to where the lad and his dad are sitting, happily playing snap. For a second, I get a flashback of my dad playing cards with me when I was a kid, but I brush it away and head back to the busy counter.

CHAPTER 12
– HELEN

Well, Jake seems to have taken our surprise pregnancy well. I felt reasonably certain he would. He came to the doctors with me and all seems to be going the way it should. The person I'm really worried about is Jenny. Not that I think she won't be lovely and support me. I know she will, but I know that it will be really hard for her. I've seen her face every time another person she knows announces their pregnancy. She's smiling but her eyes are too bright, like it's tears rather than joy that are lighting them up. I really hope her adoption assessment goes well, especially the medical which I know she's losing sleep over.

But also, and I feel a bit guilty about this, I'm really excited. I wouldn't have planned for this to happen right now – we haven't been together all that long, but I can't imagine being a parent with anyone other than Jake. I keep finding myself drifting off at work, daydreaming about babies and gazing at websites with prams and the cutest little baby clothes.

I'm bursting to tell people but I don't want to risk it getting out to Jenny before I've had time to think about how to put it to her. I really want to tell my mum and dad but again, my mum is to secret keeping what The Hulk is to needlework. Anyway, it's probably best to wait a few weeks until we have the twelve-week scan and are a bit more certain that things are okay. Though it baffles me how medical professionals think losing a baby before twelve weeks is no big deal as long as you haven't mentioned it to anyone. I saw the devastation Jenny and Kyle felt after their miscarriage and they hadn't even known they were pregnant. Mind you, that brought so many questions to the fore for them about how and if they would have a family. I fold my arms over my stomach to give myself a kind of hug. 'It's okay,' I whisper to the little person I'm carrying inside me, 'it's all going to be okay.'

I'm glad I've got work today to take my mind off things a bit. The Panto is still in full swing and everyone is happy but looking a little tired as the run continues. There have been a few of the parts needing to be filled in by understudies as seasonal coughs and colds take hold. This led to an interesting performance the other night when there were no more female members of the company left to stand in for the fairy. Derek did an excellent job but it did take a lot of last minute sewing on my part to adjust the costume. I had to dive down to the haberdashery shop and buy a job lot of sparkly netting, reduced luckily in the post-Christmas sales. We just about managed to make Derek look the part and he was brilliant with his solo, once the music director had managed to find an appropriate key for him.

Of course, this meant that someone had to fill in for Derek in the chorus. There were no lines to learn so I volunteered without looking at the stage directions properly. It was only half an hour before curtain up when I realised that I'd be wearing a dog costume. I'd glanced at the script and read that I was in a dog walking scene and had naturally assumed, that as a human, I'd be the one walking the dog. But no such luck. At least the paws and ears were comfy and if I felt a bit tired, I only had to pretend to sit on my hind legs. It was, of course, the night that my mum, dad and Jake were in the audience. I blushed red as you like as I followed the stage directions and cocked my leg against a cardboard tree, especially when I heard my dad roaring with laughter and my mum saying in what she mistakenly thought was a quiet voice, 'She'd do that in real life as a child you know, Jake, if the queue for the ladies was too long.'

At the end of the performance, I was relieved to take my costume off and we had a good time at the pub with my parents, Jake and a lot of the cast. My dad asked me if I'd like my usual wine but of course, I asked for an orange juice instead. My mum, who often seems to be on another planet, apart from when you don't want her to be paying attention, glanced from me to Jake with a knowing look on her face and then looked pointedly at my stomach. Luckily Jake managed to throw her off the scent for now by discussing how warm it got in the dog costume and said I was more of a hotdog than a poodle. My mum giggled at him like a schoolgirl with a crush and all was well. Luckily, she didn't have chance to return to her line of thought as everyone was distracted by a loud crash as Tommy, one of the ugly sisters, fell over his chair whilst trying to demonstrate one of the dance routines to some 'fans' who had come over to speak to him. It didn't hurt that Tommy was far from ugly and the two young women who had come to ask him to sign their programme took great delight in helping him up, mentioning casually that they wouldn't mind if he also put his phone number next to his autograph.

***

The performances fly by and by the time Blue Monday is finally here, we're all more than ready for the grand finale. Which means, of course, that naturally, half the cast are off sick. We really are dragging people onto the stage from backstage now. The ugly sisters are being played by the members of the chorus who had previously only had the smallest of speaking parts and the guests at the ball are played by Pete the lighting guy and Martin who usually sells the raffle tickets. Luckily, they only have a couple of lines each, but they've had to be sellotaped to the scenery, the props and in some cases, the cast members' trousers, so this should be an interesting night.

I thought we'd got away with it until just before curtain up, when there's a loud crash in the wings. Carrie comes running over to me holding a costume.

'Now,' she says, 'don't panic, but Maggie needs to go home, nothing to worry about, possibly mild concussion. No need to panic, we just need to saw you in half!'

I instinctively put a protective hand across my stomach and feel the colour drain from my face.

'Helen?' she says, looking at me, 'are you okay? You haven't caught the sickness bug as well, have you?'

'No, no, I'm fine,' I say, 'it's not that. I just… I don't feel comfortable being sawn in half today, the table looks a bit wobbly and…' I put my other arm across my stomach and feel tears prickling in my eyes.'

A look of realisation crosses Carrie's face.

'Oh my goodness, you're not, are you?' she mimes the shape of a pregnant stomach and mouths the word 'expecting'.

'Shhh!' I say, looking round, 'nobody knows, well, no one except Jake!'

'It's okay,' she whispers, 'I didn't say it out loud.'

'I know,' I say, 'but your mime act is so good I think people out of earshot would be able to guess what we're talking about…' My eyes flit anxiously about, but it doesn't seem like anyone is looking in our direction. I'm glad we're safely in the wings - Jenny is in the audience with Kyle and Jake and I still haven't worked out how to tell her.

Carrie gives me a hug.

'Don't worry,' she says, 'I think you'd better go and sit in the audience, you look a bit peaky. You've done more than your fair share for this run. I can manage this – we'll just get a woman from the audience to be sawn in half. How about your friend Jenny, she looks a good sport?' I look a bit dubious. Carrie lowers her voice again, 'She's not pregnant as well, is she?'

'No,' I say, looking down, 'no, Jenny's not pregnant.'

'Great!' says Carrie, 'Jenny it is then!' Carrie won't take no for an answer, so I go and take a seat in the audience between Jake and Jenny. Jake looks concerned.

'You okay?' he asks.

'I'm fine!' I reply brightly. 'Carrie said I deserved the night off!'

Jake doesn't look convinced. When Jenny pops to the toilet he whispers in my ear.

'Everything alright, really?' He glances

down at my stomach. I glance over at Kyle who looks at us and smiles.

'Yes, honestly, I'm fine,' I say, 'but Carrie has found out, she wanted me to be sawn in half as the cast are dropping like flies, but I hesitated and she kind of guessed.'

'What's up, you two?' says Kyle, 'my birthday's not for ages yet, so you can't be whispering about that!'

'We're just saying that Carrie has decided…' I say. Jake squeezes my hand urgently and looks in the direction of Jenny who is on her way back.

'Carrie has decided to use someone from the audience for the scene in the butchers,' I say.

'The one where the customer gets sawn in half?' asks Kyle. They've been so supportive of me that this is not exactly the first time they've seen the pantomime.

'Yes, and she wants to use you, Jen,' I say as she settles back into her chair.

'I'm going to be on stage!' Jenny says with a beam! 'Fantastic! I'm not the jealous type, but I've felt the odd twinge recently, wanting to be in your shoes.'

'How do you mean?' I say, heat starting to rise in my face.

'You know, being on stage. I wouldn't mind a go at that! I'm ready!'

'You'll be great, Jen,' I say, leaning into Jake and taking a grateful gulp of the water he's just handed me. 'It's your turn to shine!'

When the butchers' scene comes, Jenny takes to the stage as if she's been treading the boards all her life. The audience clap and cheer as she is sawn in half and she takes the biggest of bows, beaming happily. It's good to see her enjoying herself and not worrying about adoption things. Jake holds my hand all throughout the performance. We all get into the spirit of things with plenty of 'Behind you's and sign up to karaoke as soon as we get to the afterparty. Kyle gets us all up at once and chooses ABBA's 'Does Your Mother Know'. Jake and I exchange uneasy looks.

'You don't think he's guessed, do you?' asks Jake.

'No,' I reply, trying to look more certain than I feel, 'He must just love ABBA.'

'We're going to have to tell them sometime,' says Jake.

'I know,' I reply, 'but not tonight.' Jake looks unsure. 'Carrie won't have said anything,' I continue, 'Let's just be calm and keep singing. Who's choosing the next song?'

Kyle steps up to the mic again.

'And now,' he says, 'your favourite ABBA tribute act will delight you with a second song.'

'Oh god,' says Jake as the opening chords blast out of the speakers, 'what's this one?'

I bite my lip.

'Mama Mia,' I say.

CHAPTER 13
– JAKE

I thought Jenny and Kyle were onto us last night at the panto afterparty. But nothing was said and everyone seemed happy so I think our secret pregnancy is still a secret for now. We danced and sang bad karaoke into the early hours. I'm surprised any one of us have surfaced today – we've all taken annual leave to recover, but Kyle's obviously up as he's messaged me several times about the board game. He's suggested we ask Bazza, Helen's old boss if he'd like to invest in it.

Bazza is a bit off the wall, but he genuinely cared about his staff team and was sad when Helen left. Not sad enough to give her a decent leaving gift though, rather than a box of singing toy dogs that we still have in the cupboard under the stairs stuffed away with the Christmas decorations. They all sing eighties Stock, Aitken and Waterman hits in voices only slightly more artificially enhanced than those of the original artists. I suggest to Helen that we give 'Pup Astley' and 'Jason Bone-a-van' to Jenny and Kyle to put in the rooms they're getting ready for the kids. Helen looks horrified at the idea and says that the dogs' wild eyes and high-pitched singing would scare a child to pieces and she doesn't want to be single-handedly responsible for them being turned down by the adoption panel. I'm about to point out that I'm not actually suggesting that they take the dogs to the panel, but Helen looks so stricken at the thought that I change the subject and ask her what she'd like for tea.

'Jake,' she says, rolling her eyes, 'Tea is hours away! We haven't even washed up the breakfast things yet. I know I'm eating for two but that's two people, not two football teams!'

I decide I need to change the subject again. Helen is a bit moody these days, which could be the pregnancy hormones or could be her worrying about Jenny and how she will feel when she finds out we've accidentally beaten her and Kyle to parenthood. I decide to talk about the board game and ask Helen how she feels about Bazza being involved.

'Yeah, you could ask him,' she says, 'he's a decent bloke, though I don't know how much spare cash he's got at the moment. One of my old colleagues told me that he's been giving more refunds than he usually does recently, which is saying something.'

'Oh?' I say, pleased to be on safe ground. 'What's he been trying to sell now?'

'He had a batch of bath bombs in his "home spa" range called "candyfloss chaos" that were supposed to turn the bubbles pink but created more chaos than candyfloss. There must have been something wrong with the colouring because customers' baths are being stained with streaks of red.'

She shows me the photos on Facebook and they do look less like a home spa and more like a crime scene. I start to wonder whether going into business with Bazza is a good idea after all. Just as I'm thinking about it, my phone goes off with another message from Kyle. He's clearly bored, resting his leg and is asking if I want to come over now and talk over the board game ideas. I look at Helen. I know she's anxious about Jenny finding out, but it went okay last night and if we start avoiding them, they'll know something is up.

'Kyle wants me to pop to his,' I say.

'Do you think that's a good idea?' Helen asks.

'It'll be grand,' I say, grabbing my phone and keys. I walk over and give Helen a hug. 'Don't worry, I won't say anything. We're just going to talk over the board game. Now we're going to have another mouth to feed, I'd best crack on with inventing a bestseller! We can't let Hasbro to have the monopoly on Monopoly, can we?'

Helen gives me a playful shove. 'Can I

come with you?' she says.

'Yeah, sure,' I say. 'We need you to get Bazza onside anyway – to give us the benefit of his knowledge and hopefully, money.'

'You're sure he's a good person to have on board?' she says, looking quizzical, 'I mean, his stock isn't exactly reliable.'

'Exactly!' I say, 'And yet he's still in business and shifts loads of it! Imagine how much he could sell when he gets something really good on his hands!'

We make our way over to Kyle and Jenny's. Jenny is pleased to see Helen and ushers her into the kitchen where she's baking. Kyle shows me the notes he's been making.

'What's CTB forfeit mean?' I ask.

'Change the barrel' Kyle replies. 'There's a timer involved in the game – like a sand timer shaped like a beer barrel, and if it runs out during your turn, you have to do a physical challenge. If you don't do it quickly enough, you have to go back several spaces, or give up some of your wages or something.'

'Cool,' I say. 'You've thought loads about this, mate. I really appreciate it.' I see a pile of papers next to him on the sofa. 'What's on those? More ideas?'

Kyle picks up the papers and tucks them away into the newspaper rack.

'No,' he says, 'they're some of the many, many forms we have to fill in for this adoption assessment.   Jenny's read like a nobel prize winner. I don't know where to begin.'

'You'll be alright, mate,' I say to him. 'You'll be a natural father.'

'That's it, though, isn't it?' he says, lowering his voice and glancing nervously over my shoulder towards the kitchen where we can hear Jenny and Helen chatting. 'There's nothing *natural* about this, is there?'

'I thought you were alright about them not being biologically yours?' I ask, a stab of guilt piercing me.

'Oh, don't get me wrong,' he says, 'I am. That doesn't bother me one bit. It's just all this,' he gestures towards the stack of papers, 'all the questions, all the assessments, all the proving we're good enough that makes me a bit...'

'Yeah,' I say, 'it is a lot, isn't it? Me and Helen are finding it hard enough to write you decent references.'

'Cheers!' laughs Kyle, 'Are we that difficult to say good things about?'

'Not at all!' I reply, 'Helen's in the acting business, we're pretty good at lying!'

We both laugh. But then Kyle's serious face returns.

'I wish I knew someone else going through this,' he says.

'You'll get to know the people on your training course though, won't you?' I ask. 'Some of them must be alright?'

'Yeah,' he says, shifting his leg to get more comfortable, 'but it's not the same as being with your mates. I don't really have any close friends with kids. I think I'd feel a bit less worried if I did.'

I look at him, my lips twitching as if I'm about to say something. I turn behind me and look at the kitchen door.

'What?' Kyle says, 'What is it, Jake?'

I lean towards him and lower my voice.

'You're not going to be on your own, mate,' I say.

'No, I know,' he says, 'Jenny's brilliant, but I wouldn't mind another Dad to hang out with.'

'You're going to have,' I say.

'Who?' he asks, frowning. I point to myself.

'Me,' I say, 'Helen's pregnant.'

There's a gasp behind me. I turn and see Jenny and Helen looking at us with similar shocked looks on their faces.

CHAPTER 14
– JENNY

'That's fantastic!' I say, turning to hug Helen. 'Why didn't you tell me?'

'It's all been a bit of a surprise,' Helen says, 'And there's you both jumping through hoops...'

'Don't be silly!' I say, 'Champagne! We need to celebrate!'

Helen pats her stomach, 'I'd best stick to orange juice, I think, unless you've got any schloer - that feels like fizz!'

'Oh goodness, of course! How stupid of me!' I say, 'But no, we don't have schloer, I can't have it, too much sugar.'

Now it's Helen's turn to look apologetic. There's an awkward silence. Then Kyle raises himself and his bad leg carefully off the sofa.

'Well, folks,' he says, raising his mug, 'whatever your poison is, tea, beer, orange juice or diet coke, let's all raise a glass to parenting! Whether it be a surprise or something that has a tougher qualification process than the Olympics, we will ace this parenting lark, together!'

I bustle into the kitchen to grab the drinks and we toast parenthood. Then an email appears on my phone. A book I've ordered on adoption has arrived in the shop in town.

'Sorry to break up the party, guys,' I say, 'I've got to pop into Waterstones to pick up my order, it's a book I want to read before we meet with our social worker.'

'I'll come with you,' says Helen.

'Thanks, Hel,' I say, throwing some insulin, biscuits and emergency jelly babies into my rucksack and checking my bloods, 'but I've got loads of boring things to get whilst I'm out, and I don't want to drag you round in your condition. You stay here and keep the boys company. They need a female brain and your Bazza connections to get this board game of theirs going.'

Helen looks a bit crestfallen, but I can't worry about that now. I grab my keys and pull my boots and jacket on.

'Won't be long,' I call over my shoulder as I rush out the front door, 'stay for tea if you like, we can get takeaway later.'

Once in my car, I put the radio on and sing mindlessly to the songs as I drive into town. I find a place to park and go into Waterstones. As I'm waiting in a queue at the counter, my eyes are drawn to the display next to me. It's full of those story books for babies with the sensory pages that declare 'That's not my monster/kitten/

teddy, its fur is too scratchy/stripy/rough and so on. My eyes rest on one that declares 'That's not my baby...'. I can feel hot tears threatening to escape. I blink rapidly. *That's not my baby,* I think, *it belongs to my friends... That's not my baby, I've got dodgy DNA... that's not my baby, the adoption panel turned me down...*

'Can I help you?' The sales assistant's breezy voice breaks into my thoughts.

'Er, yes, thanks, my book has come in,' I reply, scrolling through my phone for the order number. I can't find it anywhere. As I search my inbox, a text notification pops up from Kyle asking if I'm okay. I accidentally press on it and exit my inbox. 'So sorry,' I say to the sales assistant, aware of the long queue behind me, 'I had it here somewhere...'

'No worries,' he says, can you tell me your name and the title of the book?

I take a deep breath and blink hard again.

'Jenny Williams,' I say, 'Parenting the Child Who Hurts.'

***

I collect my book and leave the store. I don't want to go home just yet so I walk round the town centre for a bit, and find myself in Wilkos. I come through here to get to the car park when I have work meetings in town. They have a small section of children's furniture. There's a little pink bookcase with ladybirds on it. I've stopped to look at it so many times on my way home from work that I could draw it from memory, but I daren't buy it. What if we don't get approved? We're being practical and sensible with all the other furniture, buying plain stuff that we can put to good use even if we don't have kids. Stuff that we can stick transfers and pictures on if we do. But a small pink bookcase will really give the game away. That's like admitting to the world that I've got my heart set on having children. I mean the whole adoption process is a bit of a hint, but I can pass that off as paperwork, admin, going through the system, filling in forms as if I'm on a youth work course. I can say I'm just giving it a go. But if I arrive home to Kyle, Jake and a pregnant Helen carrying pastel-coloured shelving with cartoon bugs on it, it'll be like wearing one of those 'bun in the oven' t-shirts while I'm still waiting for permission to look after the cakes.

I swallow hard. I don't want to wait for permission any more. I grab the bookcase and march to the till.

'Oh, that's beautiful,' says the lady on the counter. 'Is it for your little girl?' I clear my throat.

'Yes, it is,' I say. As I leave the store, I feel like the security guard is going to run after me, yelling that I'm a fraud and not approved to buy ladybird bookcases, but I keep walking on my unsteady-feeling legs and no one arrests me. The bookcase is quite heavy and I feel a bit out of breath carrying it. I wish I'd brought Kyle with me, I think to myself, but then remember he's hurt his knee. Maybe I should have let Helen come, I think, but then berate myself. She's pregnant! I can't be letting her carry furniture around! I need to look after her!

She's going to need our support now. I love her to pieces but sometimes I wish I could shake her upside down so all her silly worries would fall out. Her ex, Will, left her in such a state when he walked out on her that she nearly let her insecurities mess things up when she met Jake. She often says me and Kyle are like her mum and dad but without the crazy. I guess I have always kind of mothered her but at the moment, I really want to be a proper mother to my own children. And when I say, 'my own', I don't care if they don't have my DNA, my health issue is genetic after all - so much for blood being thicker than water. My dodgy DNA is not the family heirloom I want to pass down. Kyle and me are very much in the minority at the adoption training sessions in that we have been trying hard *not* to get pregnant!

Pregnant. Helen is pregnant. She didn't plan it. She didn't even have to try. It's just happened. And brilliant, funny, kind, wonderful Jake is the father. And unlike me, with my blip on chromosome seven, there's no reason to doubt that the baby will be healthy. No one is assessing them, questioning them, training them or sending them to a panel of experts to approve them.

I love Helen to bits. Always have and always will. I want everything that is good for her. I'm pleased for her. But I am ashamed to say, that for the first time in our friendship, I am really, really jealous of her.

CHAPTER 15
– KYLE

We haven't met up with Jake and Helen for a week now. They decided not to stay for tea the day of the revelation and Jenny looked relieved when she got back from town laden with some brightly coloured shelves to find just me and a takeaway menu. I think everyone needed a bit of space after it all. But I don't want it to get weird. I reckon we should try to do something to take everyone's mind off our own personal paths to parenthood for a bit, so I've booked a table at Jake's board game café this evening for us all. I checked with Jake that he didn't mind a bit of a busman's holiday, but he said he was happy to be there on his night off as long as they don't drag him behind the counter to work.

Me and Jenny arrive to find Jake and Helen are already there. Jake gives us a big wave and Helen gets up to hug Jenny. We order some drinks and nachos and ask Jake what games he recommends. They've got everything here, from snap and Guess Who to Dungeons and Dragons.

Tonight is a retro night and they've set out all our childhood games like Frustration and Game of Life.

'I think I used to play Game of Life at my cousin's house,' I say, 'what did you have to do again?'

'You kind of drive round in a car, go to university, get a job, get married, have a couple of kids…' says Jake, his voice tailing off awkwardly at the end.

'If only it was that easy!' says Jenny brightly. Helen looks down. 'Don't worry, I'm only joking,' says Jenny, 'Come on, let's play kerplunk, it's got a bit more action in it than Game of Life as far as I remember.'

'Yeah, you're right,' says Jake, 'for all its talk, Game of Life is basically just spinning the spinny thing and driving around the course. Our game we're inventing will be much more exciting than that, won't it Kyle?'

I agree wholeheartedly, and dive happily into a conversation about the game we're hoping to make.

'So basically, it's a board game about a pub?' says Jenny.

'Yeah, what could be better?' laughs Jake, 'Games and pubs! Two of my favourite things!'

'Hey!' says Helen, nudging him in the ribs.

'Sorry,' he says, putting his one arm round her and gently placing the other hand on her stomach, 'you know you two are my actual favourite things.'

Helen looks across at Jenny and blushes.

'Look, guys,' says Jenny, 'you've got to stop feeling awkward about the fact that you're pregnant. If we all flinch every time someone mentions children, it's going to get ridiculous. We're over the moon for you, aren't we Ky?'

'Course we are,' I nod enthusiastically. 'This way I don't have to be a Billy no mates at the swings! We're made up for you both.'

'Cheers, mate, cheers Jen,' says Jake, raising his glass to us. 'How is everything going with the adoption stuff anyway? What's happening next?'

I look at Jenny. She gives a stiff smile. 'We've got our medicals this coming week,' I say.

'You'll be grand, Jen,' says Jake.

'Your specialist is writing you a letter of support – that'll reassure them – and you're really well and you look after yourself brilliantly,' says Helen, 'That has to count for a lot.'

Jenny smiles but it doesn't reach her eyes. 'I hope so,' she says, 'Anyway, let's get Kerplunking!!'

As the evening develops, we all start to chill out a bit. Jake is on form, winning most of the games hands down. Helen is a bit quiet at first but warms up when Jenny sits by her and gives her a gentle squeeze. Soon we're playing a particularly raucous game of Guess Who with me and Jenny on one team and Jake and Helen the other.

'It's a bit like the adoption forms,' I joke, 'all these questions and all this choosing!'

'What,' grins Jake, 'has he got a moustache? I know you're looking past the baby stage, but surely that's going a bit far?'

Jenny laughs, 'Sure, but they do ask you about whether you want girls or boys and preferred ages though. But I don't think they mention whether they'll be wearing a hat…'

'Glasses, possibly,' I say, 'they do ask you how you feel about dealing with disabilities.'

'We score pretty highly on that one,' smiles Jenny.

'Maybe we should develop an adoption Guess Who game for the social workers to use,' I say, 'it'd make a change from all those forms and be something to do whilst we wait for the biscuits at the training days.'

'Yes,' says Jenny, 'and one of those card games where you match the pictures for the matching panel!'

'Is that where you go to be approved,' asks Helen, 'the matching panel?'

'No, approval is the first panel,' says Jenny, 'we have to be approved to adopt and they will specify how many children and what age range we're approved for.'

'And then you get kids?' asks Jake.

Jenny shakes her head. 'No, then the matching starts. There's like huge databases of approved adopters and separate databases of the children needing parents and social workers have to try to match the right parents with the right kids.'

'Blimey, how do they know what's right?' asks Jake.

'Well, they just look at us and realise we're brilliant!' I say.

'Obviously,' say Jenny and Helen at once. They laugh.

'Seriously, though, I'm not a hundred percent sure as yet,' I say. I think it's things like matching our experience and skills to the needs of the kids, isn't it Jen?'

'And what football team they support,' she says. 'Heaven forbid Kyle gets asked to adopt an Arsenal fan.' She rolls her eyes and grins at me. 'And of course, they have to assess the kids' ability to tolerate bad jokes.'

We order some more nachos and dive into a game of Rapido but it doesn't last long. Helen starts to go as green as the play dough and rushes outside for some fresh air.

'Was it something I said?' I ask.

'No, it'll be the smell of the playdough,' says Jenny, getting up to go after her. 'At least I don't have to put up with morning sickness!'

Jake waits until Jenny has followed Helen outside then asks me how Jenny is.

'She's okay,' I say, 'she'll be glad when the medicals are done and dusted. She's convinced she's going to fail and the whole process will grind to a halt. No amount of reassurance from her specialist can reassure her.'

'I'm sure she'll be sound,' says Jake. 'How's she taking it with us being pregnant though?'

'Alright, I think,' I say, 'She's not said anything negative about it. I think she's focussing on getting the house sorted for the social worker to assess. If anything, she's intensified her sorting out. I'm worried if I stay on the sofa resting my knee too long, she'll take me to the tip along with my old CDs.'

Jenny and Helen return. Helen looks a bit less peaky now, thank goodness. Jake has moved the Rapido out of smelling distance. He grabs a pack of cards.

'Now,' he says, 'let's embrace this new stage of our lives!'

'What you got there?' I say,

'Happy Families,' he replies.

'Here's to Happy families,' I say, and we all raise our glasses.

A few days later, the meeting with Bazza comes around. He certainly lives up to his reputation.

'Jake, my man! Superlative to speak to you! I'm beyond flattered that you've thought of me to enhance your enterprise!'

Bazza hasn't calmed down at all since Helen worked for him. The opening of his email reads as if we've just written to tell him he's on the new year's honours list, not that we'd like him to invest on a board game we're trying to produce. He's also attached a photograph to the email of him beaming, surrounded by his staff, all holding what I can only assume is his latest big idea – Vegetable Easter eggs. Not, according to the link he's kindly put underneath the photo, easter eggs for vegans, no, actual vegetables, packaged in easter egg boxes and wrapped in foil. Surely they're all going to go off before Good Friday?

'It'd be great to have you on board,' Jake replied to him, copying me in, 'I've shown Helen the photos of your new 'Easter Veg' range and she says it makes her sad she's no longer part of the team.' According to Jake, that's not exactly what Helen said. She used to work in customer services for Bazza and spent most of her days giving refunds to understandably dissatisfied customers. I think she actually said something along the lines of 'Thank god I don't have to deal with all those returns, we'd have been eating rancid stew for weeks!' and then ran off to the bathroom to throw up.

Me and Jake arrange to meet Bazza at his office later on today. We don't mention to Helen that we're going into her old work. Her ex-friend Katie still works there. She's the one that was having an affair with Helen's ex-boyfriend Will behind her back. Katie and Will are apparently still engaged, though they don't seem to be anywhere close to setting a date. Hardly surprising really, seeing as Will isn't capable of committing to anything other than his dodgy covers band and his own ego.

Jake picks me up and we head into Bazza's. As the receptionist takes us through the customer services department to Bazza's office, Katie looks up. The expression on her face when she sees us is classic. Jake gives her a nod and a grin and I wave one of my crutches at her with a smile.

'That'll confuse her, killing her with kindness,' Jake says as we are shown into the boss's office, 'and she'll be desperate to know why we're here.'

'She probably thinks we've come to avenge Helen,' I chuckle.

'Gentlemen!' booms Bazza, arms open wide as if he's an ancient King greeting a triumphant returning army, 'Come, come, sit yourselves down!' He gestures towards my crutches, 'Good grief, has Jake here been fouling you at five-a-side?'

'No, just a disagreement with a mountain board,' I say, wincing as I position myself in one of the chairs. 'I thought I was in charge of the mountain board and let's just say, it disagreed.'

'Have a Vit-o-Fit!' says Bazza, holding out a tin half-full of sweets shaped like dumbbells. I look at them hesitantly and wrinkle up my nose. Jake takes one and sniffs it dubiously.

'What's in them?' I ask.

'Er, you know, all the good stuff,' says Bazza, 'a trace of vitamin C, gelatine, colouring...'

'And?' says Jake, 'I can't quite place the aroma.'

'Oh, don't worry about that,' says Bazza with a beam, 'Get it down ya, both of you, it'll heal that leg in no time! You're not allergic to pilchard are you?'

We shake our heads, exchange a glance and swallow the Vit-O-Fits as quickly as we can.

'Hmmm,' I say, 'do I detect a hint of Marmite in there?'

'Spot on!' says Bazza, 'full of goodness and vegetarian!'

As I'm pondering the vegetarian qualities of pilchard, the receptionist places a pot of tea on the table and we thank her and pour ourselves a cup. Surprisingly for Bazza, this seems to be normal tea, rather than some kind of novelty beverage but even so, it does little to take away the taste of the Vit-o-Fits.

'So, gentlemen, what can I do for you?' asks Bazza, 'Your email said you had an investment opportunity for me, some kind of board game you're inventing?'

'Yes,' Jake says, handing Bazza a file of sketches and plans for 'Last Orders.' He looks over them, a smile spreading across his face.

'Very interesting,' he says, 'I think you might be onto something here. May I suggest a name change?'

'Of course,' Jake says, glancing across at me. I nod in agreement, 'That's just a working title at the moment. What did you have in mind?'

'Oh,' says Bazza, getting up out of his chair and pacing grandly back and forth, for all the world as if he were the CEO of Apple about to announce the new iphone with personal robot attachment, 'how about "Bazza's Boozer"?'

Jake and I look at each other.

'Great idea,' Jake says, 'but let's not rush into anything, we have plenty of time to decide on the name later. What we need to think about is if we can go into partnership so that we can fund it being made and get beta test editions out there.'

'So, you're after my money not my monika, you'd say, boys?' he says. We've been demoted from 'gentlemen' to 'boys', not a good sign.

'I was thinking the landlord image could be based on yourself,' I say hastily.

'Yes, and a picture of the cartoon you on the box?' Jake adds.

Bazza perks up at this suggestion.

'Okay gentlemen, let's talk money,' he grins.

CHAPTER 16
– HELEN

After worrying about going, once I got into it, I really enjoyed the games night at the café and was ever so pleased when Jenny asked me to go shopping with her the following weekend. She wants to get some bits and pieces to do up the rooms for the children and some storage boxes to squirrel away all the stuff she and Kyle can't bear to get rid of that has to go in the loft.

We meet at the retail park outside B & Q. Now that I'm feeling queasy in the mornings, I have a taste of what Jenny has to put up with every day. I can't predict exactly what time I'll be able to meet because as soon as I think I'm ready, I get the urge to throw up again. Sometimes I can stave it off with some fresh air and a digestive, other times, there's no stopping it and then I have to clean my teeth all over again and if it's been really bad, change my clothes. Poor Jen has to go through similar daily with her physio – she can never tell how long it's going to take and she needs to clean her teeth afterwards and wash her face to feel fresh and ready to face the world. I think this is the first time she's arrived before me. I get out the car biting gingerly on a dry cracker and give her a hug. We go into the store and gaze up at all the signs hanging over the aisles.

'God, you need a map to find anything in here,' I say, 'it's massive!'

'I know!' says Jenny, 'Let's try this way, by the wallpaper.'

Sure enough, along with enough wallpaper to cover a small village full of houses are some pictures and transfers. I'm instantly drawn to Peter Rabbit.

'How about these?' I say to Jenny. She shakes her head.

'I'm not going for anything specific as yet,' she says, 'we don't know what age they'll be or if they will be girls or boys, or if they will like pink even if they are a girl or what they'll like at all really.' She holds one of the Peter Rabbit transfer packs out to me, 'You could get these though. You'll need to be thinking about turning your spare room into a nursery!'

'I don't like to jinx anything just yet,' I say quietly, stroking my stomach.

'Of course,' Jenny replies, giving my arm a squeeze. 'I guess we're in a similar boat there, in a weird way, here I am decorating two rooms and we have no idea if we'll get approved for two children, one child, or any at all.'

'What kind are you looking for?' I ask.

'I don't mind, as long as I can be a mummy to them,' Jenny says.

'Of course,' I say, 'and you'll be a brilliant one, but I actually meant the transfers...'

We both collapse in a fit of giggles. It's good to laugh together. I know Jenny is being great about my surprise pregnancy, but I still can't shake the guilty feeling that I've beaten her to it. I mean I get to start from the beginning with our baby whereas she and Kyle will be thrown into parenting two little people who will, by the sound of what Jen has told me, have experienced far worse trauma than someone decorating their room with the wrong stickers.

'I quite like these,' says Jenny, picking up a packet of transfers with smiley sunshines, fluffy clouds, rainbow-coloured umbrellas and stars and moons on them. 'Cheerful and bright, versatile and friendly looking,' she says.

'Hang on,' I say with a grin, 'I'll just write that down – it'd make a great description of you both for your reference!'

'And I suppose I can always get rid of them if they don't suit.' She looks at me, 'The transfers, I mean, not the kids.'

I don't know if I'm supposed to laugh or not.

'Come on Hels, loosen up,' says Jenny, 'we've got to have a bit of a giggle about it all or our minds will explode. You should see half the stuff these kids might have experienced before coming to us.'

I look serious again. I can feel tears threatening to come. My emotions are all over the place at the moment. I don't know whether it's hormones, the surprise baby or worrying about Jenny and Kyle.

'Still,' says Jenny, determined to be light-hearted, 'at least it'll make Kyle's terrible jokes and bad taste in TV programmes seem like a breeze!'

'How is Kyle?' I ask, 'Jake said he's not a huge fan of the forms.'

'He just needs to get on with them, really,' Jenny says, 'He writes massive reports at work. I don't know why he's got such a mental block over these.'

'I suppose you're more used to that kind of thing than him, though,' I say, 'you know, with all your youth work experience, he's not so used to all the self-analysis as you are.'

'True,' she says, 'he does tend to use sarcasm and football as a substitute for emotions at times.'

'He's a good egg, though, isn't he,' I say. Jenny is brilliantly strong and can achieve anything she sets her mind to, but she sometimes lacks patience for those who do things differently to her or at a slower pace. 'He'll get there Jen, don't worry.'

'I know,' she says, 'but I wish he'd hurry

up, I don't want the social workers thinking we're not keen if he turns up with half the prep stuff not filled in. If I took as long as he does, by the time I'd done all my physio and taken my meds in the morning, it'd be time to start my evening routines and we'd never get anywhere.'

'How about this?' I ask her, deciding I'd best change the subject. I hold up a clock with pictures of the sun and moon on it. 'It says here it helps the kids know when it's time to get up.'

'Let's go for it,' says Jenny. 'It's got an alarm setting too, I can set that to get Kyle to finish his forms on time!'

CHAPTER 17
– JENNY

Kyle's full of the meeting with Bazza when he returns. Helen's old boss is happy to back them financially so they can get some help with the design and get some prototypes produced and tested. There are a few strings attached, mainly to do with how heavily Bazza features in the design, but it seems they are negotiating things well. Apparently, they saw Katie whilst they were there.

'I don't know how you managed to smile at her, I'd have wanted to put her hand in the paper shredder the way she betrayed Helen!' I say as Kyle positions his leg on the sofa. 'Having an affair with Will behind her back whilst pretending to be her best friend! That rotten pair deserve each other!' I continue.

'You alright, Jen?' asks Kyle, 'you seem a bit wound up.'

'I'm fine,' I say, 'Katie just annoys me, you know? Why didn't you say anything to her?'

'Well, I didn't really think Helen would

want us having a good old catch up,' he says, getting out his board game notes and starting to pour over them. Again.

'Kyle!' I say, 'Can you put those down for five minutes! I need help with the top shelves of the cupboards in the kids', I mean *spare* rooms.'

'My leg's aching a bit,' he says, 'Don't worry, I'll do it later.'

I sigh. 'You've overdone it gadding about with Jake and that bloody board game!' I say. 'Did it not occur to you that I need your help here? I'm knackered doing everything myself. By the time the social worker gets here I'm going to look so wrecked, they won't give us a goldfish to look after, let alone two kids!'

'I just want to rest my leg for half an hour, Jen,' he says, 'I'll give you a hand with the cupboards before I make the tea. I'll still manage to feed us both and do all the washing up, no doubt, despite being on crutches!' He picks up the board game notes again.

'Don't you dare make out you're hard done by!' I hiss at him. I can feel the heat rising now. Is it stress or are my blood sugars a bit low? I grab my phone and scan the diabetes sensor on my arm. Sure enough they are dropping too low and it's not helping my mood. It's like being hangry to the power of ten. I stomp into the kitchen and grab some jelly babies. 'I do as much as I can here,' I say, shoving two of the sugary sweets into my mouth, 'Unlike your ligament, my CF won't heal in a few months. I'll still be proving myself every single day when your crutches are a distant memory!' I walk over to him, snatch the papers out of his hands and put them on the table. Then I grab his adoption forms out of the paper rack where he's stuffed them and thrust them onto his lap. 'If you're so exhausted you can't move, try filling these in at last! At the rate you're going, any toddlers we might get a chance at adopting will be leaving home for university by the time we get approved!'

'I'm doing the best that I can!' he shouts at me. 'It's a lot to deal with! Despite my leg - an inconvenience to you, I know, but not exactly a delight to me - I'm still working, looking after the house and you as much as I can, not to mention trying to work out how we're going to fit in looking after two traumatised kids as well!'

'Well, that's not going to be an issue if you don't fill the bloody forms in!' I yell.

'I'll do them tomorrow afternoon!' he says, manoeuvring himself off the sofa and going into the kitchen. He shuts the door and I can hear cupboard doors slamming. I slump down at the table and eat another couple of jelly babies. I hate feeling like a burden. I can't help it that I can't do as much around the house as other people do. But then again, just because I have less energy than others, that doesn't mean Kyle has been given superpowers, although I can't say it wouldn't be handy if he had. No wonder he's looking tired. As a tear rolls down my cheek, I take my blood sugars again. They're going back up again and I start to feel calmer, if a little bit wiped out. I'd go out to clear my head, but you're not allowed to drive for an hour after a hypo and it's no use me walking anywhere and my blood sugars dropping again with the exercise. Now the fast sugars are taking effect, I need to go and get myself some food with slow release carbs in so they don't drop again. But Kyle's in the kitchen and I don't feel like talking to him at the moment.

Just as I'm searching through my rucksack for snacks, the living room door opens. Kyle comes back in, limping without his crutches and carrying a plate of toast. He walks over, kisses me on the head and places the food in front of me.

'You get that down you,' he says, sitting on the chair next to me, 'and then perhaps you can help me nail these adoption forms.'

I wipe a tear away. 'We can't do them tomorrow afternoon,' I say.

'I know,' he says, 'I just looked at the calendar. 'It's tomorrow, isn't it. Sorry, it slipped my mind for a second.'

'How could you forget?' I ask, taking huge bites of the toast as the hypo hunger grips me. 'I've been counting down for ages.'

'I guess I just wanted to put it to the back of my mind, I suppose,' he says, 'a bit like these wretched forms. I'm sorry, I'm just worried I'm going to let you down. I don't know what to write to convince them that we can handle everything.'

'Kyle,' I say, wiping the crumbs off my top, 'You just hobbled out in the middle of a row and made me some toast to rebalance my blood sugars. I think we've got this. I'm sorry it's all so complicated with me.'

'I wouldn't have it any other way,' he says.

'Really?' I say, 'You wouldn't like it to be straightforward like it is for Helen and Jake?'

'No,' he says, 'because then I wouldn't have you.'

'Me, who you have to do so much for?' I say.

'You, who tackles more before breakfast than most people tackle in a day and still with a smile on your face,' he says. 'Besides, what better way to prove to the social workers that we are adaptable and resilient than by living the life that we do together?'

'True,' I say, 'I think parenthood might come as a bit of a shock to Jake and Helen, but we're well versed in things like eating and leaving the house being something that needs a bit of careful planning!'

'Exactly!' says Kyle, 'Preparation is your secret weapon! Now, let's use some of that to get my forms sorted. Then we'll sort that cupboard you mentioned, relax with a takeaway and a film and get an early night ready for tomorrow.'

Tomorrow. The day of my adoption medical. I rest my head on his shoulder as we hold each other.

***

The next morning, I remember what day it is the moment I wake. I get ready as quickly as I can, despite all my health routines meaning it takes an age compared to most people.

Sitting in the waiting room, my eyes flit from one poster on the walls to another. I don't even notice I'm jiggling my leg up and down until Kyle puts his hand on my knee to try to reassure me. This just results in me jiggling my leg and his arm up and down until we look like we're about to leap out of the plastic chairs and burst into a Diversity style hip hop routine.

'Don't worry, you'll be fine,' Kyle says. I try to smile at him, but someone has frozen my face muscles.

'Jenny Williams to Dr Abbot, please,' says a voice over the tannoy.

I grasp Kyle's hand and stand up. Then, realising he needs both arms for his crutches I release it again. We head off towards Dr Abbot's room.

'Good afternoon, Jennifer,' says Dr Abbot with a smile.

'Hello,' I say.

'Now, adoption medical,' says the Doctor. 'I remember you discussing this with me not so long ago. Excellent, how is everything going?'

'Okay,' I say, 'We've been to some information sessions and we're filling in some forms in preparation for the training and the home visits.' I look down. 'I just want to get my medical approved so that I can relax a bit.'

'Of course,' says Dr Abbot. She is a friendly woman and usually puts me at ease. Today, however, I'm not sure anything could.

Dr Abbot goes through the questions and procedures needed. It's a lot quicker and easier than we'd both imagined. I think I was expecting to be put through a kind of army style assault course, but it's just standard, unobtrusive tests like taking your blood pressure and some fairly run of the mill questions about our lifestyle. As neither of us are huge drinkers and we don't smoke, we seem to tick the right boxes there. We discuss family history for hereditary diseases.

'Well,' I say, 'ironically, there aren't really any illnesses as such other than the one that is leading me to adopt so that I don't pass my genes on.'

'And does no one in your family have cystic fibrosis other than you?' asks Dr Abbot. I shake my head.

'No,' I say, 'Just carriers. I guess I hit the jackpot.'

'There we go, then,' says Dr Abbot after a few more questions about diet and exercise. 'I'll send all this off to your adoption agency, they will look at my report and the one from your specialist and you should hear their decision shortly.'

'Is that it?' I ask.

'Well, you've still got to go through the full adoption assessment, but that's all I have to do for your medical, yes. Kyle, yours is next, would you like Jenny to leave or stay?'

Kyle replies that he's happy for me to stay and he gets taken through more or less the same questions as me. They discuss his leg and Dr Abbot confirms that she has received the reports from the hospital and physio.

When it's all finished, we thank Dr Abbot and go out into the sunshine.

'Well, how do you feel now that's done?' Kyle asks. I wince.

'I can't really relax until I hear what the agency say,' I say. 'But I suppose it's like doing your GCSEs, I can't do much more about it now until we get the verdict.'

'Let's take our minds off it, shall we?' Kyle says, 'What would you like to do now?'

'I think,' I say, 'after all that talk of healthy eating, I'd like to go to the pub and have as chocolatey a pudding as my insulin can handle!'

'Consider it done,' says Kyle, 'the unhealthy food is on me.'

CHAPTER 18
– HELEN

Now we've had the 12-week scan and everything is going to plan, I can't put off telling my parents any longer. Don't get me wrong, I want to tell them and I know they're going to be over the moon, but I am worried that telling this amazing news to my mum and dad is going to be hard for Jake as it will highlight the absence of his.

We arrange to go round for Sunday lunch. It's a good job I'm eating for two as my mum has, as usual, cooked enough food to feed her whole street. I wonder if she thinks we don't eat properly or something. But I've only just sat at the table when she comes out with one of her five-star lines.

'Len,' she says to my dad, her eyes resting on my stomach, 'can you see if we've got any of that half-fat cream in for the gateau, instead of the full cream stuff?'

Jake squeezes my hand. 'Lovely spread you've done for us, Mary,' he says, 'I hope you haven't been toiling over a hot stove all day on our behalf.'

'It's an absolute pleasure, my dear,' my mum beams at him, then calls into the kitchen where my dad is clattering about and muttering something about 'diet cream', 'On second thoughts, Len, keep the full cream out as well, Jake needs feeding up. Helen, the poor lad is wasting away! I hope you're not feeding him salads and sandwiches all the time!'

'Not at all, Mary,' says Jake, seeing my face, 'Helen looks after me very well indeed.' Dad comes back into the room and Jake continues, 'In fact, now that Len is back with, I see, *four* kinds of cream, we have something exciting to tell you about Helen's nurturing abilities.'

My mum's eyes sparkle. My dad looks mystified. Jake gives me an encouraging smile.

'Mum, Dad, we're having a baby,' I say.

'I knew it!' cries my mum in delight, 'We're going to be grandparents, Len! You know what this means!'

'That Helen's pregnant?' says my dad, looking proud but still a bit confused. I'm not sure he's ever really accepted that I'm not a little girl anymore, so I suppose the concept of his little girl having a little one of her own is something he'll need time to adjust to.

'Obviously, Len, how else would they be having a baby?' mum says, rolling her eyes.

'Well, actually,' I say, 'Jenny and Kyle are going through the adoption process at the moment and so there are many different ways of having children these days.'

'Yes,' says my dad, 'George from the post office's son is married to a man and they've just had a baby using a suffragette.'

'A suffragette?' says mum, 'one of those women's rights campaigners?' Dad frowns but Jake comes to the rescue.

'I think you mean surrogate, Len,' he says, 'The two words are easily confused and besides, being a surrogate is probably quite a feminist thing to do if you think about it, so not far removed from the suffragettes really.'

Dad nods and says, 'Is there anything you need? A cot? A pram? Just let us know if you need a hand with anything.'

'Thanks, Dad,' I say and go over and give him a hug. Mum joins in and so does Jake until we all look like we're in some kind of rugby huddle. Mum breaks away first.

'Well, we'd best eat this dinner before it gets cold,' she says, 'Can't have you wasting away now you're expecting! Len, I told you I should have made two gateaux – they will both need extra helpings!'

As we eat, mum reels off a bewildering list of 'essentials' we'll need for the baby that she's just found on an american 'Mom' site. These include a 'diaper genie', a changing table and a highchair. It all sounds like something from a fantasy novel to me - What is the genie going to change the table into and why does the chair need to be high? Babies are quite small – how do they reach it?

'What did you mean earlier, Mary?' asks my dad, 'when you said, "you know what this means?". You had that look in your eye.'

'Oh, you know,' mum says, 'I'll be able to enter the glamourous granny competition when we all go on family holidays together.' I'm sure I can see the colour draining from Jake's face.

'I'm not certain we're thinking of holidays just yet, mum,' I say.

'Of course you are,' mum continues, undeterred, 'and we'll need to book early if we want a caravan big enough to take us all!'

'All of us in the same caravan?' says Jake, 'oh, we couldn't do that... to you, the baby might disturb your beauty sleep and we don't want the other holiday makers stealing your glamourous grandma crown!'

'Well, okay then, the caravan next door,' concedes mum. 'You'll need us for the baby sitting!'

'So, how are Jenny and Kyle getting on with the adoption lark, then?' asks dad. 'Will they be having their baby the same time as you do?'

'Ooh, how lovely!' says mum, 'You'll be able to go to bouncy baby gym time together and little squirrels!'

Mum is certainly well versed on baby

things. She must have been on to me when I stayed off alcohol the last time we saw them. Or I've been showing more than I'd realised. I thought my baggy jumpers had done the trick.

'Jenny and Kyle are hoping to adopt a pair of siblings,' I say, 'and they most likely will be toddlers or infant school age.'

'Don't they want a baby, then?' asks my dad.

'Well, it's not so much that they don't want one, I think,' I say, 'just that there aren't actually that many babies needing adopting but there are a lot of slightly older children who desperately need a new mum and dad.'

'Why are people giving these children up?' asks dad.

'Where are all the babies going?' asks mum. I look at Jake. My hormones are making me emotional and I'm not sure I can bear to go into the realities of the reasons a lot of children are in care and how old they often are by the time they're removed from their unsuitable birth homes.

'It's complicated,' Jake says. 'It's often the case that the children have been taken into care because they haven't been looked after properly, going hungry, neglected, or... worse.'

Mum and dad look horrified.

'Right,' says mum, getting her tablet out and putting her reading glasses on, 'we'd best order you some of the things off my list, we don't want anyone thinking you're neglecting my grandchild!'

'And I'll get the gateaux out,' says dad, 'got to feed you both up!'

I decide it's no use fighting and besides, squeezing Jake's hand, I realise again how lucky I am to have my parents here, fussing over me like this. Even if I have no idea where I'm going to put a changing table and a diaper genie.

CHAPTER 19
– JAKE

After we've finished eating, Helen's dad takes me out to his shed.

'Now Jake,' he says, 'I know your dad and mum aren't with us, with your dad being on the other side of the world and your mum, sadly... well...' he reaches out awkwardly and squeezes my arm, 'but I want you to know that Mary and me are here for you and Helen, whatever you need, just come and ask.'

'Thank you,' I say, 'that means a lot to us.'

'Well,' says Len, clapping his hands together and looking round the shed frantically for something else to talk about, 'best get these potatoes planted now we'll have another mouth to feed. Pass me that old recycling box, will you?'

I'm not sure the baby will be ready for Len and Mary's mash for a good while yet, but as he works away, I spend a good half hour passing Len various bits and pieces, feeling like I'm on the amateur veg grower version of ER. Once that job is done, we go back indoors where Mary immediately puts on the kettle and tries to get us to eat some more cake. She and Helen have been looking at the old baby albums and I enjoy the opportunity to gently tease about the hair styles and multi-coloured baby clothes.

When I pop up to the bathroom later, I hear footsteps on the stairs as I'm drying my hands. I open the door to see Helen walking into her old room. I go up to her and ask if she's okay.

'Yes,' she says, gazing at the shelves still half full of her childhood books and dolls, 'just seems a bit strange that I'm going to be a mum. I mean, a mum is, well, like my mum, fussy and funny and coming out with all sorts of mad stuff, and I'm…'

'… Ticking all the boxes, I'd say!' I grin. She gives me a playful shove.

'Cheeky,' she says, laughing. Then her face turns serious again, 'No, but how am I going to know what to do?' she says, 'It seems five minutes ago since I used to sleep in this room, dropping off staring at my posters and dreaming of marrying a heart throb and being in a girl band! And now I have to be all mature and nurture a new tiny human and keep them happy and well fed. What do children even eat?'

'Food?' I say, putting my arms around her. 'Potatoes, if your Dad has his way and lots of them if your mum does.' I give Helen a gentle squeeze. 'Don't worry, we'll work it out and I'm sure your mum and dad will be on hand to answer any questions we have. Not necessarily in a logical way, but you turned out alright so they can't have done that bad a job!'

Helen hugs me back. We go back downstairs to see her dad setting up a game of monopoly on the table. He looks at me hopefully.

'Quick game, anyone?' he says.

'I'm in,' I reply, 'but first, I'd love to get your take on an idea for a board game that me and Kyle are working on. It's called "Last Orders" and is set in a pub.'

'Sounds good,' says Len, 'tell me more.'

I pull up a seat and show him the design ideas on my phone. Helen and her mum go off into the kitchen. Undoubtedly Mary feels it's been too long since the last cup of tea so I loosen my belt a little in anticipation of the accompanying biscuits.

Several cups of tea and biscuits later, it's time for us to leave which is a good job as I don't think my waistband could take much more. At this rate, I'm going to have to borrow some of Helen's maternity trousers for our next visit. We hug our goodbyes and load the car with wool, knitting needles, catalogues and a ridiculous amount of tuppaware that Mary has spirited out of nowhere and thrust upon us for our 'nesting'.

When we get home Helen asks me if I'm alright.

'Yes,' I say, 'why wouldn't I be, spending a lovely afternoon with my wonderful fiancée, our baby to be and my nearly in-laws?'

'Just, you know,' she says, nestling into my arms, 'I feel sad I didn't get to meet your mum so I can only imagine how you must feel.' Her eyes start to fill with tears.

'Hey, now, it's okay,' I say, wiping her face dry, 'You look shattered, why don't you go and take a nap whilst I find somewhere to put all the nesting paraphernalia.'

Helen looks at me for a second, then nods her head, gives a little yawn and goes upstairs. Whilst she rests, I sit down and get out my board game file again. I stare at the pages, but can't focus. Instead, I scroll through the photos on my phone of my mum. She's laughing and smiling in nearly every single one. I gaze at one where she is beaming at the camera, with one of my cousin's children on her lap. She doesn't even seem to care that there is ice cream down her top and in her hair. She would have been over the moon to be a grandma. And she'd have known what to say to all the parenting questions Helen has that I'm pretending to know the answer to. I reach into my pocket and take out mum's wedding ring. I slip it on my little finger and open up Facebook and type in my dad's name. We're Facebook friends, whatever that means, but we haven't been in touch for ages. I hover over the messenger icon then change my mind and shove my phone under a cushion.

I grab the board game papers again and

start scribbling down question ideas for the pub quiz trivia section. I don't know what to do about the distinct lack of Freeman Grandparents but I do know a lot about capital cities and football stats and right now, that's going to have to do.

CHAPTER 20
– JENNY

We've hoovered, dusted and tidied the house to within an inch of its life. It's as if we're expecting the TV crew from that show where the B&B owners visit each other's places and complain because they found a speck of dust in a locked box under the towels in the back of the airing cupboard. Part of me wishes it was one of those TV crews instead of our social worker coming to do his first home visit.

I've told Kyle to rest his leg today so that he's looking as fit as possible when the social worker arrives. The doorbell rings and kyle winces as he manoeuvres himself off the sofa.

'No, no, don't wince!' I say, 'I'll get it, you do some warm-up exercises or something. You've been sitting too still and it'll have seized up!'

'But you told me not to move!' he says. The doorbell rings again.

'Oh god, he'll think we've changed our minds!' Jenny says, frozen to the spot. 'What do we do?'

'Opening the door will be a good start,' Kyle says, striding as confidently as he can manage to the front door. I follow him and we put on our best smiles.

'Jenny and Kyle Williams?' says the man at the door on crutches. We nod. He holds up an ID card. 'Mike Cartwright,' he says, 'Nurturing Families Social Worker.'

We show Mike to the living room where he props his crutches next to Kyle's and Kyle goes to make us some drinks. I perch on the edge of the sofa opposite Mike, smiling. I can hear the cupboards opening and closing in the kitchen. Kyle pops his head round the door.

'Do you take sugar, Mike?' he asks. 'We don't, obviously, Jenny's diabetes...'

I glare at him. Why is he bringing up my health problems before we've even started. I see Mike looking at me, the corners of his mouth twitching.

'Er, I mean, it's not good for anyone, is it, extra sugar,' says Kyle. 'We have herbal tea if you'd prefer?'

'Tea, strong, two sugars, thanks,' says Mike, smiling, 'and don't worry Jenny, you having health issues needn't be a problem, it's how you'll handle them whilst parenting that I'm here to help you with.'

'She handles everything brilliantly,' says Kyle.

'I'm sure she does,' says Mike with a smile, 'and we have plenty of time to find all that out over the coming weeks and months and present your situation to the panel. I'm not here to catch you out, folks, I'm on your side. I'm on the children's side too. And my absolute wish is that we can form a happy new family here, whilst ensuring that everyone's needs are being met.'

'Thank you,' I say.

'And talking of needs,' says Mike, 'If you have any biscuits to go with that tea, I'm sure it'll gain you a few brownie points.'

Mike winks at us as he says this. I know he's joking, but all the same, I do hope Kyle uses the good biscuits.

I excuse myself and go into the kitchen to help Kyle with the drinks tray. He can manage without his crutches some of the time now, but the last thing we want is his knee giving way and him covering Mike in hot tea and M&S digestives. Once we're all back in the living room, Mike takes a slurp of his tea and gets out his folder. He looks over at Kyle's crutches in the corner of the room.

'Ah, yes, they told me we were peas in a pod,' he says. 'Was yours a skiing accident too?'

'Not quite,' says Kyle, 'Mountain boarding with a mate. Stupid idea. I don't usually go around taking risks like that.'

'I do,' says Mike, smiling, 'I go skiing on the dry slopes by us as often as I can. Just didn't count on the actual snow-covered ones being a bit trickier to negotiate.'

'Oh, he didn't mean you were taking silly risks, did you Kyle?' I say.

'Not at all,' says Kyle, 'How's your physio going?'

'Pretty good now, thanks,' says Mike, 'and yours?'

'Great, yes,' says Kyle, 'should be up and about pretty normally by the time we are at the stage of having kids, you know, if you all say yes, that is.'

'We don't want to assume,' I say, 'but we are very keen and I think you'll agree we have a lot of experience. I've been a youth worker for most of my working life, dealing with kids from all sorts of backgrounds with all sorts of needs.'

'Yes, your applications are very impressive,' says Mike. I smile. 'But let's not get ahead of ourselves, today is really about getting to know each other a bit, me telling you what is going to happen over the next few months and hopefully putting your mind at rest.'

Mike goes over the topics we will be discussing over the assessment visits. We'll be talking about our families and friends, support networks, our own childhoods, our careers and how we will be fitting children into our working weeks. Then of course, there's discussions on our health and how I will continue to manage my conditions whilst also looking after two children who have experienced trauma. We'll also be covering parenting, family lifestyles, specific needs of adopted children and many more things which are whirling round my overfull mind.

We're having to book time off work to attend these sessions and I'm so pleased that we are finally getting down to business. But despite handing in my annual leave request last week, it doesn't feel like much of a holiday. But at least Mike seems like a decent person and, as he says, he's certainly on our side and rooting for us to be approved by the panel. I think he liked us. He certainly liked the biscuits and between us we got through a whole packet. I hope it wasn't a secret test on healthy eating and self-discipline.

After he's finished, our heads are spinning with all the things we're going to be covering with him and the group training sessions over the coming months. We both wave him goodbye, with cheery enthusiastic looks on our faces. The second he's out of sight, we flop onto the sofa and stare into space.

'What do you want to do now?' Kyle asks.

'Er...' I say, staring into space a bit more, 'perhaps we should get on with clearing out the bedrooms?'

'I was going to suggest the pub,' Kyle says hopefully.

'We really should get things sorted,' I say, grabbing my notebook.

'Jen, over the next few months, we're not only going to turn our home into a haven for two children, we're also going to answer questions about every experience we've ever had and be asked to predict how we will cope with situations we can only imagine. I think we can give ourselves a couple of hours off now and go to the pub,' he says.

I flick through my notebook. Then rub my eyes.

'I am a bit drained,' I say, 'Okay, let's go to the Oak and have tea there as well. I don't feel like cooking or washing up.'

I can tell by the look on Kyle's face that he's about to joke that there's nothing new about that but fortunately, he thinks better of it. After the last two hours I'm even more hyper aware of my health conditions than normal. He grabs his wallet, keys and phone, whilst I load my rucksack up with insulin, snacks and anti-bac gel and we head out to the pub.

'Shall we ask Jake and Helen if they want to join us?' he asks as I park the car. 'No worries if you'd rather it be just us, though.' I think about it for a moment. He looks worried he's said the wrong thing so I give him a big smile.

'Yeah, good idea,' I say, 'It'll bring us out of ourselves a bit and we can have a bit of a laugh, hopefully after all that heavy stuff.'

I whatsapp our group and Helen replies just as we're sitting down.

'They'll be with us in quarter of an hour,' I say.

Sure enough, fifteen minutes later, Jake and Helen come through the pub door. Me and Helen hug and we all settle down, ordering food and drink.

'How did the social worker session go?' asks Jake.

'Not bad,' Kyle replies, 'bit exhausting thinking about it all, but he seems a nice bloke.'

'Did he say anything about your medical?' says Helen, giving my hand a squeeze.

'No, no news on that yet,' I say, 'They have to get the adoption agency's medical adviser to look over the reports from our doctors and my specialist and then they'll let us know.'

'You'll be grand, Jen,' says Jake. 'Now, who's for another drink?'

We all accept and Jake goes to the bar. Kyle goes up with him, managing the short distance without his crutches.

'How's everything going with you?' I say to Helen. She looks a bit tired.

'It's good,' she says, 'We've told my mum and dad now.'

'I bet they're excited,' I say.

'Yes, very,' she says, 'but I feel a bit for Jake, not having his here.'

'Your folks are good with him though,' I say, 'They'll be there for you both.'

'Oh yes, my parents are full on enough for both of us,' Helen giggles, 'but he must feel it, even though he says he doesn't.'

Jake and Kyle return from the bar, laden with drinks. Just as they sit down, the food arrives and I rummage in my rucksack for my insulin and tablets.

'Extra insulin, I reckon,' I say with a glint in my eye, 'I've just seen the pudding menu!'

As we're finishing off our food, the barman comes over to ask if we'd like to join the pub quiz. We all decide we're up for it. The first round is pictures which results in the usual discussions.

'It's her, from that thing, you know, the one in the village with the retired policeman who finds the body in the lake and has to arrest his own son,' says Helen.

'No,' says Jake, 'It's her from the thing by the coast with the grumpy policeman who gets arrested when they find the body in a beach hut.'

'I think it's Angela Merkel,' says Kyle.

'No,' I reply, squinting at the photo and turning the paper upside down, 'It's Nicola Sturgeon in a bad light.'

Luckily, we do somewhat better on the music round and Jake and Kyle ace the football anagrams. We end up tying for first place with 'Quiz Team and the Queens' and everyone nominates me to answer the tie break question. I make my way nervously to the bar.

I smile at Fred, the captain of the Queens and he nods back. Brian the quizmaster does a drum roll on the corner of the bar, nearly knocking Fred's pint over in the process.

'What is the name of the film starring Mark Wahlberg and Rose Byrne about a couple adopting a family of three children?'

I know this. Kyle and me watched it the other day. It's on the tip of my tongue. I look at Fred. He doesn't look too sure. I look over at our table. Kyle's eyes are sparkling, willing me to get the right answer. Jake gives me a big thumbs up in encouragement. Helen shifts in her seat, trying to get comfortable. Her bump is already starting to show. Before we know it, there will be a little baby in our group. And hopefully two little friends for it to play with if we get approved. Suddenly the answer comes to me.

'Instant Family,' I say.

CHAPTER 21
– HELEN

The prize pot was quite good for the quiz, so I have some spare cash in my pocket when I meet my mum in town the following weekend. She wants to take me shopping for maternity clothes. I'm four months pregnant now and quite happy wearing comfy leggings and big hoodies at the moment but I expect she'll want to buy me a t-shirt with the words 'Grandma's first grandchild' emblazoned across it with a huge arrow pointing to my bump.

We meet in the maternity department of Next. There are adorable baby clothes in here but I'm trying to resist buying anything until a bit closer to the time when we know everything is most likely okay. I spot mum as I walk in. She's caressing a stripey red and white maternity dress as if she's a stable hand stroking a horse. It's not exactly my style as I wasn't planning on going for circus-tent chic. I'm half sure that if I unzipped it, a couple of elephants and a trapeze artist would appear. I greet mum with a hug and steer her gently to the leggings and long shirts.

'Look mum,' I say, 'these have got little daisies on them.'

She smiles, takes the maternity leggings off me and pops them in her shopping basket.

'Oh, no, I'm not sure whether to get them,' I say, turning over the price label and taking a sharp breath in, 'they're quite expensive.'

'Nonsense!' says mum, 'Only the best for my daughter!' She reaches out and pats me gently on the stomach, 'and my grandchild! Don't you worry, Me and dad are paying for you to have some nice outfits to wear whilst you're expecting.'

'Oh, mum,' I say, tears welling up in my eyes, 'that's really kind of you, but you don't have to.' I don't know why I'm crying at some clothes. But then again, I cry at jingles on the radio these days.

'I know I don't have to, but I want to,' she says. 'Now come on, silly, there's no need to cry! Let's find you a nice pair of maternity socks.'

'Maternity *socks?*' I say, 'My feet aren't pregnant!'

'No, but you'll thank me once you get swollen ankles,' she says, leading me to the underwear and holding up some pants which look as if they might double up as a baby sling once I've given birth. She throws a couple of pairs in her basket and starts rifling through the socks. 'They've got looser tops, you see – they're also good for people with diabetes - your Jenny probably wears them.'

I feel a twinge of guilt at the mention of Jenny. Partly because it has never occurred to me that she might have to wear special socks and partly because I still feel bad about the rather less complicated route Jake and I seem to have taken to parenting. I pop an extra set of socks in the basket and tell mum I'm buying them for Jenny as a present.

After about half an hour, we seem to have filled her basket with half the contents of Next and mum has handed over most of her savings to the sales assistant.

'Where next?' she says, 'Café?'

I nod enthusiastically. I'm feeling a bit overwhelmed with all the maternity clothing she's bought me. It feels more real with each oversized shirt, voluminous tunic top and brightly coloured pair of dungarees. Besides, if mum is right, I'd best take the weight off my ankles before they start ballooning and burst out of my boots. We settle down in the Costa that forms part of the Next store and take a sip of our drinks. Mum slides a slice of her shortbread towards me.

'Go on,' she says, 'you're eating for two.'

For once, I decide not to argue with her and bite into the sugary shortbread. Mum starts buttering her toasted teacake.

'So,' she says, placing the knife back on her

plate, 'I suppose you and Jake will be bringing the wedding forward now. Not that you've actually set a date.'

My sip of hot chocolate goes down the wrong way and I cough into my serviette. Once I've composed myself, mum continues.

'Well, now you're going to be parents, you'll want to have everything above board, won't you?' she says, her now thickly-buttered teacake remaining untouched on her plate.

'Eat up, mum,' I say, 'it'll get cold.'

She takes a bite but rifles in her bag with her free hand and passes me a leaflet from a local hotel, detailing their wedding packages.

'Mum,' I say, 'Jake only proposed at Christmas. We're not in any rush. Besides, we haven't got money to be spending on a wedding now. We need to focus our finances on the baby. Neither of us earn that much and I'm not sure yet how long I'll want to take off when the baby is born.'

'Well, it doesn't have to cost the earth,' she says, taking the leaflet back and placing it carefully in her bag, where I'm sure I spot another bunch of similar flyers, 'but you'll want the baby to have Jake's surname and therefore, you'll need to have Jake's surname as well.'

'Not necessarily,' I say. 'We could combine surnames.'

'But our surname is already double-barrelled,' mum points out, 'If you add Jake's name to the end of yours, you'll be Helen Weston-Smith-Freeman. You'll never be able to embroider that onto the poor child's pump bag.'

I'm not sure I could even embroider initials onto school bags, especially not if we land the child with that many.

'You have a point,' I say, 'but Jake might take my name, or we could ship our names.'

'Ship?' says mum, 'What have boats got to do with anything?'

'It's where you take part of your name and combine it with your partner's,' I say, trying to think of some celebrities she'd know, 'You know, like when Brad and Angelina became "Brangelina."'

'You can't give the baby a surname that sounds like a brand of window cleaner!' mum says, looking alarmed.

'No, well our baby wouldn't be "Brangelina" though, would it? We could merge our surnames into something like "Westman" or "Freesmith."'

'But "Freesmith" sounds like a campaign to release someone falsely accused of murder!' says mum, the horrified look increasing.

'Don't worry mum, I think you're getting ahead of yourself, we have plenty of time to get married after the baby is born,' I say, glancing down at the large bag of clothing she's brought. My eyes rest on the pack of babygros she manged to sneak past me. 'And just think of the cute little outfits the baby could wear to the wedding,' I try. But it doesn't work.

'You won't have a minute once they're born,' she says, wiping her hands on a serviette, 'You'll end up still not married when you're waving them off to university!'

I take a steadying bite of shortbread. I haven't even got my head round having a baby yet and now I'm welling up at the thought of them leaving home. Mum must notice I'm looking flustered as she changes tack.

'Don't worry, love, me and dad can help with the wedding costs,' she says.

'But I don't want to take loads of your money, you should be saving it, not spending it on me,' I say.

'Well, it doesn't even have to cost much,' she says. 'Barbara's daughter got married in the scout hut. The girl guides made her origami table favours from old copies of the *Woman's Weekly* and they stayed in a youth hostel on their honeymoon.'

Hopefully not with all of the girl guides, I think to myself. My mum continues to have access to a world of information that I've never heard of. Did I miss a class at school where they taught us about changing tables, wedding favours and how to negotiate massive ankles in pregnancy?

'Look, mum,' I say, 'I don't want to honeymoon in a youth hostel, but I suppose Jake and me should at least discuss when we're going to get married.' Mum starts to smile. 'Don't get overexcited,' I continue, 'I'm not saying we're going to do it right away, it might be a few years down the line yet, but I'll talk to him tonight.'

'That's wonderful, love,' she says, beaming, 'and no pressure from me.'

'Thank you,' I say, feeling my shoulders relax a little. 'Where would you like to go now?'

'Let's go to Marks and Spencers,' she says, 'I've seen a lovely maternity frock in there that would pass for a wedding dress in a good light.'

CHAPTER 22
– JAKE

Whilst Helen is shopping with her mum, I get a bit of work done on the board game. I meet Kyle in the pub and we go over what we've got already. It's coming along nicely. Kyle has been looking into local shops that might stock it and online options for selling it. I've found an indie games competition we can enter it into. It only has to be in the planning stages to enter and the finalists get to go to an event in a posh hotel which is under an hour's drive away. Plus, if you win, your game gets made and promoted with the help of the competition organisers who are big names in the board game industry.

'It's definitely worth a go,' says Kyle, looking over the details of the competition.

'Yeah, I think so,' I reply. 'and it'd be a good night out for us all if we get through to the finals.'

'Yeah, and a chance of getting our game made without us and Bazza having to bear all the financial burden,' says Kyle, 'Plus a free night out would be a bonus at the moment with all the extra mouths to feed popping into our lives soon!'

'How's it going with your social worker?' I ask.

'Not bad,' he says, 'there's a lot of questions to answer.'

'What, like about bringing up kids and stuff?' I say, looking at our board game cards, 'Like a kind of quiz?'

'Not really,' says Kyle, 'though there will be a bit of that, I suppose, asking us what we would do in certain situations, but more so questions about our lives, our childhoods, our past relationships...'

'What, your exes?' I say, 'What have they got to do with it?'

'I think it's just checking that you know how to form functional relationships,' he says, 'I haven't got any dark secrets, so that's not a problem. Jenny's got a few exes but nothing awful there either.'

'So, they haven't unearthed a secret family of triplets in the Cotswolds then?' I say before kicking myself. 'Sorry mate, I didn't mean to be insensitive.'

'Don't be daft,' says Kyle, 'I might have lost half my annual leave to the assessment meetings and training days but I haven't lost my sense of humour. Good job, really, I think I'm going to need it if we get two kids.'

'Two at once, eh?' I say, raising my pint to

him, 'I salute you, mate.'

'Thanks,' says Kyle, raising his glass as well, 'Going from zero to one kid is quite a leap but zero to two... well, in for a penny, in for a pound, and like Jenny says, it's better to adopt two at once and keep some siblings together. Plus, this way, we only have to go through the panels and everything once.'

'You'd have to do it all over again, then, if you adopted them one at a time?' I say.

'Yeah, they have to assess how you're coping and how the first child would cope with the addition of a new one and if they'd get along and if we'd cope with the change.'

'But no one will do that with me and Helen if we decide to have another one in a few years,' I say, 'Doesn't seem fair that you two are jumping through hoops to do what me and Helen have quite literally done without thinking about it.'

'True,' says Kyle, 'but they've got to make sure the kids are going to be looked after properly. They'll have already gone through a hell of a lot before landing themselves with yours truly as a dad.' He takes another sip of his pint. 'But don't worry, Jake, you two will be great parents, it's the people who churn them out one after the other without bothering to look up from their phones that rile me.'

I'm just thinking what to say when my phone beeps. It's a message from Helen: *Worn out from shopping with mum. Are you still in the pub? I could join you for a drink.*

Sure, we're in the Anchor I message back, *I'll get you a double orange juice.*

I tell Kyle that Helen is going to be joining us and he messages Jenny to see if she's free. She's been working on a youth parliament session but has just finished and says she'll join us. In about ten minutes Helen arrives, looking exhausted. I get her settled onto one of the more comfy chairs the Anchor has to offer and she sips gratefully at her orange juice and rips open the bag of smokey bacon crisps I got her.

Jenny arrives a few minutes after Helen, grabs a diet coke from the bar and comes to join us. She looks at Helen, concerned.

'You look wiped out, you okay?' she asks.

'Yeah,' Helen replies, 'fine, just been shopping with mum. She's bought me a bewildering amount of maternity clothes, including a bump covering dress she has heavily implied she'd like to see me get married in within the next few months.' She looks at me as I swallow my pint the wrong way and start to cough. Kyle wallops me on the back. 'Don't worry,' Helen continues with a smile, 'I told her we weren't planning on setting a date in the near future. We've got other priorities at the moment. We can't go spending money on hotels and wedding stuff.'

'It doesn't have to cost that much, you

know,' says Jenny, her eyes sparkling, 'I'm not saying you have to, but just that if you did want to get married soon, I've got a friend at work who had her wedding in one of the village halls and it didn't cost much more than a tea party. And we could make some of the food, couldn't we Ky?'

'Yeah,' Kyle says, 'I could make the sandwiches and stuff and Jen is a whizz at baking – as long as her blood sugars are okay when she does it, otherwise she eats all the chocolate before it gets a chance to go in the cakes.'

'We'd still need a place to do it in, though,' Helen says, 'and anyway, I'm not pressuring you into it Jake, it's just mum going on. She made me promise I'd mention it to you so I said I would and then I can report back to her that we're going to wait until after the baby and then she should get off my back.'

I think for a moment. My boss at the board game café has just started a plan to hire out the café for parties and things. He was asking the other day if anyone wanted it at cut price rates for a trial run. He was even going to throw in some drinks at trade prices. I get off my chair and kneel at Helen's feet, by the mountain of shopping bags. Jenny gasps and her face lights up as she watches Helen to see her reaction.

'Jake,' Helen giggles, 'what are you doing? You've already proposed at Christmas and besides, that floor's filthy!'

'Helen,' I say, 'will you marry me, in the

144

next few weeks or so, in a dress your mum has just brought you, in the board game café, so that you can make an honest man of me, ready for BWSF?'

'BWSF?' grins Kyle, 'I don't think you should be taking up wrestling in your condition, Helen!'

'Baby Weston-Smith-Freeman,' I say, 'What do you say, Mrs WSF?'

'I say we need to decide on a shorter surname,' says Helen, 'but other than that, it sounds perfect!'

CHAPTER 23
– JENNY

We're getting used to our visits from Mike now and over the weeks he's been visiting us, he seems to be getting used to us. But even so, he looks slightly surprised when he arrives this time to see a massive inflatable unicorn in the hall, wearing a bridal veil.

'Don't worry!' I say as I help him manoeuvre round it on his crutches, 'it's not ours - our friends are getting married.'

We go into the living room and I manage to find him a seat amongst the hen night sashes, baskets of sweets tied up in pink netting and a large box of bubbles with 'just married' written on them.

'Looks like you're busy!' he says.

'Yes, but we're not too busy to focus on adoption,' I say. 'Always ready, Mike, that's us!'

'I'm in no doubt,' Mike says, wincing then pulling a now-broken plastic fairy wand from underneath him and placing it with the others on the coffee table.

'So sorry,' says Kyle, 'that's mine. I wondered where it had gone.'

Mike smiles and opens his folder. 'Well folks,' he says, 'today we were going to plan your family books.'

I whip out a couple of brightly coloured folders with plastic pockets in and plonk several pieces of pastel coloured card on the coffee table. Mike mentioned in our first session that we have to make a kind of scrap book for the children to prepare them for living with us. Whilst it seems a bit bizarre doing this when we don't even know if we're going to be approved to have any children, it doubles, I suspect, as an exercise for us in getting used to thinking of ourselves as parents and our home as a family home. That's the advantage and disadvantage of having a background in youth work – every time we're asked a question by Mike or we have to take part in an activity at the training days, I can imagine the way the workers are analysing our responses.

'Brilliant,' says Mike, a smile pulling at the ends of his mouth, 'I see you're prepared as always, Jenny. Top marks!'

'So,' says Kyle, 'What sort of photos do you want us to stick in the books? Do I need to get a better haircut?'

Mike smiles at Kyle's joke as he replies, 'Pictures of yourselves, pictures of the children's bedrooms, your garden, stuff like that.'

I'm so relieved Mike gets Kyle's sense of

humour.   One of the more serious potential parents at the training thought Kyle was serious when he suggested we could adopt three children if we turned the cupboard under the stairs into a box room. 'What else shall we pop in the book?' I ask. 'Can I decorate it with stickers and things?'

'That would be lovely, Jenny,' says Mike, 'and you can put photos or leaflets of some places you might take them to,' says Mike, 'Nothing fancy, we don't want to set up unrealistic expectations – you're not going to take them to Alton Towers every weekend - but it would be good for them to see things like photos of the local parks you'll take them to.'

My heart swells at the thought of going with our children to the park. It's something I'm sure a lot of parents take for granted. I've seen loads of them scrolling through their phones as their children call in vain for them to look at them on the top of the slide. But having spent so long worrying that it'll never happen, a trip to the swings seems like a holiday at Disneyland to me. And I love the way Mike just said 'parks you *will* take them to' – as if it's actually going to happen. I know we're a long way off being approved, but it's wonderful to hear someone in authority speak as if we are going to be parents, even if it was probably a slip of the tongue.

'So, is it just us you want to see in the book?' asks Kyle, 'or other people too?'

'Well, it's okay to have a few close family and friends in there,' says Mike, 'but you don't want to overwhelm the children with too many faces. Mainly we want them to focus on you both but if there are any potential babysitters in mind – and I'd choose those carefully – you could pop a photo of them in there and write a little caption underneath to explain who they are and something fun about them.'

'This is Jake,' says Kyle, gesturing towards a photo of the four of us on the wall, 'he will never let you win at Monopoly.'

'Jake's great,' I say 'and his fiancée Helen. They're the reason we have the bridal unicorn in the hall. They're getting married. It's all been rather brought forward as they recently found out they're pregnant.'

'How is that for you both, having pregnant friends?' asks Mike.

'It's great!' I say. Kyle looks over at me. I force a smile.

'It's okay to say if you find it difficult,' says Mike.

'Well,' I say, 'I suppose it just makes me even more determined to join them in parenthood.'

'It was a bit of a surprise for everyone,' says Kyle, 'It's an unplanned pregnancy, you see. And of course, you could say that adoption is the complete opposite of an unplanned pregnancy. Not that we mind that, of course.'

'We're really pleased for them!' I say.

'Of course you are,' says Mike, 'you both seem like very compassionate people to me. But it's okay to acknowledge that things are in many ways more complicated for you both than for your friends. But that doesn't mean to say that you can't support each other with your new families.'

'Yes, we'll be able to brave the soft play together,' says Kyle.

'You will,' says Mike, 'but you also need to realise that you will face very different challenges and must remember that what's right for them as parents, isn't necessarily what you will need. You will be *re-parenting* your children, dealing with emotional reactions and behaviours that have resulted from the difficult lives the children have lived before coming to you. And when they do come to you, it isn't going to be all happy ever after. You will be gaining two children and they will be gaining two parents, but don't forget, they will also be experiencing loss.'

'Loss?' says Kyle, 'We'll make sure they have everything they need.'

'I'm in no doubt about that,' says Mike, 'but they will have left behind their foster home, their friends and of course, their birth families.'

'Won't they have already left their birth families when they went into foster care?' asks Kyle.

'Not necessarily,' says Mike, 'they will most likely have been having regular weekly contact with their birth parents whilst in foster care. Some children continue to have contact with birth family members after they are placed for adoption.'

'They still see their parents?' I ask.

'A small number do,' says Mike, 'most have what's called 'letterbox contact' where letters are sent at agreed times of the year, via our letterbox contact department. Plus, there's also children who are placed separately to their siblings and then we will ask the adopters to meet up with the siblings' families.'

'We'd like to adopt two siblings,' I say, 'to keep them together.'

'Absolutely,' says Mike, 'and that's wonderful, but often there may be large sibling groups needing adopting but the courts may decide that they need to be placed in two or more families.'

'But we could perhaps take more than two?' I say.

'Er, yes,' says Kyle, trying to hide his look of surprise, 'I suppose we could get bunk beds.'

'Don't worry folks,' says Mike, 'It's a little more complicated than increasing the number of beds you have. Let's stick with two for now and take things one step at a time. Sometimes the courts will decide that the children will thrive better in separate families to their siblings even if there are families willing and able to take on two or more children.'

'But why?' I say, 'If they've already lost so much. Isn't it better to keep them with their brothers and sisters?' I feel like I'm going to cry. I may not be experiencing Helen's hormones but like hers, my tear ducts are on a hair trigger.

'Not always,' says Mike, 'sometimes the children have experienced such trauma or birth parents have treated them so differently from each other that their relationship is quite destructive and remaining together in a family will result in them retraumatising each other and being unable to settle and grow. In those incidences, it would be better for them to be placed in separate families that can meet their needs and to work on building positive and manageable relationships for them through carefully planned sibling contact. Not forgetting, of course, that they may not end up living in the same part of the country to each other.'

'That's so sad,' I say in a whisper.

'That's where the sibling contact arrangements become the right way forward though,' says Mike. 'Initially with the help of the social workers, the adoptive families will meet each other so that the children can develop a healthy relationship with each other.'

With my mind reeling from all this new information, we continue the session with Mike.

He takes us through what safety devices we will need to equip our home and we agree to make a start on the family book to show him next time. I try to smile and be positive and excited about getting to this stage, but I keep thinking about poor little children saying goodbye to their brothers and sisters and not seeing them for months on end.

When the session is over and we let Mike out past the bridal unicorn, I wonder how it can possibly be that the more I learn about adoption, the less I feel I know.

***

Later that day, Kyle says, 'Well, the latest session with Mike was certainly an eye opener.'

'The thought of the kids being split up from their brothers and sisters…' I reply quietly.

'Yes,' says Kyle, 'I pride myself in taking things in my stride, but I must admit, I found that a bit of a difficult one.'

'I know we don't have brothers and sisters ourselves,' I say, 'but the thought of being separated from friends we're close to is upsetting enough, let alone a sibling.'

One of the reasons we wanted to adopt two kids was that we've both felt it would have been nicer growing up with a brother or a sister and the thought that us forming our new family might still mean we're separating the children from their other siblings is quite a jolt.

We decide to throw ourselves back into

the wedding preparations. Kyle, I suspect, would like to sit, have a cup of tea and let it all sink in whilst he stares at some repeat on the television, but I prefer to get on with things. Having a plan and getting stuff done makes me feel better. And after all, Jake and Helen are getting married very soon. As soon as they decided in the pub that day, they went to the Register Office, gave the 28 days notice and booked the Registrar. That was nearly four weeks ago now and the last month has been spent planning a wedding that's as simple as possible on as small a budget as we can. I'm sure it would be a lot easier planning a huge wedding if we had a load of money - it's the keeping it simple and within budget bit that's tricky.

Jake spoke to his manager and the board game café is over the moon to host their gathering and refuses to accept any fee from them. They are getting married in the Registry Office. Helen's mum was a bit upset at first that they weren't going to a grand hotel, but she soon came round when Helen spent an hour or so looking at baby catalogues with her and talking about how much nicer the prams and cots they could afford would be if they didn't waste money on a wedding venue. Helen's dad was excited that the event would be taking place in a café with so many different kinds of Monopoly and there was a moment when it looked like he and Jake were going to suggest it be a Monopoly themed wedding, but one look from Helen's mum nudged them back to a more traditionally romantic theme.

Me and Helen have made decorations out of craft materials with the help of one of my youth groups, who happily took the craft challenge on as part of one of their achievement certificates. The theatre company where Helen works has lent her all sorts of props and accessories to make the place look like it was built to be a wedding venue.

As best man and woman, Kyle and me are in charge of organising the stag and hen nights as well. Obviously, Helen doesn't want anything too wild, so the ladies are gathering at our house for some drinks, nibbles and party games and Kyle, Jake, his friends and Helen's dad are just going for a few drinks around town. It should all be fairly simple, if everything goes to plan.

'Have you sorted everything for the entertainment for the after-wedding party?' I ask Kyle, notebook and pen in hand.

'Yep,' he says, 'Jake has collected the speakers we can connect our phones to and karaoke stuff from your youth club and delivered them to the board game café and I've written the quiz all about Helen and Jake and bought prizes to give out to the winners.'

'Great,' I say, ticking off things on my list, 'Did you get the answer sheets printed out?'

Kyle taps the side of his nose and winks

at me. 'Sneakily used the photocopier at work to print out answer sheets which double up as wedding souvenirs,' he says.

'Perfect,' I say, 'Helen's work came up trumps, lending us loads of hats and props and a big chest to put them in and it's all set up like one of those photo booths. Carrie and Lacey, have volunteered to take the photos of everyone at the makeshift photo booth and Jake's boss has set up the printer from the office to print them out.' I continue ticking my list. 'I've ordered a load of cards for us to slip the photos into so people should be going home with more souvenirs than a coach trip to Blackpool.'

With the help of Julie, I've baked a three-tier chocolate wedding cake and we've been making sandwiches and preparing buffet food like there's no tomorrow.

'It's certainly been a busy month,' Kyle says, 'veering between wedding prep and adoption assessments. It's a good job I've been able to ditch the crutches.'

'Yeah,' I grin 'and at least you're finally pulling your weight a bit more again at home.'

But just for 24 hours or so, we have given ourselves permission to switch off from all the adoption stuff and focus on our two best friends and their wedding. Tomorrow, two of the nicest people we know will be married, celebrating their love, surrounded by friends, family and twenty-five different kinds of Monopoly.

But first, tonight it's the stag and hen parties.

CHAPTER 24
– HELEN

I can't believe I'm about to go to my hen party. If you'd have told me this time last year that I'd be five months pregnant, about to get married and wearing a sash that says 'Bride and Mummy to be' I wouldn't have believed you.

It's been a hectic month, but a good one. I've really enjoyed going into Jenny's youth club and making all the decorations with the group there. I'd got a book on origami and we all sat in the craft room folding, sticking and drawing patterns on bits of paper and stringing them together to make wedding decorations. The kids Jen works with are great, but they did ask a lot of questions.

'So, did you want to marry Jake anyway or are you just doing it cos you're pregnant?' asked one of them.

'We were planning on getting married,' I replied, 'this unexpected treat just sped things up a bit.'

'So you didn't plan to have a baby then?'

asked another.

'Well, I think we would have had a family one day,' I said, 'but, a bit like the wedding, we hadn't realised it would happen quite yet.'

'Didn't you use condoms then?' asked one of the girls.

'Or didn't you use them properly?' added one of the lads. 'Jenny can teach you all about that if you need her to. Bit late now though,' he added as an afterthought.

'Hey, you lot,' Jenny called across from where she was grabbing some more paper out of the craft cupboard, 'less nosing and more folding! Helen might not want to tell you all her private information!'

'Okay then,' said my inquisitor, 'let's talk about you, Jen, how's the adoption going? When are you going to bring the baby into the youth club? Hey, maybe you can ask them if you can adopt your baby on the same day that Helen has hers, so you can be mummies together?'

I'd looked over at Jenny, concerned, but she took it all in her stride. 'I don't think I can dictate exact dates to them,' she said, 'There are a lot of stages to go through first and nothing is definite yet as we've discussed. Now let's focus on getting these decorations right or Helen will look like she's getting married in a paper recycling centre.'

Jenny had said this all with a big grin and her group had respected our privacy then. I was half expecting them to ask me if I'd had to start wearing maternity underwear yet. They'd even made a papier mâché pinata for me which they'd covered in silver stars and horseshoes and filled with sweets for us to use at the hen party tonight.

We're having the hen do at Jen's house as I didn't feel like traipsing round town. It's just a small gathering with my mum, Jen's mum, Carrie and Lacey and some of the girls from work and some of my cousins and friends. I've also invited Jake's mum's friend Julie who runs a lovely little café and insisted on bringing a load of gorgeous fairy cakes tonight as well as helping with the catering for the wedding tomorrow. Julie is lovely and looks out for Jake. Since his mum passed away, she's the closest thing he has to a parent really. You can't overly count his dad in Australia - he hasn't seen him much at all since he walked out on them when Jake was a teenager and they're hardly in touch. Jake hasn't invited him to the wedding. When I asked him if he was sure he didn't want to, he said that it wasn't practical as he'd never be able to arrange flights with such short notice, but I think he was relieved at having an excuse. He goes quiet when I ask him about it and says he'll talk to his dad sometime between the wedding happening and us having the baby, but I'm not sure if he will when it comes down to it.

The hen party gets off to a good start as

we all tuck into the buffet and devour Julie's delicious cakes. Jenny has arranged a quiz called 'To Helen back' which involves funny scenarios that we have got into over the years and asks the guests to remember or guess what happened.

'So,' she says, standing in the middle of our ring of chairs, 'How did Helen meet Jake? Was it a) He was working behind the counter at the Games café and she had got one of the Monopoly dice lodged in her bra and had to borrow another one because she couldn't get it out in public? Or b) He was demanding a refund at customer services at Bazza's when Helen worked on the phones there because the Poppa Pig wellies he'd bought for his nephew had a warning on the box that they should not be immersed in water or c) His ex-girlfriend was throwing his belongings out of the top window of their house and he asked Helen for a bag for life so he could rescue his battery operated minion?'

'C! C!' shouts Julie.

'Jake had another girlfriend when he met you?' says my mum.

'Correction, Mrs W.S,' says Carrie, 'Jake had just broken up with his girlfriend when he met Helen.'

'Absolutely,' says Julie, 'Our Jake is a true gentleman. His relationship with Joanne was completely over before he started to romance Helen!'

'I didn't think a minion would be the battery-operated device we'd be arguing over at a hen do!' says Lacey and collapses in a fit of giggles. Luckily, everyone else does too, including my mum.

CHAPTER 25
– JAKE

Kyle has organised a decent stag do. Thankfully, he's listened to me when I said I didn't want anything wild. Seeing as we're holding it the night before the wedding, I can't risk getting too drunk and ending up tied to a railing outside the train station.

'It's a good job I didn't let you take over, Phil,' I say to my mate, 'we'd have been knee-deep in strippers by half eight!'

'I can think of worse places to be,' grins Phil.

I glance over at Helen's dad, Len but he just winks at me. He's getting into the spirit of things, happily wearing his 'I'm with the groom' cap and 'father of the bride' t-shirt. Jenny insisted on kitting us all out in t-shirts.

'So, you're about to be an old married man, eh Jakey-boy?' says Phil.

'Yep,' I say, 'and a dad.'

'You've always been like a dad to us lot,' slurs Phil. He must have started drinking way before we arrived.

'What you been up to today, then Phil?' Kyle says, 'You seem to have got a head start on us in the drinking stakes.'

'I started on the coach,' Phil says.

'But you live within walking distance of town,' I say, 'what were you doing on a coach?'

'You know Becky?' Phil says.

I nod. 'Vaguely,' I say, 'I think she was at the mountain boarding.'

'That's the one,' says Phil, 'great legs. Well, better than yours were after the mountain boarding, eh Kyle?' Phil laughs heartily at his own joke. Kyle smiles but doesn't laugh. 'Anyway, Bec and me went away for a couple of days but it just wasn't working, you know. She was getting too clingy so when we weren't far from home, I told her it was over.'

'On the coach?' I say, 'That's a bit harsh, mate.'

'Lighten up, Jake,' says Phil, 'You bring more guilt to the party than a mini-bus full of priests with no road tax.'

'Easy now, gents,' says Kyle, 'So how did Rebecca take it?'

'It would have been fine,' Phil says, 'Only problem was, just as we broke up, the bloody coach broke down and we were stranded together in a layby in the arse end of nowhere for half an hour.'

'Couldn't happen to a nicer bloke,' says Kyle

in a low voice so Phil can't hear him. But he needn't have worried as Phil has gone back up to the bar again.

'Listen, mate,' I say to Kyle, watching Phil and the others downing shots, 'Do you mind if we make a move soon – I don't mean to be dull, but it looks like Phil and co are going all out and my heart's just not in it. I want to be able to enjoy my wedding day tomorrow, not be nursing a hangover and I don't know what them lot might do if we stay much longer. I don't want to wake up with a tattoo and a nose stud.'

'Course,' says Kyle, 'but I can't let you just go home before ten on your stag do. You're going to be a dad soon, and you'll regret cutting short a night out when you're up to your eyes in nappies.'

'We could go back to yours?' I say, 'Take Len with us?' We look over at Len who, like a zoo animal released into the wild has fully embraced the evening and is sitting by his collection of empty pint glasses, smiling happily to himself.

'No problem, I'm sure that'll be fine,' says Kyle, 'I'll just message Jen to let her know, just in case they need to hide the kissograms and wash off the chocolate body paint before we get there.' He messages Jenny but gets no reply. There's a loud crash from the bar. I look over and sure enough Phil and co have bumped into a waiter carrying a tray of drinks which are now all over the floor.

'Come on, let's slip out before they see us,' I say, 'Come on Len, we're off to join the ladies at their party.'

Len finishes his pint in one go and rises unsteadily to his feet. Kyle grabs his arm and we hail a taxi outside and give it Kyle's address. In under fifteen minutes we're walking up the path, Len singing something unrecognisable to himself.

Kyle rings the bell but there's no reply, so he searches his pockets for his door key. When he finally finds it, we open the door. We can hear squeals of laughter coming from the living room.

'Maybe we should leave them to it,' Kyle says, trying to steer Len towards the kitchen. But it's too late, Len has already got his hand on the living room door. He leans heavily on the handle for support and it swings open, revealing Helen's mum, wearing a see-through black lace nightie over her leggings and mother of the bride t-shirt, doing something indescribable to large inflatable man with a mask of my face on it.

'Mary!' says Len, his face a picture. 'What are you doing to Jake?'

The ladies roar with laughter and Helen runs up to me and gives me a hug. 'What are you doing here?' she says, 'I thought you were going to enjoy your last night of freedom?'

'We thought we'd come and see you,' I say, trying not to look at Helen's mum who is attempting to put the t-shirt and shorts back on my doppelganger. 'Is that my football kit?'

'Sorry Jake,' says Jenny, appearing beside us and giving Kyle a kiss, 'we couldn't bear to be without you and we thought we'd give Helen some honeymoon tips.'

'Well,' I say, 'that's very kind of you, but we need to watch the spending so we're not really going on honeymoon.'

'Yes, you are,' says Julie, appearing next to us, 'we all chipped in and got you a long weekend by the sea. We can't have you getting married without at least a little break. And I'm sure Mary will give the nightie back in time for you to pack it.'

'That's okay, Mary, you keep it,' I say, taking in the sight of my future mother-in-law wrestling with a pair of my shorts, 'I think Len has taken quite a fancy to you in it.'

Sure enough, Len has staggered over to his wife and thrown his arms around her. There is a loud bang as the inflatable version of me bursts and everyone falls about laughing again.

CHAPTER 26
– JENNY

The day of Helen and Jake's wedding is here. I'm over at their house helping her get ready and Jake has been packed off to ours.

'How you doing, are you nervous?' I ask her.

'A little bit,' she says, 'but excited mainly.'

'And rightly so,' I say, 'Jake will make a brilliant husband and father.'

'He will,' she says, 'Thank you for lending me your necklace, Jen, it's beautiful and with the turquoise stone, it counts as something borrowed and something blue.'

'You're more than welcome,' I say, 'now, what have you got for your something old and new?'

'Well, the old is my mum's bracelet she lent me which was my nan's and the new is here!' She indicates her baby bump.

'Of course!' I say, 'wonderful, a new baby! I'm so happy for you both, Helen.'

'Thank you,' she says, 'and I know it'll

happen for you guys soon - children, I mean. We've sent off our references for you and your social worker is going to come and interview us soon.'

'That's great,' I say, 'it's lovely of you both to do that for us. Hey, and good thinking of yours to get pregnant so they take you doubly seriously in your ability to recommend us as potential parents.' We chuckle. 'Now, let's get going so we don't keep Jake waiting at the registry office!'

Helen's dad and mum drive us to the registry office. There's a small group of the youth club kids who helped us make the wedding decorations standing outside and they give whoops and cheers as Helen gets out of the car. She looks beautiful. I have to give her mum credit, she might be a bit pushy, but she chose a lovely dress for her. It's white with little turquoise flowers on it, in a sort of empire line style and Helen looks like someone out of a Jane Austen novel. Polly from her work who does the hair for the theatre productions came and did her make up and styled her hair for her and has put it up and woven little turquoise and white fabric flowers into it.

Helen's dad takes her arm and we walk into the Registry office, with me and Mary following behind. I'm wearing a lemon-coloured dress with little yellow flowers in my hair, curtesy of Polly and Mary has a lemon two piece suit and matching hat on. Helen's dad is wearing a suit and a tie matching Jake and Kyles. The ties are silvery-grey with thin turquoise stripes on and they have yellow carnations in their button holes. Helen's bouquet is a beautiful bunch of delicate yellow and blue flowers.

When Jake sees Helen his eyes light up and his face breaks into the biggest, happiest smile imaginable. It's all I can do not to start blubbing with emotion there and then. Kyle looks at me and mouths 'I love you,' and I mouth the same back. I remember our wedding like it was yesterday. I'm so glad our best friends are getting married. I only hope that we will follow them into parenthood. I'm still waiting to hear back from the medical advisor at the adoption agency. They said they'd email when they have assessed my medical report but I must put that to the back of my mind for now. Today is all about Helen and Jake.

The ceremony is short but sweet. The words are simple but perfect. No messing, just love and commitment. Which is quite fitting really when you think about it. Jake has always been straightforward with Helen. Much better than her boyfriend before him, Will, who left her via a short but sour note and turned out to have been having an affair with her friend Katie. Jake is honest and decent and caring and kind. He's perfect husband and father material. I look at Kyle. So is he. I do hope my genes don't stop him from being a father. He would make the best dad.

It's soon my turn to do a reading. I quickly check my blood sugars before stepping up to the front. I've written a short piece to read for them. I didn't want to use something everyone has, today seemed too special for that.

'Helen and Jake,' I say, 'your romance was whirlwind and your wedding was planned in a month, but when love is as pure as yours, why wait? I will keep this speech as brief as your courtship but with words as loving and meaningful as your relationship. Today you are starting your new life together as a married couple, and soon you will be joined by your beautiful baby. All of us here have no doubts that you will be the most loving and happy family ever. We love you and we are here for you, to help you when you need us and to celebrate with you. May life bring you as much joy as you bring to those around you.'

I look over at Helen as I take my seat again. She's welling up whilst beaming at me. The Registrar completes the service and it's time to sign the register. Kyle and I are witnesses and we all pose happily for photographs. As everyone is clicking away, I can feel my pocket buzzing with a phone notification. I can't look at it now as I'd ruin the photos but I can't help but wonder what it is. Once the register is signed and we all walk out to one of Helen's favourite songs, I get chance to have a sneak peak at my phone. I can see the notification on the screen and the first few lines of the email. It's the adoption agency telling me that their medical advisor has had a chance to look at my medical report. My heart leaps into my mouth.

Whilst everyone is posing for more photos, I whisper to Kyle. 'My email has come from the adoption agency's medical officer.'

'What does it say?' he whispers back.

'I don't know,' I reply, 'I haven't dared open it.'

'Come, on,' he says, 'we can do this, let's open it now whilst everyone is busy.'

'But what if it's bad news?' I say, 'I don't want to spoil their day.'

'We won't,' Kyle says, 'we'll party and celebrate love and we know we'll find a way to make everything okay whatever it says, but Jen,' his eyes sparkle, 'what if it's good news?'

'Okay then,' I say, opening the email. The signal isn't great here and it takes an age to load. But even when it does, I can't believe the words I'm reading.

'We are pleased to be able to tell you that the medical officer is satisfied with the results of your adoption medical and the letter from your specialist and we look forward to continuing your adoption assessment journey with you both.'

'Oh my god,' I say, 'I feel like I've just cleared the biggest hurdle ever.'

Kyle lifts me up and twirls me around.

Then he gives me the biggest of kisses.

'Hey,' calls Jake with a grin, 'it's *my* wedding day, I'm the one who should be giving all the public displays of affection!'

'I've passed my medical!' I say. Helen and Jake rush over to me and squeeze me tight. Kyle joins in. As we envelop each other in a huge group hug I feel invincible. Now we can continue the adoption assessment with lighter hearts and a spring in our step. They've cleared me medically and so we can relax and show them how perfect we will be as parents. I have all my youth work experience and have spoken to human resources about taking adoption leave and reducing my hours to look after the children and Kyle has his well-paid secure job to support our new family to be.

CHAPTER 27
– KYLE

Getting the great news about Jenny's medical has put me in even more of a mood to party than I was before. We all tumble into the cars and make our way to the board games café for the after-wedding celebration.

The café looks amazing. The decorations have transformed it and the food and drink is quite a spread. As we go in, Jake's boss plays a fanfare on the speakers and we walk under an archway of yellow and blue balloons.

Jake and Helen greet all their guests and then we sit to enjoy the food. After a while, it's time for the speeches. Jake stands up first.

'I'd like to start by thanking everyone for coming here today to celebrate the marriage of me and my wonderful wife, Helen,' he says as everyone claps and cheers. Helen beams.

'I'd also like to thank everyone who helped us organise everything so quickly so that we can be an honourable married couple before the arrival of our baby.' There's more cheering and some gentle jibes from Jake's mates about it taking more than a marriage certificate to make him honourable. Jake continues, 'When I met Helen, I never imagined that in so short a time we would be here together, surrounded by friends and family, wearing matching wedding rings and getting ready to welcome a new little Weston-Smith into the world.' More clapping fills the room. 'Yes,' continues Jake, 'I've decided to take Helen's name, so will you raise a glass to my wife, Mrs Weston-Smith.'

Everyone toasts the newlyweds and Jake sits down. Helen stands, a huge smile on her face and raises her glass of orange juice.

'As my husband said,' she begins but is drowned out by more cheering and whooping at the word 'husband.' She smiles happily and waits for the noise to die down. 'As my gorgeous husband just said, thank you so much to everyone. Mum, Dad, Jenny, Kyle and everyone here, we love you all and are so happy you could celebrate with us. And you're all on baby-sitting duties once this little one arrives!' She pats her stomach affectionately. 'Jake, you have made me happier than I could ever have imagined. I love you so much.'

Helen sits down, her cheeks flushed red and it's Len's turn to do the father of the bride speech. To my surprise, Mary gets up with him and they read together from a speech they've prepared.

'Helen, you have brought us joy from the day you were born,' says her dad.

'And we can't wait for the joy our first grandchild will bring,' says her mum.

'And Jake,' continues Len, 'welcome to the family, son, we couldn't wish for a better son-in-law.'

'And daddy to my grandchild!' says Mary.

'Anything you both need, we are only a phone call away,' concludes Len.

'To Mr and Mrs Weston-Smith!' says Mary and everyone echoes the toast.

I stand up, 'Now it's my turn to speak,' I say, 'but in true tradition of this wedding, I'm sharing the best man duties with the best woman in the world - apart from you Helen, of course - my wife, Jenny.' Everyone claps.

'We won't keep you long,' Jenny says, 'we just wanted to congratulate our very best friends and wish them all the happiness in the world.'

'We're so glad that Helen found a man who deserves her,' I say 'and that Jake found someone to love who isn't a battery-operated minion.' There is laughter and murmurs around the café whilst those that know the story of how Jake and Helen met fill in those who don't. I continue, 'I'm so glad we welcomed Jake into our quiz team and into our hearts and that Helen and he have won the top prize by finding each other. If I can trouble you to take another sip of your drinks, please raise your glasses once again

- To Jake and Helen!' Everyone toasts the happy couple again.

'And now,' says Jenny, 'seeing as we first got to know Jake properly at the pub quiz, what could be more appropriate wedding party entertainment than a quiz! Kyle, over to you!'

I pop on a glittery trilby that Carrie has provided for me from Helen's work and put on my best tv quiz show host voice. Jenny runs round putting pens and answer sheets on the tables.

'Now ladies and gentlemen, and Jake and Helen,' I say with a wink, 'which will be the winning table? Who knows the most about our lovely newlyweds? Who will win first prize of a beautiful photo of the happy couple and who will win the booby prize of two photos of the happy couple!' Jenny holds up some photos we have framed of Jake and Helen pulling silly faces, both looking a bit worse for wear during a night out a while back. 'Question one,' I say, 'What is the name of Jake's minion that he was rescuing when Helen and he first met? Is it a) Kevin, b) Jake2, or c) Bob?' Everyone starts scribbling down their answers. 'Question two, what was Helen wearing on her feet during her first on-stage role with 'All the World's a Stage' where she usually works safely in the office? Was it a) ruby-red slippers, b) roller skates or c) nothing, she was barefoot?'

The quiz continues and is a great success,

with only a small argument erupting over whether 'servicing customers' counts as Helen's old job title in customer services. The quiz is won by the table from Helen's workplace.

'Congratulations to 'All the World's a Stage' for winning the quiz,' Jake says, taking the photo I'm holding out to him to present to the winning table, 'and Helen, we'll talk later about just how much you tell everyone about me...' He winks at his new wife and she giggles happily.

There's no time for the party to lull as the karaoke starts up. Bazza, does an excellent Tom Jones impression and then Helen's mum and dad dive up there and start singing 'We are family,' beckoning Helen and Jake up with them. Helen goes straight up but Jake hangs back.

'You alright, mate?' I say. He's looking down at his wedding ring and takes his mum's out of his pocket and places it in his palm. The disco lights glint off both the rings. 'She would've been so proud of you,' I say. He smiles at me and puts his mum's ring safely back in his pocket.

'I wonder if I did the right thing not telling my dad about all this,' he says.

'Don't worry about that now,' I say, 'you can always give him a call once you're back from your honeymoon. Perhaps tell him about the baby?'

'Yeah,' he says.

'Come on Jake!' calls Helen's mum over the

mic, 'come and sing with your mum-in-law!'

Just as I'm worrying the situation will turn awkward, Julie, Jake's mum's best friend appears beside us. She hooks her arm gently in his and kisses him on the cheek.

'You can do it, Jake,' she says to him kindly, 'I'll come with you.' Jake's shoulders relax a bit and the two of them join Helen's family in the little stage area and sing their hearts out. Jenny goes up to join them and waves at me to as well. I feel a buzz in my pocket and look down at my phone. I mime to Jen that I'll be with her in a minute. They carry on singing as I open the email. It's a memo from the council department I work for. I'm about to lock my phone again when I spot the heading: *Redundancy*.

I scan through the email. My job, and most of those of my colleagues are at risk. Just when we were ready to show the social workers how strong and secure we are to welcome two children into our family. Just as Jenny has cleared her hurdle, another one has been set up. Jenny works part-time because of her health and was going to cut back her hours even further once the children come, as well as taking the best part of a year off for adoption leave. How is that going to all work out when my job is hanging by a thread?

CHAPTER 28
– HELEN

When I wake the next morning and rub my eyes, I notice the unusual feeling of my wedding ring as I rub my face. I spread my fingers out and look at it and then turn to look at Jake. My *husband* is sleeping next to me. We have stayed the night in the honeymoon suite at a lovely hotel in our hometown. It was a perfect wedding day and we partied into the early hours. When we got to our hotel room, Kyle and Jenny had left chocolates and drinks there and little love heart sweets. They'd helped us to pack our stuff for our mini honeymoon on the morning of the wedding so that we can set off from here after breakfast.

Jake stirs beside me and opens his eyes. A smile spreads across his face. 'Morning Mrs Weston-Smith,' he says. I giggle.

'I keep thinking you're talking to my mum when you call me Mrs,' I say.

'Ooh, don't remind me of her in that nightie!' he says, doing a mock shudder as he recalls the scene he walked in on at my hen party.

'Serves you right for crashing my hen do!' I laugh.

'How was I to know what debauchery you ladies would be up to?' he says in mock protest. Then he pulls me towards him.

'Wait!' I squeal, 'I haven't cleaned my teeth yet!'

'Oh, we're an old married couple now,' he grins, those niceties have gone out the window!'

We nearly miss breakfast, despite waking quite early. When we arrive late, the stern looking waiter asks our room number.

'The honeymoon suite,' Jake says.

The waiter's expression softens and his eyes twinkle. 'No problem, do follow me, I'm sure the chef will have kept something aside for you. Would you like extra sausage and eggs?'

Giggling like school kids, we are shown to our table by a bay window and enjoy a traditional English breakfast, as well as cereal and croissants. At this rate, we won't need to eat again until the honeymoon has finished.

Afterwards, we load up our car that Kyle thoughtfully parked at the hotel yesterday and set out for our mini-moon at the coast. The sun is shining and we sing along to the radio as we drive. A few miles down the road, we pull into a petrol station and Jake gets out to fill up the tank. He pops inside to pay and grab some snacks for the journey, even though it's not a long one and we've eaten such a big breakfast that I think I'm going to need to lend Jake some of my maternity trousers.

Whilst he's inside, another car pulls up at the pump alongside us. It's a family with two small children. The kids are full of energy and demanding sweets and the parents look like their heads haven't hit a pillow for months. The mum sees me looking at them and I blush.

'Sorry,' I say, 'didn't mean to stare!' I don't mean to overshare but my need to explain myself always seems to result in me doing just that. 'I'm pregnant, you see,' I say, 'and I was admiring how full of beans your two are! Where do such small people get so much energy from?'

'They syphon it from us while we sleep!' says the dad, filling the car up with petrol.

'Not that we get to do much sleeping,' adds the mum. 'Come on you two, calm down or you won't be having those sweets daddy promised you.'

The family disappear inside to pay for the petrol and no doubt stock up on sugar. I swallow hard. I look down as I stroke my bump thoughtfully and see my new shiny wedding ring. It looks too big and solid and somehow out of place on my hand. I try to imagine cradling the baby the way I'm cradling the bump. How am I a wife and nearly a mother? Five minutes ago, my biggest responsibility was freshening up the costumes at work after the matinee and now I'm about to be in charge of a tiny human life.

I don't think we can Febreze the baby and spot clean it with a wet wipe.

The car door opens and Jake gets in, popping a bag of sweets on my lap and a couple of bottles of water into the cup holders.

'What's up?' he asks, 'you look a bit green. Morning sickness?'

'Yes, that must be it,' I say as the children re-emerge noisily from the petrol station, armed with about a thousand pounds worth of comics, sweets and drinks.

'Don't you worry,' he says, 'the sea air will do you the world of good, won't be long until we're there. You alright to get going, or do you need some fresh air?'

His look of concern and lovely smile make me feel a bit better. I catch sight of his wedding ring glinting in the sun. It looks right on him. I look back at mine. They match perfectly. We match perfectly. It's all going to be okay. I concentrate on opening the bag of sweets, turning my head so the manic children are no longer in my eyeline and we head off on our honeymoon.

CHAPTER 29
– JAKE

It was strange booking into our room under my new surname. Not a bad strange, but a bit weird, nonetheless. I don't mind losing my dad's surname, even though it's one of the few things he's given me and taking Helen's makes me feel part of her family. I couldn't have asked for nicer in-laws, despite Mary's antics with 'Inflata-Jake' as Jenny christened him.

Talking of christenings, being married has made me feel like I've taken a step closer to fatherhood. Like I've gained a few Adult-Points. Not that you'd think we were adults the way the two of us have been giggling this morning at breakfast. After we've eaten enough for the week, we head out to walk along the beach. As I hold Helen's hand, I can feel her wedding ring on her finger. I stop walking and pull her into a hug.

'Hello, Mrs Weston-Smith,' I say.

'Hi, Mr Weston-Smith,' she giggles back.

'So, how's married life treating you?' I ask, brushing her hair out of her eyes. The sea breeze is quite strong.

'Not bad, so far,' she says, 'At least, I'm not bored yet!'

'Just wait til I unpack my pipe and slippers,' I say, 'and start doing the crossword in bed.'

'At least it'll give you something to do whilst I'm knitting,' she says.

'Ooh, trying new things in the bedroom,' I say, 'now you're talking.'

'Actually,' she says, 'I am trying to knit a cardigan for the baby, but I think I'm using the wrong sized wool.'

'Isn't all wool the same size?' I say, 'Or did yours come from a particularly enormous sheep?'

'It's chunky,' she says.

'Hey, stop fat-shaming the flock,' I reply. She laughs. I love seeing her happy.

'Maybe it's the knitting needles that are too big,' she says. 'So far, I've only done an arm and I think the baby could use that as a cocoon.'

'Don't worry,' I say, 'I'm sure your mum can help.'

'But what if it's a sign?' she says.

'What kind of sign?' I reply, 'A sign you shouldn't go on the Great British Sewing Bee?'

'That's sewing, not knitting,' she says. 'No, what if it's just the first of many things that I get wrong for the baby? What if I don't know what to do? When I first started work at the drama studio, I got stage left and right mixed up all the time. I kept leaving the props in the wrong place. One night during the run of *Hamlet,* I put the skull and the poisoned chalice on each other's props tables in the opposite wings. Hamlet ended up standing in a grave, emoting over the wrong thing.'

'Alas poor Yorick, he had a head like a goblet,' I laugh. Helen joins in but still looks worried. 'Come on,' I say, 'we'll muddle through.'

'But we can't muddle, Jake, it's not a dress rehearsal, it's our child.'

'We've got lots of people to help us,' I say, 'and there are books. We have months to go yet and we can read up on all of this. And we'll get some practice in – we've got friends with kids, we'll offer to babysit.'

'I'm sure they'll love that,' Helen says, 'Excuse me, we're about to become parents and we haven't the faintest idea what we're doing. Do you mind if we practice on your offspring?'

'Well, when you put it like that, it's not as appealing an offer as it was in my head,' I say, 'but parents always look so tired, I'm sure they'll be glad of a break. Let's read up on it and then tout our babysitting services.'

'Okay,' says Helen, 'it's a plan.' She takes her phone out.

'What are you doing?' I ask.

'Googling the nearest bookshop,' she says, tapping away at her screen.

'What, right now?' I say, 'but we're on honeymoon!'

'Well, it says here the bookshop is next door to a department store, maybe they'll have a nice underwear department,' she says with a twinkle in her eye.

'So, we'll get an early night?' I say hopefully.

'Yes,' giggles Helen, 'I need to get a head start on my reading.'

We find the bookshop and sure enough, it has an entire set of shelves dedicated to babies and children. There are books on getting pregnant, being pregnant, exercising whilst pregnant, having the baby, exercising with the baby, feeding the baby, feeding yourself whilst feeding the baby, teaching the baby, teaching yourself about the baby and every stage of development you can imagine, right up to books on what to do when your child leaves for university. We stand side by side and stare at the shelves.

'Where do we begin?' I say, reaching for Helen's hand.

'The beginning, I suppose,' she says, picking up a set of four books. I glance at their titles: *Conception to cord cutting*, *Birth to first birthday*, *One to two, don't forget about you* and *Terrible twos, tantrums and training pants.*

'The lesser known installments of *The Fast and the Furious* franchise,' I say. To my relief, Helen laughs. It looks like we're going to need all the laughs we can get if the photos of screaming toddlers on the front of the last book are anything to go by.

We pay for our bundle of books and decide to head to the pub. Helen isn't drinking, of course, but I could do with a pint. My head hurts just reading the books' covers. But we find a lovely pub on the pier and once we're settled by the window, looking out over the sea, things start to feel a bit better again. On the beach below, we can see a family building sandcastles. The older child, a girl, is carefully patting the upturned bucket full of sand and making neat turrets to the castle as the toddler roams around, chubby legs sticking out of a suspiciously bulky nappy, brandishing a spade and bashing the turrets to pieces. I keep thinking the older child is going to get upset or retaliate, but she just patiently starts over again. The mum scoops the little one up and takes him away from the newly formed turrets whilst the dad helps the older girl rebuild the ruined castle. By the time Helen and I have finished our drinks, there is a moat and flags and the mum and toddler are returning with ice lollies.

'There, you see,' I say to Helen, 'it doesn't look that difficult.'

'You're right,' she says, giving me a kiss. I hold her tight and steer her away from the window as the toddler rampages through the freshly constructed castle, the older child finally succumbs to tears and the dad's ice lolly falls off its stick and onto the mum's white trousers.

CHAPTER 30
– JENNY

'Oh look,' I say, leaning over to show Kyle the photos Helen has just messaged me of her and Jake on the beach, 'they seem like they're having a brilliant time!'

Kyle smiles at the photos. 'I suppose this might be their last holiday together before the baby comes,' he says.

'Yes,' I reply, 'Maybe we should try and get a few days away after the adoption panel. You never know how quickly we might be matched with children.'

'Fingers crossed,' Kyle says.

'We've got to think positive,' I say, 'Let's assume we will be approved and then if we're not, well, I suppose we'll need a holiday to recover.'

'Who could refuse us?' he says and wraps his arms around me. I have a feeling both of us are trying to sound more positive than we actually are.

'It's kind of like... it feels a bit more

definite now we've had a few sessions with Mike, though, doesn't it?' I say.

'Yeah,' Kyle nods, 'I like his down to earth attitude and he seems to get us.'

'Is that a good or a bad thing?' I ask.

'Good, definitely good,' says Kyle, doing that positive voice again which doesn't quite match the look in his eyes. 'And we've got the friends and family event coming up soon. Have we decided who we're taking with us?'

The adoption agency are having an information evening for prospective adopters who have started their assessments to take their friends and family to. It's to give them an idea of the things that we will be going through and to help them to understand the different needs of adopted children and what support we might need. Plus, it will explain to them why things like 'the naughty step' would be really inappropriate and might backfire on children who have experienced the kind of things adoptees have.

'Well, we're taking Helen and Jake,' I say, 'and my parents. Do you think we need anyone else?'

'I don't think so,' Kyle says, 'But didn't they suggest we bring about half a dozen people?'

'Yes, but they also said when the children are placed, you mustn't overload them by introducing them to too many people all at once,' I say, as if reciting it from a handbook.

'Yes,' says Kyle, 'so we'd best choose the right ones to take with us– the ones who we can line up for a bit of help! Not much point in taking my folks, even if they could get over here that day.'

'True, they're not exactly going to be able to pop by to babysit,' I say. Kyle's mum and dad retired to Spain a few years ago. They're great and I hope we can take our children out there for holidays so they get to know both their sets of grandparents, but it's a bit much to expect them to pop over for the evening for a meeting. And as much as I love them, I don't really feel like having them to stay here at the moment when there's so much to do with sorting the house out and all the assessment meetings. What with all that and trying to fit in work and Helen and Jake's wedding, it's all been a bit hectic.

By the time Helen and Jake arrive back from their honeymoon a few days later, I'm so excited to see them that I nearly knock Jake over in the rush to hug them both. Bless them, they've come straight over to ours to see us and then we're all travelling together to the friends and family evening tonight. It's so good to have them here. They look happy and relaxed and even slightly suntanned.

'It's a marvel what a few days at the coast will do for you,' Kyle says, 'You look like an old married couple!'

'Did you do anything exciting?' I ask.

'Everything is exciting with Mrs Weston-Smith,' says Jake with a grin, 'and we got to go baby book shopping!'

'How lovely,' I say, 'you can tell me all about it!'

'You both sit down and put your feet up,' Kyle says, 'I'll get us all some lunch, we can have a relax here this afternoon, order a pizza for tea and we'll set out to the adoption agency about 6pm if that's okay?'

'That's sound,' says Jake, 'I'll give you a hand with lunch.'

They take off into the kitchen and me and Helen sit next to each other on the sofa and she shows me more honeymoon photos.

'So, what was the most romantic moment then?' I ask, 'or is that private?'

'We watched the sun come up on the sea front,' says Helen.

'Wow, was that a late night or an early morning?' I ask.

'Early morning,' she says, 'neither of us could sleep so we decided we might as well make the most of it.'

'Weren't there other things you could have been doing on honeymoon?' I say with a grin.

'Yes, but that night I think our minds were whirling – we'd been reading the baby books and it's just so much to take in. I do recommend the sunrise though, I expect we'll see a few of those when the baby is born!'

'True,' I say, 'I don't think I'd be much good waking up for the sunrise though. As soon as I get up, my chest demands its physio and my blood sugars demand their breakfast. By the time I've attended to all that, we'll have missed it all! It's probably a good job we won't be adopting a baby. Let's hope our two can manage some coco pops in the morning whilst I juggle my meds and nebulisers!'

Helen gives my leg a squeeze. 'You'll be great, Jen, and Kyle will be there to help, won't he? Has he still got flexi-time at work?'

'Yes,' I say, 'thank goodness. And my blood sugars are pretty much under control and I've got my physio off to a fine art. I'm hoping the kids will enjoy jumping around with me to get some exercise. We're thinking of getting a trampoline – the kids will love it and it'll be great physio for me.'

'Isn't it great when you can buy something nice because of the kids?' says Helen, 'Jake is trying to convince me that the baby will benefit from a PS5.'

We all have a lovely afternoon together. As it gets closer to the time of the friends and family session, I get a bit anxious and badger Kyle into ordering the pizza so early that we've barely digested lunch when we're starting on tea. But once we've thrown away the pizza boxes and I've checked three times with Kyle if I look healthy and smart enough, we all pile into the car and set off. His knee is much better now and he's up to driving.

My mum and dad are meeting us there. I printed out the directions for them and wrote down all the information of where they have to go when they get in the building. As we pull up, twenty minutes early, Kyle turns to Jake.

'Look at the cars!' he says.

'Not this again, Ky,' I say, rolling my eyes and grinning at Helen. 'Kyle has a thing about how everyone's car here is bigger and better than ours.'

'Got a complex about your engine, mate?' grins Jake.

'No, it's just they're all so new and expensive looking,' says Kyle, 'I'm worried they will think we're the poor relations.'

'Their fancy cars won't look so fancy with biscuits and squash mashed into the upholstery,' says Jake, 'don't you worry!'

As we are about to go into the building, my mum and dad arrive, my mum waving her arm out of the window and my dad beeping the horn as if he's about to take part in a road race. I look around anxiously, convinced the social workers will be watching us.

'Louise, Dan, lovely to see you,' says Kyle, 'You've met Jake and Helen, haven't you?'

'Of course, congratulations on your wedding and your new little one!' says my mum, giving Helen a hug as my dad shakes Jake by the hand. 'Now, let's get inside and get Jenny and Kyle a couple of children to keep your baby company!'

'They haven't actually got the children here today, mum,' I say.

'I know that, darling,' mum replies, 'but they'll be yours soon, don't you worry, now let's get in there and show them how capable we all are.'

'Team Williams, let's go!' says my dad and we all march inside.

CHAPTER 31
– KYLE

The usual receptionist is on duty and greets me with a knowing smile as she asks for my car registration.

'No problem finding a space to fit it into?' she says, her lips twitching with a smile.

'Perfect, thanks,' I say, steering Jake through into the meeting room before he can join in with the teasing.

We find a row of six chairs together and shuffle around taking our seats. Bridget, one of the social workers I recognise comes over to greet us and I introduce her to everyone.

'Ooh, are congratulations in order?' she says to Helen, looking at her baby bump.

'Oh, thank you, er.. yes,' says Helen, blushing and pulling her coat around her, despite it being rather warm in the room.

'It's alright, Helen,' Jenny says, 'you don't have to feel guilty about being pregnant, we won't make you stand outside in the car park.'

Helen continues looking unsure, but Jake

puts his arm around her and hands her a drink of water he's grabbed from the refreshments table.

'Jen's right,' I say, 'hopefully we're all going to become parents more or less together, it makes no difference how we become mums and dads, it's all pretty much the same.'

'That's a beautiful sentiment,' says Bridget, 'and I admire you for it, but actually, the point of tonight is to explain to your friends and family about the difference between biological parenting and re-parenting - as we often call adoption.'

I can feel my cheeks reddening now. At this rate, they'll be able to save on electricity and light the hall with the glow from Helen's and my faces.

'We're ready for that,' says Jenny, 'I think Kyle just meant that we will love the children just the same as if we'd gone down the same route as our friends have.'

'Wonderful,' says Bridget, 'now, do help yourselves to refreshments everyone and we will be getting started in a few minutes.'

'Thanks,' I whisper to my wife, 'sorry, I didn't mean to put my foot in it. Do you think Bridget will keep me back after class?'

'No,' Jenny says, 'not unless you eat all the biscuits again.'

The evening starts with a PowerPoint presentation, covering the stages of the adoption process.

'So, you see,' says Bridget, 'although you're not experiencing a nine month gestation period, you will be 'expecting' to wait a similar amount of time for the home visit assessments, the adoption training sessions, gathering of references and medical reports and finally the day of the adoption panel. Any questions before we move on?'

Jenny's dad's hand shoots up. 'So do the children come home with them after the adoption panel, then?'

'No,' says Bridget, 'the adoption panel is simply to say whether you are approved to adopt. It is very unusual to have even been matched with children at that stage. The panel will make their recommendation on the day, which your social worker will pass onto you there and then. Then the panel's recommendations have to be reviewed by the decision maker which can take up to a week or two.'

'The decision maker?' whispers Jake, 'sounds like something from a marvel film. Hope he hasn't been hanging out with Thanos!'

'Shhhh!' says Helen. I wink at her and she relaxes a bit.

'And then,' continues Bridget, giving Jake the kind of smile usually reserved for an endearing but hyperactive toddler, 'you will receive official confirmation as to whether you have been approved to adopt. It's very unlikely that the decision maker will disagree with the panel but we have to wait for them to make things definite. You will hopefully go on to receive official approval to adopt, along with the age and number of children you have been approved for. Some of you, will of course be applying to adopt a sibling group.'

Louise, Jenny's mum, sits up proudly. As does Jenny. Helen slides down further into her chair and I feel like lying on the floor. Although I totally get the logic of adopting siblings together, going from having zero children to two children is quite a leap.

'So, when do the children actually come?' asks Louise.

'Well,' says Bridget, 'After the panel's decision has been confirmed by the decision maker,' – I see Jake making a superhero gesture out of the corner of my eye – 'then social workers set about finding a good match. Our prospective parents will receive phone calls and information about children we feel they may be suited to. Sometimes we will be considering more than one potential family for the children. The children's social workers will do home visits to find out more about the families. When they feel they have found the right parent or parents for the children, another panel will happen – this time the matching panel. And when or if that panel approves the match, that's when things start to happen quickly.'

'Quickly?' Dan mutters in a voice much

less quiet than he thinks it is, 'It all sounds like it's taking longer than Helen's pregnancy to me!'

'Well, you see, Sir,' says Bridget, 'these children will have been through a lot and will have already experienced the loss of their birth family. They will be about to move on from their foster family who they will possibly have been living with for quite some time. In some cases, they will be placed separately to their siblings. So, we need to do all we can to ensure that the match is a solid one and that we will be placing them with a forever family.'

'Yes, of course,' says Louise, giving Dan a glare which reminds me scarily of Jenny when she's in one of her determined moods.

'But as I say,' continues Bridget, 'once the matching panel says yes, it will be all systems go. Things will usually already be in place for the introductions to the children to start the same week. Having endured a long wait, things will suddenly be racing ahead. This is partly why you will probably have seen the spare bedrooms in our potential adopters' homes turning gradually into children's rooms, despite there being no children in them!'

'See,' says Jenny to Jake with a grin, 'I haven't lost the plot!'

'You've done a great job, Jen,' says Jake, 'and I'm always happy to help with any furniture building you need.'

At about the halfway mark we have a

break. Jenny and Helen are in deep conversation with some other potential mums-to-be they've met in the ladies' toilets and me and Jake pop outside to get some fresh air.

'How you doing, mate?' asks Jake.

'Alright,' I say.

'Sure?' he asks, 'You can say, it's just me.'

'Well, yeah,' I say, 'It's just a bit... you know.'

'Yeah, it is,' he replies. 'All these panels and,' – he puts on a voice like the commentator from a wrestling match – 'The Decision Maker!'

'I do feel a bit like my future is in the hands of a bunch of strangers, all deciding if I'm good enough daddy material.' I say, looking over my shoulder to check no one can overhear us.

'It is a bit like that, isn't it,' says Jake, 'I mean, I don't get much of that at the pre-natal classes. Helen gets more of it than me, I suppose, being advised what to eat and what not to eat and stuff, but nothing compared to the scrutiny you guys get.'

'I know why it has to be this way,' I say, 'the kids need us to be prepared and we need to be the right people for them. But sometimes it seems a little unfair that we have to do all this when your route to fatherhood was...' my voice tails off. I don't want to seem crass.

'A bit more fun and a lot less form filling?' says Jake, 'Don't worry mate, you're entitled to feel a bit worn out by it all every now and again, but we're here for you. Anything you guys need, just ask, okay?'

'Okay,' I say, 'Thanks. It's scary though, isn't it, all this talk about what they will have been through and how they will behave differently to other kids, need different stuff. I'm just a bit worried I won't be up to it.'

'Mate,' says Jake, 'when Jen told you about her Cystic Fibrosis, what did you do?'

'How do you mean?' I say, 'I just listened really. And thought about how bloody strong she was.'

'It didn't make you not want to be with her?' Jake says.

'No,' I say, 'of course not, if anything it made me love her more. She's amazing. Strongest person I know.'

'Exactly,' says Jake, 'and so will your kids be and they'll have you and your amazing wife to look after them. You've both already proved you're not remotely fazed by things that most of us haven't dreamed of coping with.'

'Yeah, you're right,' I say, 'cheers mate. But two kids at once…'

'No worries,' says Jake, 'we're here for you and your double arrivals. You'll take it in your stride and there will be support. You won't be able to get rid of us and Jen's parents are scarily capable. And it's great you can keep the kids together rather than them being split up.' I nod. Jake gives me his trademark grin and continues, 'now we'd best get back inside before Bridget gives us a late mark. What's part two all about then? How we charm the decision maker?'

'I think we're workshopping about the needs of the children and the kind of support we will demand from you all,' I say, 'so chop, chop, get your furniture-building-babysitting-butt back in there!'

CHAPTER 32
– HELEN

The workshops in the second half of the friends and family meeting are really quite fun. They turn it into a kind of quiz show and we all have to work together as a team. The social workers lay out examples of the support the adopters will need, such as a baby doll needing its nappy changing and volunteers from the friends and family groups have to run up and do the activity and points are awarded for the best efforts. Jake is a whizz at changing the nappy, although he does hold the baby doll above his head like the world cup trophy when he wins. I'm hoping that's just exuberance rather than something he intends to do with our child.

It's Jenny's mum's turn next and she's really good at her challenge. One of the social workers pretends to be a toddler throwing a tantrum and the friends and family members have to try to calm her down. Some of the teams lead the tantruming social worker to a time out area, like the naughty step but that is frowned upon. We're told how the children may have experienced too much isolation, maybe being left alone through neglect or excluded from friendship groups at school, so the social workers suggest a 'time in' approach where you sit calmly with the child and show them that they are safe without overwhelming them. Jen's mum remains calm and in control even when the social worker toddler starts to throw things. To top things off, Kyle catches one of the cuddly toys she throws.

'Whoop!' he cries, holding the toy above his head like a football trophy as Jake did with the doll. Sometimes I wonder if our husbands realise that it's children we're about to welcome into our homes, not the England squad.

Jen's dad thrills everyone by winning the school parents' evening task. This time, the social worker pretends to be the child's class teacher, explaining to the adopters why the child is not allowed to go on the school trip due to their behaviour in class.

'Oh dear,' whispers Kyle, 'this could be uncomfortable. I think Dan is about to give the teacher a piece of his mind.' But to our surprise, Kyle's concerns are unfounded.

'My grandchild,' says Dan, politely but firmly, 'has experienced enough unfair exclusion in their life already and I am not willing to see them miss out on this school trip as well. I, as their grandad, would be happy to accompany them and take personal responsibility for their behaviour. Or, my daughter, their mum will and she is a highly experienced youth worker and could manage your trip with her eyes shut.'

Jenny blushes with pride and the social worker is highly impressed. Kyle shakes Dan by the hand on his return to our group and I'm sure Jake wells up, though he claims he has something in his eye. I want to talk to him about it when we get home, and ask him if he's thought any more about involving his dad in our new family, but I'm so tired that I fall asleep in the car on the way back and go straight up to bed when we get in. I try to bring up the subject of dads and grandads the next day, but he shrugs it off and says he has to go on a zoom call with Bazza and Kyle about the board game because they're entering it in some kind of competition.

But although I'm really thrilled that Jenny and Kyle invited us to the friends and family event, I'm relieved it's done. My back is aching from the plastic chairs and I think I must have been sitting funny, trying to hide my baby bump. I know Jenny said not to worry about it, but I kind of felt like I was flaunting my pregnancy in front of everyone there.

The week flies by and now it's already time for Mike, Jen and Kyle's social worker to visit us. We're acting as referees for them and he needs to interview us face to face. I feel ever so nervous and worried I'm going to stick my foot in it. We're being interviewed separately, like some kind of scary Mr and Mrs game. Jake goes upstairs to carry on with painting the spare room which we are going to turn into a nursery and I sit opposite Mike, trying not to fidget.

I answer all the basic questions like how long I've known Jenny and Kyle and how often we see them. Then we move onto the more in-depth ones. Mike asks me what kind of couple they are.

'Oh, the best kind,' I say, 'They've always been sort of like parents to me, in fact I've largely got them to thank for the fact that I'm about to become a parent myself.'

'How so?' says Mike, 'If that's not too personal a question.'

'Not at all,' I say, 'Well, they looked after me when Jake and I had a misunderstanding and nearly broke up. He hadn't really done anything wrong, you see, it was just because I'd been so hurt when my previous boyfriend, Will, left me via a rather short note. I'd met Jake far too soon afterwards really and was still a bit of an emotional wreck, especially after finding out about how he'd been cheating on me with my friend Katie...'

'Really?' says Mike, 'and did Kyle know this Will? He and Jenny haven't been unfaithful to each other, have they?'

'Oh goodness, no!' I say in alarm, 'They'd never cheat on each other! They helped me to see that Jake was a decent person, unlike Will and to build my confidence so that I could have a functional relationship.' Mike is frantically making notes and I'm mentally kicking myself. Why am I saying all this and making myself sound like a complete mess? Why should the adoption agency take the word of a neurotic woman like me as a referee? I'm doing Jen and Kyle more harm than good.

'So,' says Mike, looking up from his notebook, 'you were saying that Jenny and Kyle helped you?'

'Yes,' I say, 'they always make me feel safe and they helped me to get my thinking straight, stop overreacting and to repair my relationship with Jake. And now, we're having a baby.' I look at Mike, 'Sorry,' I say, 'I'm talking about myself again. This can't be of any use to you.'

'On the contrary,' says Mike, reading from his notes, 'being able to make someone who is emotionally distressed feel safe, get their thinking straight and react logically to situations sound like perfect qualities in adopters. Just what children will need who have experienced trauma.'

Whilst I'm very relieved that I seem to have said the right thing somehow, I'm not sure how I feel about having my behaviour compared to a child who has experienced trauma. I'm glad when my interview has finished and it's time to call Jake downstairs.

CHAPTER 33
– JAKE

Helen looks a bit pale when she calls me down for my turn in the hotseat.

'Do you need anything?' I ask her, 'you look a bit off-colour.'

'No, I'm fine,' she whispers, 'I'm just worried I kept sticking my foot in it.'

I give her a quick hug and stride into the living room, trying to give off a confident, calm air.

'Good to see you, Mike,' I say, 'So, how do we do this? I feel like I should lie on the couch or something!'

'No need, Jake,' says Mike, smiling, 'I'm just here to find out a few things about Jenny and Kyle – how you see them coping with the demands of parenting and so on. So, how did you meet them?'

'Through my girlfriend, I mean wife, Helen,' I say.

'Oh yes, congratulations are in order, I hear. Double ones, a marriage and a baby.'

'Cheers,' I say. 'I met them mainly at pub quizzes – not that they spent an excessive amount of time in the pub, you understand, just that's where we used to all go together when Helen and I were first dating.'

'And do you get on well?' Mike says.

'Oh yes, great,' I reply, 'apart from I got a bit of a warning from them both when they saw my mate Phil had got two women on the go at the same time. They gave me a bit of a talking to that I wasn't to behave that way towards Helen. Not that I would, of course. My relationship with my ex, Joanne, was well and truly over when I started dating Helen. Admittedly, I did ask Helen out the same day that Joanne threw me out, but there was no crossover.'

Mike starts making notes. Oh god, I think I've gone as pale as Helen was.

'And so Kyle and Jenny were looking out for Helen, then, in a protective way?'

'Oh yes, and once they realised I wasn't some two-timing idiot, they have been great mates to me as well. You couldn't get a nicer couple and you couldn't ask for better parents. They look after everyone with warmth. Jenny does an amazing job at the youth club. I don't know how she puts up with half the stuff she copes with there.

'Does she tell you the details of the youth club?' says Mike, 'I ask because the children will have complicated backgrounds and some of the information may not be Jenny's to share widely.'

'Oh no,' I say, 'Jen knows all about confidentiality. As does Kyle. He is all up on data protection and such, with his job at the council. He has the patience of a saint too – no idea how he puts up with everything he has to at work as well. No, they're a great pair. They'll help anyone. And they're solid, a brilliant team.'

'And can I ask, how you feel Jenny will manage to maintain her necessary health routines whilst looking after two lively children?' Mike says.

'Well,' I say, 'I know cystic fibrosis and diabetes seem like big hurdles to us, but Jenny just takes it in her stride. I suppose it's all she's known really and she injects her insulin, for example, when we're out for a meal, without missing a beat. You and I might flinch at measuring a dose and sticking a needle in ourselves, but it's natural for her. And she's got Kyle.'

'Does Kyle support her a lot?' Mike asks.

'Brilliantly so. All the time.' I say.

'Jenny needs him all the time?' Mike asks, raising an eyebrow.

'No, I didn't mean that,' I say, 'I mean he's a rock for her. She copes brilliantly and is very independent. It's just that she knows he's there if she needs him. They make a great team. He does the heavy lifting housework and hoovering etc, so that the dust doesn't get on her chest, things like that. He'll make the meals which helps her manage her blood sugars.'

'And who supports Kyle?' Mike asks.

'We do, and Jen's parents. And he has mates at work. Everyone loves Kyle.'

'What about his parents, do they support him?'

'They do, it's just they live in Spain' I say, 'but you can chat and everything over zoom these days and they have occasional visits. But he gets on well with them and the kids will have lovely holidays in sunny Spain.'

'That's good,' says Mike. 'Support of our parents is beneficial to us when we become parents ourselves.'

'Yes, it is,' I say.

'Do you and Helen have a couple of sets of grandparents knitting and building cots for you?' Mike says. I look down.

'Helen's mum and dad are great,' I say. 'Mine… er, I lost my mum and my dad… isn't on the scene.'

'I'm sorry to hear that,' says Mike. 'I do apologise for intruding. I'm not here to spy on you all, just to ensure that any children placed with Jenny and Kyle will have a secure home in which to thrive.'

'Of course,' I say, 'well, you've come to the right place with the Williams's. The kids will be lucky to have them.'

'It definitely seems like it,' smiles Mike.

'And I think they are very lucky to have you both as friends as well.'

'Thank you,' I say, relaxing a bit.

The rest of the interview goes well and at the end, Mike chats to me and Helen together whilst we all have a much needed cup of tea and some biscuits. We see him out once he's gathered all his notes together.

'Phew!' I say to Helen as Mike drives away, 'I don't know how Kyle and Jen do this, being grilled every week, I'm exhausted!'

'Me too,' she says, 'I kept thinking I'd put my foot in it. I started rambling about Will having the affair with Katie.'

'Oh god,' I groan, 'I started going on about Phil and those two girls he was seeing at the same time – you know, the one that threw the drinks over him at the pub quiz.'

'Fine referees we are,' says Helen, 'we've made us sound like a dodgy late-night film!'

'I'm sure it was alright by the end though,' I say, 'He seemed happy and he said they were lucky to have us supporting them.'

'And I told him how much they'd supported us,' Helen says, 'so I reckon if he does think we're a mess, then at least he knows Jen and Kyle will love the kids no matter how they behave!'

We both laugh at ourselves and flop on the sofa.

'So, Mr Weston-Smith,' says Helen, 'What

are we making for tea?'

    'Let's ask our old friend Ronald,' I say.

    'Ronald?' Helen asks.

    'Ronald Mcdonald,' I grin, taking out my phone.

CHAPTER 34
– KYLE

'Six months!' Jenny says, showing Helen's Instagram post to me. 'Can you believe she's six months pregnant already?'

I glance at the photo. 'She looks happy,' I say. 'Did she say how they both got on with Mike? Did he shine a torch in their eyes and get his lie detector test out?'

'No, silly,' laughs Jenny, 'they said it was fine. Everything above board. You make it sound like we've got something to hide! We've told him all our deep dark secrets like your addiction to Star Wars and my love of Countdown.'

'And not even the cool version with the comedians on it,' I tease, 'the afternoon one the pensioners use to keep their brains active.'

'You'll thank my active brain when we're at the adoption panel,' she says, 'it's only a couple of months away.'

'July 15th, isn't it?' I ask.

'Yes!' Jenny says, rolling her eyes at me, 'Haven't you put it in your diary? You have booked it off work, haven't you?'

'Yes, of course I have,' I say.

'Good,' she replies, 'I've been waiting for this for so long, I don't want anything to go wrong or delay it.'

'It won't,' I say, going over and giving her a hug. 'Before you know it, we'll be dad and mum to two children.'

'Yes,' she says, holding on tight to me. When I don't squeeze her as tight in return, she pulls back and looks at me quizzically. 'What's the matter?' she says.

'Nothing,' I reply, 'come on, let's go get those bedrooms sorted, we need to get rid of some more books and CDs before we have to fill the shelves with lego and teddy bears.'

'That can wait a minute,' Jenny says, 'What's wrong? You don't look right.'

'I'm fine,' I say, 'There's lots to do, that's all.'

'We're going to have to get used to that,' she says. I force a smile.

'Kyle!' she says, giving me a gentle shake, 'What is it? You can tell me.'

'Well,' I say, 'it's just... I wonder sometimes if I'm up to it. Having two children all at once.'

'But you're wonderful at looking after people,' she says, 'What would I do without you?'

'But will we be able to manage to look after ourselves and two little ones, do you think?'

I say. 'I don't want to let you down and it end up effecting your health.'

'I think you need to talk to someone,' Jenny says, taking out her phone.

'Who do you mean?' I say in alarm, 'Not Mike? Honestly Jen, don't say anything to him, I'll be alright. It's just cold feet.'

'No, not Mike,' she says. She presses dial and puts her phone on speaker. It rings out a few times then we hear Jenny's mum's voice.

'Hi Jen, just give me a minute, I'm just chasing the chickens,' she says.

'Hope that's not some kind of kinky new afternoon activity you and Dan have going on,' I say. Louise laughs.

'Cheeky!' she says. 'Casserole! Kiev! Bacon Club Sandwich! Come here! Hang on Jen, I'll put your dad on.'

We can hear squawking in the background and then Jen's dad appears on the line.

'Hello Jennifer!' he says, 'Your mother is up to her eyes in feathers at the moment. What can we do for you?'

'I just need you to reassure Kyle, dad,' she says.

'What about, that his mother-in-law isn't the village madwoman who thinks it's a good idea to career round the garden after crazy chickens when there's a perfectly good corner shop selling eggs less than five minutes' walk away?' says Dan, 'No can do, I'm afraid.'

'No dad, Kyle is worried about being a dad and how he's going to look after me as well as the children,' Jen says.

'Have you got the children coming soon, then?' Dan bellows above the squawking.

'No, dad,' Jen says, rolling her eyes at me, 'as they said at the friends and family meeting, that all comes much later. We have to go to the adoption approval panel first. But at least that's only a couple of months away now.' The squawking dies down and her mum comes back on the line.

'How can we help you, Jen?' she says.

'Kyle's worried about how he'll look after me with my health issues and the kids,' Jen replies. 'Can you tell him how you managed to look after me when I was a kid with cystic fibrosis.'

'We just did,' says her dad. Louise must have put the phone on speakerphone as they are both there, but thankfully they seem to have gone back in the house as I can no longer hear squawking. 'We didn't really have time to think about it.'

'Well, that's not strictly true, Dan,' says Louise, 'we thought about it a lot before Jenny was born, Kyle - of course, we didn't know she had CF then, but I was still worrying. Reading all the books, attending all the antenatal classes and asking all my friends questions. But once she actually came, there was so much going on, there wasn't that much time to worry and we just sort of got caught up in everything and got on with it.'

'Yes,' says Dan, 'she came with a whole extra set of circumstances we weren't expecting, but she was still our little girl and we loved her. We did worry about her and it was an awful lot to take in, as, I expect it will be for you both, with two little ones who have had all this stuff happen to them, but when they smile at you and call you 'daddy', you'll have the strength to move mountains.'

'Dan is, for once in his life, speaking a lot of sense,' says Louise. 'It's good to be as prepared as you can, but nothing will really prepare you for everything. All you can do is listen to the social workers, attend the training and take as much time for yourselves as you can to relax together before they come.'

'Because you sure won't be doing a lot of relaxing after they arrive!' says Dan, chuckling heartily. 'I don't think I've relaxed for a moment since we had you, Jen!'

'Thanks, dad,' Jen says, 'you're supposed to be making Kyle feel better, not worse!'

'Ignore him,' says her mum, 'he's only teasing. You two will be fine and we're always here to help. And your friends will be going through parenthood as well, so that will help, and you've got the social workers. I'd be lying if I said parenting was easy, but it's also a wonderful thing. You will have difficult times and I would imagine quite different challenges with the route you're taking. But you will also have wonderful times and a full life.'

'Thank you, Louise, thanks Dan,' I say.

'Have we helped you, Love?' asks Louise.

'Yeah,' I say, 'I think you have. If you two could bring up this monster, then I reckon we have the right grandparents in our corner and I have the most amazing wife to do this with.'

'Thanks mum, thanks dad,' Jen says, 'speak to you again soon.' She hangs up the phone. 'Do you really feel better?' she asks me.

'Yes,' I say, 'I do.' And we have the biggest kiss we have had in ages.

I do feel less concerned after talking to Jenny's parents. They're a good example of how you find the strength to deal with the unexpected in parenting. And Jake was a great help at the friends and family thing, he spoke a lot of sense about how I wasn't fazed by Jen when she told me about her health. It's just part of her and I wouldn't be without her for the world. I suppose once the kids are real, once we've met them, it'll seem less scary. At the moment it's all statistics and training and worse case scenarios but once it's real little people and ice creams and picnics and story times, I reckon it'll feel better. Mike has suggested we get some practice in, so I'm going to have a word with Dev at work and ask if we can possibly look after his twins one day.

I've still not told Jen about the redundancies at work though. My manager reckons I'm in a good position to get one of the remaining jobs I've been ringfenced for but what will I do if I don't? I've been searching the job ads just in case and I've managed to send off some applications. Maybe me and Jake will make our millions with the board game, but I doubt it.

We went to meet with Bazza again the other day. He's very excited and has put quite a wodge of cash into it. This has enabled us to get a designer on board who has helped us to produce a mock-up of the board. We've hammered out the ideas of how it works and developed the questions for the quiz section. At the moment, we've been using bits and pieces as counters – spare dice from other games, old key rings and things from Christmas crackers, but Bazza says he knows someone who can make us proper ones in the shapes of beer barrels, wine glasses, and packets of crisps and things. We've printed the challenges and quiz questions on cards made to look like beer mats and we found a bell in a charity shop we're using when you have to ring last orders. 'Last Orders' is now the official name of the game and refers to the final round when everyone races to the finish line, having to complete a series of quick-fire questions and challenges to be crowned the winner. Jake, me and Bazza have officially formed a company called 'Halojen' which is a combination of 'Helen', 'Jenny' and 'Alice' which is Bazza's wife's name. Jake has found an indie games company who are inviting people to pitch their game ideas. He's filling in the paperwork to enter 'Last Orders' and the top twenty entries get invited to an awards night where they announce the winners. The top three games get made into a real board game, sold by the company via their website and some pretty big shops. I offered to help Jake fill in the paperwork, but he said I had enough of that sort of thing to do with the adoption forms, so I happily left that all up to him.

Talking of forms, Jen is a bit stressed as she's had an email from Mike saying he needs to pop by this afternoon and discuss one of her references with her. I'm sure it'll be something and nothing, but she's not been able to relax since she got it this morning.

By the time Mike arrives, Jen practically drags him through the door. She marches into the living room and is asking Mike what the problem is before he's even had a chance to manoeuvre himself and his crutches into an armchair.

'I'm sure it's just an admin error,' says Mike, trying to shrug his jacket off whilst Jen jiggles up and down in her seat. 'but we can't find the record of your specialist's letter. You did tell us that he was in full support of your application?'

'Yes, of course he is!' says Jenny, her face flushing, 'I wouldn't lie about something like that!'

'No one is saying you are lying, please don't worry,' says Mike, 'It's just an admin error, I'm sure, but we have to make sure we have all the paperwork in place before we go to panel.'

'I'll phone him now,' says Jenny, leaping up and grabbing her phone.

'No need,' says Mike, 'our office will contact him directly and they'll get another copy of his report.'

'That's alright, then, isn't it?' I say.

'Yes, of course,' says Mike, 'it's no problem at all, it just means that we have to make a small adjustment to the panel date.'

'What small adjustment?' says Jenny.

'Well, we were due to go to panel July 15th, but we won't meet the deadline for submitting all the paperwork now, so I'm afraid we will have to wait until mid August.'

'But if you just let me phone him, I can get a copy of his letter emailed to you today!' says Jenny, her eyes bright with tears.

'I'm afraid that isn't soon enough, Jenny,' says Mike, 'I'm really sorry, but the deadline was yesterday but it was only last night when double checking the documents that we realised the omission.'

I put my arm around my wife. 'Come on

Jen,' I say, 'another month doesn't make much difference does it? I mean you've been thinking about adopting for years, a few more weeks isn't much in the grand scheme of things, now, is it?'

'No,' says Jenny, sitting bolt upright on the edge of the sofa, 'do let me know when it's sorted, and if you need me to chase it up.'

'We will, of course,' says Mike, grabbing his crutches. 'Now, I'll leave you in peace.'

'Do you need anything else sorting, whilst you're here?' asks Jenny, 'We might as well double check everything – we don't want anything else holding things up again.'

'No, no, everything else is in order,' Mike says, 'unless you have any other changes? No change in your job circumstances or anything?'

'No,' says Jenny, 'not at all.'

'I'll show you out, Mike,' I say.

Once Mike has left, I turn to Jenny. I'm going to have to come clean to her about the redundancies. Then, once she's calmed down, we'll let Mike know. Just so everything is above board. I'm about to open my mouth when her stiff upper lip stance crumples and she sinks into the sofa like a rag doll losing its stuffing. Tears start to roll down her cheeks.

'Hey,' I say, sitting next to her and putting my arms around her, 'it's alright, it's only another month, we'll get there.'

'I know,' she says, wiping her nose, 'it's just I've waited and worried about not having children for so long and we seemed to finally be getting close. I know it's not long in the grand scheme of things, but another month before we know if the panel even approves us feels too much to bear.'

'The time will go before we know it,' I say. 'Maybe we'll have time to have a few days away at the beach or something.'

'I just can't bear to go through another year, another summer, another Christmas without knowing if we'll be parents,' says Jenny, a fresh crop of tears rolling down her cheeks.

I hold her tight and rock her gently back and forwards. 'It'll be alright, Jen, it'll be alright,' I say softly.

I repeat the words over and over to Jen until her tears subside. But even when she's calmed down and we're watching one of her favourite comedies on the telly, the words are still echoing round my head.

It'll be alright.

CHAPTER 35
– JENNY

I ring Helen to tell her about the panel being delayed and she tries hard to think of something to cheer me up.

'I know,' she says, 'you said you both wanted to get some babysitting practice in – why don't me and Jake help out?'

'You haven't had the baby yet, have you?' I say, managing a little laugh.

'No, but we're going to need some practice too,' she says, 'didn't Kyle say his friend from work has twins?'

'Dev? Yeah, he's got twin toddlers,' I say, 'we've met them a few times at work get togethers, they're adorable little things.'

'Blimey, two terrible twos?' Helen says, 'it might be a good idea for all four of us to take them on!'

'You could be right there,' I say, 'I'll ask Ky to ask him.'

'If I had twins, I think I'd have dropped them off at yours before Kyle had finished his sentence,' Helen says. There's a silence on the other end of the phone. 'Oops, sorry Jen,' she continues hastily, 'I'm not saying that having two children at once is impossible.'

'Don't be silly,' I say, 'I know you aren't. And ours are unlikely to be twins, anyway. One of them is probably going to be nursery or school age, by the looks of the children needing adopting in sibling groups.'

'Have you been looking at the children's profiles again?' she asks, 'That must tug at the heart strings.'

'It does a bit,' I say, 'their names get in my head and I start talking to them when I'm sorting out the bedrooms. Kyle must think I'm mad. There's nothing like having two empty furnished children's bedrooms to make you feel like the parenting version of Miss Haversham.'

'Well, let's go practice with Dev's little devils then,' Helen says.

Kyle contacts a tired and grateful Dev and the following week, the four of us are standing nervously at his door. We look round at the carnage of the front garden. There are discarded toys everywhere, something that looks like it was once a shoe and an upturned sandpit with its contents tipped into the flowerbed.

'Are you going to ring the doorbell, Kyle?' I ask.

'No, you go ahead,' says Kyle.

'He hardly knows me, compared to you,' I

say.

'Jake?' says Kyle.

'Helen?' says Jake.

'I'm pregnant,' Helen says, 'I can't go doing heavy lifting.'

'What, like ringing doorbells?' asks Jake.

'No, like lifting twin toddlers,' she says, 'that's why you three are here, I'm just coming along for moral support and to observe. See me as having a managerial role.'

'Well, no backing out now,' I say and press the doorbell.

There's a noise in the hall like the velociraptors scene in Jurassic Park and the barely audible sound of a tired male voice attempting to be heard over the stampede.

'How many kids did you say Dev has?' asks Jake.

'Two,' Kyle says, 'Hopefully he'll still have the same amount at the end of today.'

The door opens and Dev smiles at us, wiping something that I hope is custard off his jeans.

'Kyle, my friend,' he says, 'welcome! Kids, you know Kyle and Jenny and this is…'

'Helen and Jake,' I say, 'thank you for letting us babysit.'

'No, thank *you*,' says Dev, 'Molly and me are really grateful.'

'Have you got any nice plans this afternoon?' I ask.

'Sleep,' says Dev, 'just sleep.'

Dev's wife Molly appears beside him, looking like she's been partnering him in a sponsored sleeplessness challenge.

'Hi, good to see you again Kyle, Jenny,' she says. She turns to Helen and Jake, 'and to meet you guys. You're our saviours! Thanks so much all of you. We're really grateful.'

'Pleasure is ours,' I say as Molly hands me two enormous bags, bulging at the seams with drink bottles, changes of clothes and goodness knows what.

As Kyle takes one of the bags off me, two little faces poke between their parents' legs. They are grinning and pointing at us. Then the little girl whispers in the little boy's ear and they both fall about laughing.

'I'm not sure whether to be bowled over by their cuteness or scared stiff by these balls of energy wrapped up in Disney clothing,' I hear Helen whisper to Jake.

'Here we are then,' says Dev, crouching down to the twins' height and pointing to us one by one. 'You already know our friends Kyle and Jenny and these are their friends Helen and Jake,' he says, 'Do you remember we talked about how they are going to look after you this afternoon and you're going to have a wonderful time.' He turns to us, 'Thanks ever so much guys, Maya and Sam, are going to be as good as gold for you, aren't you?'

I can see Kyle trying not to look disconcerted by the slight laugh that escapes from Molly's lips as Dev says this. She sees the look of concern flash across his face and composes herself quickly.

'They'll be fine,' she says, 'and any problems, just give us a call, I'm sure we'll wake up – I'll put the phone on loud.'

'By the look on her face, I reckon she's more likely to put it on silent,' I hear Jake whisper to Helen.

I walk over to the twins and crouch down.

'Hello Maya, Hello Sam,' I say, beaming at them and producing two colouring books and packets of crayons for them. 'It's lovely to see you.'

'What do you say, guys?' says Dev to the toddlers who are excitedly trying to rip the boxes of crayons open.

'Thank you!' they chorus, plonking themselves down on the floor and starting to scribble frantically at the pages.

'Come on, you two,' says Molly, 'Jenny and everyone are waiting for you. Let's get you in the car and you can start your exciting afternoon.'

'And mummy and daddy can start their exciting sleep,' says Dev under his breath.

Molly and Dev grab the car seats and show me and Kyle how to strap the excited twins into them. Jake and Helen are going to follow in their car and meet us at a play place not far from here.

'Should we go and see how the car seat's done?' Helen asks Jake.

'No, too many cooks spoil the broth,' says Jake, 'it seems like you just have to wrestle a hyperactive wriggling bundle of crayons and chocolate buttons into a contraption that looks like a dentist's chair, whilst bending at an angle not made for adult humans and guaranteed to make you bang your head on the roof of the car.'

'Ow!' says Kyle, right on cue.

'See,' says Jake, 'nothing to it.'

Once both the children are strapped safely in our car, we wave goodbye to Dev and Molly and set off down the road in convoy. It doesn't take long to get to 'Archie's Adventures' - a play park with indoor and outdoor areas. I'm familiar with it, having been there with some of the younger youth groups. It caters for a wide age range, but we won't be on the high ropes today and we join the noisy queue for the toddler zone.

We seem to have fallen into gender stereotype roles already, with Helen and I having hold of one of Maya's hands each and Jake and Kyle each taking one of Sam's sticky little mitts in theirs. Maya is chatting away happily to me and Helen. telling Helen earnestly that 'mummy lets me wear make-up' when she spots lipstick in her bag.

Sam isn't quite as much the conversationalist as his sister, preferring instead to focus his energies on attempting a daring escape every two seconds. When Kyle got him out the car he tried to make a run for it, having spotted an ice cream stand placed strategically by the slow moving queue. Luckily, we'd been able to park next to each other and Jake stepped in and grabbed his little hand whilst Kyle banged his own head on the car roof again. We have been in the queue for quite some time now and Kyle and Jake have hold of Sam's hands so tightly that I have to fight the urge to check they're not cutting off his blood supply.

'So, Sam,' Jake says, 'I see you're wearing an incredible hulk T-shirt there, a big Bruce Banner fan, are we?'

'No,' says Sam, screwing his eyes up at Jake as if his stupidity physically pains him, 'I don't like Blues Banner, this is the credding-bill Hulk, silly!' and he puffs his little chest out proudly so that Jake can see the picture on his T-shirt properly.

'You're right, Sam,' says Kyle, 'Jake needs pictures to help him learn. Maybe you can let him help you with your new colouring book.'

Sam stops in his tracks and his eyes widen. 'Oh no!' he shouts. People in the queue look round, wondering what we've done to torture our little companion. Maya sighs, fixes Jake with a stare and says 'Have you wound Sam up like daddy does when it's bedtime-calm-time?'

Jake is about to defend himself when Sam

starts wailing. 'My colouring book! I lost my colouring book!' he cries, 'It's gone *forever*!'

'I'm sure it's not lost,' says Kyle, looking around, 'it must be in the car.'

'Should I go back and get it?' Jake asks, but no sooner do the words come out of his mouth, than the queue moves and we're finally at the front.

'Bumper value family entry, is it?' asks the young girl in the ticket kiosk.

'Yes please,' I say, 'but one of us,' I say, glaring at Kyle, 'needs to go back to the car to get something.'

'You'll have to all re-join the queue then, I'm afraid,' says the girl, 'I'm only allowed to give you the special entry price if you all go through the turnstile together.'

'Surely you can make an exception?' I say firmly, as Sam's wails increase in volume.

'Sorry, the system is automated,' says the girl, who seems to be pretty automated herself.

'How much is individual entry?' Kyle asks, obviously figuring it'll be worth an extra fiver to stop the wails which are now threatening to burst everyone's eardrums.

'Twenty-five pounds,' says the girl.

'I'm not paying another twenty-five pounds for the sake of a colouring book,' says Kyle, 'come on Sam, matey, we'll get you something else from the gift shop once we get inside.'

'Don't want something else,' shouts Sam, pulling his credding-bill Hulk t-shirt up and over his face and wiping his nose on it.

Leaving Maya with Helen, I go over to Sam and crouch down to his level. I gently pull his t-shirt straight, wipe his nose with a tissue from a pack in my pocket and give him a Jelly baby out of my huge emergency stash for when my blood sugars go low.

'Now, Sam,' I say in the calm but firm voice I use in the youth club, 'if we go back to the car for your colouring book, we won't be able to go into this lovely place and do lots of playing because we will have to wait in a long queue again. So, we are going to go in now, do lots of lovely things and your colouring book is going to stay safe in the car, ready for when it's time to go home.'

Sam sniffs a bit and looks like he's deciding whether to cry again. I wipe his tears with another tissue and pop another jelly baby in his mouth. Helen and Maya appear at my side and I give Maya two jelly babies as well. The little girl starts chewing on them both, her eyes wide, watching her brother to see what he's going to do.

'Yeah, mate, Jenny's right,' says Kyle, 'you won't be able to go on the swings and all the cool stuff if you're carrying a colouring book, will you?'

Maya leans towards Sam's ear to whisper

in it again, so loudly that we can all clearly hear her say, 'They're right Sam, and I want to go on the swings. And I want a big wee-wee.'

I stand up, take Sam by the hand, leaving a grinning Maya to hold onto Jake and Helen's and with Kyle bringing up the rear and making sure we've got everything, we all go through the turnstile together, like one big happy (ish) bumper value family.

Once we've negotiated actually getting into the play centre, the rest of the day goes pretty well. There are tears and tantrums, and not all of them from the toddlers, but all in all we manage and between the four of us, we make a fairly good crew.

Maya aligns herself with me and Helen, telling us that we are the 'three ladies' and that we have to make sure the boys don't do anything silly. Sam is happy with the flashing dinosaur that Kyle buys him and Maya loves her fluffy toy cat. I'm not sure if we're doing the right thing by reinforcing gender stereotypes and try to address this.

'Are you sure you want a fluffy pink cat, Maya?' I say, 'Look, there are lots of light-up dinosaurs!'

'No, Jenny,' Maya says, using my name in a way that reminds me of being told off at primary school, 'Princess Diamond Whiskers needs a new home and it's my job to be her mummy. You know what I mean, cos mummy says you are going to be a new mummy to some children who need a new home.'

My heart thuds as her serious little face sums up the complicated adoption system so simply. 'Yes, sweetheart,' I say, 'you're quite right. Let's go and pay for Princess Diamond Whiskers right away.'

'Do you have to pay for your new children?' asks Sam, waving his light-up dinosaur around so frantically that Kyle has to duck out of the way, knocking over a display of grinning garden gnomes as he does so.

'No, Sam,' I say, 'we don't need to pay for the children, we just have to love them and look after them.'

'If I love and look after my flashy dinosaur,' says Sam, 'can we keep the money and buy ice creams?'

'I'll get you an ice cream later,' says Helen, and the twins hug each other in delight.

'Maya,' says Sam, 'you order the choclit one and I'll get the storebeddy one and then we can have choclit-storebeddy-mash-up ice cream!' Maya nods in excited agreement. I glance round to see Jake and Kyle attempting to return the scattered gnomes to their pyramid formation as Helen helps me shepherd the twins and their overpriced new possessions to the till.

When it's time to make our way home later, I'm expecting tears at having to leave, but the twins are so tired from all the running around and activities that their eyelids droop and they are both asleep in their car seats before we've driven out of the car park. I look round to see them sleeping peacefully, flashy dino and Princess Diamond Whiskers tucked next to them.

'I think we did a good job,' I say to Kyle. He smiles and glances at them in the rear-view mirror.

'We did,' he says.

The next week there are a couple of back-to-back adoption training days. Emboldened by the successful afternoon out with two children, I'm feeling more excited than nervous about this one. We sign in and the receptionist gives Kyle a big smile again as she asks for our car registration. 'Same car as before, Kyle?' she says.

'Yes,' he replies, 'just slightly more biscuit crumbs in it than last time and a couple of crushed crayons on the upholstery, but other than that, no change.'

Bridget leads the session. Today we have to stand in a circle and take on roles of the people in the children's lives before they are placed with the adopters. These include birth parents, grandparents, several sets of foster carers, teachers, siblings and best friends. Then we are asked to stand round Bridget who is playing the child. She gets us to stand a distance away from her that represents how important we are to the child. I am playing her best friend from school and Kyle is her sibling who is to be placed in a different adoptive family.

'But why aren't they being placed together?' I ask Bridget.

'There are many reasons for this, Jennifer,' says Bridget, 'now, if we could…'

'But we're happy to take a sibling group of two,' I say, 'three possibly, if it stops them from being separated.' I ignore the surprised look on Kyle's face as I increase our adoption offer by fifty percent without consulting him.

'And that's wonderful,' says Bridget, 'but sometimes there are large groups of siblings needing to be adopted and it is very difficult for the adopters to meet all their needs at once.'

'But they need to be with their siblings, surely?' I say, 'they've already lost so much, they don't want to leave them as well.'

'It's not that simple, Jennifer, I'm afraid,' says Bridget, 'their needs can be very different and it may well be better for them to be placed separately where their forever families can dedicate themselves to meeting those needs, rather than being spread too thin.'

'But I run a youth club with dozens of young people in it, all different,' I say.

'But that's for a few hours at a time,' says Bridget, 'this is 24/7 and in your home and family. Besides, some of these children will have had such traumatic experiences and been treated very differently to each other or reacted very differently to their trauma, meaning that if placed together, they may retraumatise each other and be unable to heal and move forwards.'

I feel like the wind has been taken out of my sails. One minute I was riding high on the success of the afternoon with the twins and now I feel like I'm about to be given detention for interrupting the class. I can see the other attendees shuffling about as we all stand in our misshapen circle around Bridget.

'We can have a chat later, Jennifer, if you'd like to,' says Bridget, confirming my detention fears, 'but now, let's look at how contact might be maintained with some of the people in the children's pre-adoption life and how they might manage the goodbyes to those whom they have to let go. Kyle, you're playing my brother and you're going to be placed in a different family.' Bridget gives me a look which tells me that this is not up for debate. 'How often do you feel there should be contact between you and your sister and should it be direct face to face contact or "letterbox" where cards and letters are sent from one family to another via our letterbox coordinator?'

'Er,' says Kyle, 'I suppose that they'd like to be able to play together at least once a week.'

'Two or three times a week,' I interject. 'They're used to living together after all, you can't expect them to go from that to once a week.'

'Anyone else?' says Bridget, smiling kindly

but firmly in my direction. No one says anything.

'Well,' continues Bridget, 'as lovely as it would be for the children to be able to see each other that regularly, and it is wonderful that you are prepared to make such an effort for sibling contact, the reality of it is, that it is unlikely to be more than twice a year.' I see Kyle swallow hard and look across at me as Bridget continues, 'You will have lots to adjust to in your new families – new schools, new routines, new roles and you may live quite some distance from the siblings.'

I want to challenge this, but I don't trust myself not to cry. All I can see is Maya whispering in Sam's ear to reassure him. Hot tears fill my eyes as I think of their little faces covered in a mixture of their shared chocolate and strawberry treats. How will adopted brothers and sisters manage if they only get to share choclit-storebeddy-mash-up ice cream twice a year?

CHAPTER 36
– KYLE

By the time the training weekend has finished, I'm pretty worn out and put the radio on in the car as I focus on driving us home. Jenny wants to talk about it all though.

'I don't think they're trying hard enough to place siblings together,' she says.

'Well, it's like she said, isn't it?' I reply, 'Sometimes it's better for them to be placed apart.'

'Is it, though?' she says, 'or are they just saying that because there aren't enough adopters willing to have more than one child at a time?'

'I think they know what they're talking about, Jen,' I say.

'Couldn't we say we'll adopt three?' she says.

Just then a car overtakes me and cuts in front of us so I have to slam the breaks on in order to not go into the back of them. 'Jen,' I say, 'I'm tired. I've got to focus on the road.'

We don't talk much for the rest of the

journey. When we get in, I ask her what she wants for tea.

'I don't want anything,' she says.

'Come on, you've got to eat,' I say, going to put my arms around her. She moves away from me and goes upstairs. I hear the bedroom door slam shut. I'm exhausted, hungry and know Jen's blood sugars will be dropping soon so I go into the kitchen to put some pasta on. When it's ready, I call up the stairs. No reply. I put the lid on the pasta to keep it warm and go upstairs. Jenny is lying on the bed, her face puffy from crying.

'Come on, sweetheart,' I say, 'it's just been a tough day, that's all. You'll feel better after some food. You don't want to have a hypo, come on, come and eat something.'

'It's not fair,' she says, a slight smile coming through her tear-stained face, 'you can't even have a proper sulk with diabetes, you've always got to go and have your dinner!'

I take her hand and we go downstairs and eat. We pop the television on and watch a silly comedy whilst we do. After we've finished, Jen looks a little better.

'I know we can't adopt three children,' she says quietly, 'I just can't bear to think of them being split up from their brothers and sisters.'

'I know,' I say, 'and we'll be keeping two of them together, but we've got to be realistic. It's no use us biting off more than we can chew and us all ending up in a mess. We've got to focus on the good we can do and try not to worry individually about every single child in care. We'll drive ourselves mad.'

'You're right,' she says, 'I just can't help it though. They're not statistics, they're real little people, each and every one of them.'

'And two of them are going to have the best mummy in the world,' I say, putting my arm around her and kissing the top of her head. 'But we've got to look after ourselves as well. Let's watch a film where we don't have to think. Something with Dwayne 'The Rock' Johnson in it. There's a new one of his on Netflix.'

'What happens in it?' she asks me.

'No, idea,' I say, 'but it's got The Rock in it, so I reckon that's all that matters at this moment.'

The next evening Jen is at the youth club. I'm supposed to be reading one of the books she's bought about adoption but I can't take any more in after the full-on training days. I'm glad of an excuse not to do my homework and grab my phone when a message from Jake arrives. He says he's got good news and asks me to go over to his for a meeting of Halojen. When I arrive, a very excited Jake opens the door.

'You look like the cat that got the cream,' I say, 'what's the story?'

'Can't tell you until Bazza gets here,' says Jake, 'don't worry, he should arrive any minute.'

Sure enough, I've just made myself comfy in the living room and said hello to Helen when there's a repeated ringing on the doorbell. Jake leaps up and opens it. Bazza walks in, larger than life as always. He's carrying a huge bunch of flowers.

'Bazza, you shouldn't have!' grins Jake.

'These are for your beautiful wife,' says Bazza, giving the flowers to Helen with a flourish.

'Oh, thank you,' says Helen, 'I'll go and find a vase. That's very kind of you.'

'It's the least I could do, for one of my most wonderful ex-employees,' Bazza replies. 'and I also have a gift basket for you, well, rather for your soon-to-be new arrival – I couldn't carry it all at once, I'll just pop and get it from the boot.' He disappears out to his car and Helen and Jake exchange concerned looks.

'What's up?' I ask.

'We've still got Bazza's last gift basket shoved under the stairs,' says Helen, 'from when I left. Let's just say, if the quality is up to his usual standard, I doubt I'll be letting the baby anywhere near it.'

Just then, Bazza reappears, or rather his legs do. The rest of him is hidden behind the largest, brightest gift basket I've ever seen. There is so much luminous yellow netting in it and so many matching synthetic feathers that it looks like he's murdered Big Bird and dressed his carcus in a tutu. Bazza puts the basket down and straightens himself back up, beaming.

'Oh,' says Helen, 'thank you so much. Jake, look what Bazza's bought us!'

'Oh,' says Jake, 'yes, thank you, er, Bazza, what *have* you brought us?'

'Just a few essentials for mother and baby!' he says.

Helen gingerly starts to look through the basket, 'oohing' and 'ahing' with increasingly faked enthusiasm at the fluffy toys that look like they'd scare rather than soothe a baby and the set of dummies in the shape of garden bugs - not brightly coloured ladybirds, but slugs and caterpillars. I can't imagine Helen is going to want her baby to look like it's devouring a hoard of creepie crawlies. In the middle of the basket is a gigantic rabbit which glows an eerie shade of green when you squeeze its stomach. Jake reads the label.

'A Fright light?' says Jake, 'Maybe we should save this until the baby is old enough to go trick or treating.'

'That's just a typing error,' says Bazza, taking the hideous rabbit off Jake and ripping the label off it. 'It's supposed to say "night light". You know, the little one cuddles it and it stops them being afraid of the dark.'

'Presumably because the dark is preferable to seeing, if that rabbit is anything to go by,' I whisper to Jake.

'Well, I truly don't know what to say,' says Jake, 'Kyle, I feel guilty keeping all this to ourselves, would some of it be useful for when you and Jenny adopt, do you think?'

'Oh, no, no,' I reply, 'the social workers have to approve all our toys and accessories.'

'Really?' says Helen, shocked, 'I'm going to give Jen a ring, I've been given some bits and bobs for older children by a friend at work and I'd best check if that's okay. What time does she finish work, Kyle?'

'Oh, round about now, I'd say,' I say, checking my watch. Helen goes off to the kitchen to call Jenny.

'Well folks,' says Jake, 'I've got great news! Halojen are through to the semi-finals of the indie board game awards.' He waves a handful of tickets at us, 'and we're all invited to the ceremony in just over a month's time. Helen will be just over 8 months pregnant then, so all being well, we can have a good night out together before the baby comes!'

'That's fantastic, mate,' I say.

'Hoorah!' says Bazza, we are on the up!! The prize is in the bag! I wonder if they need any gift bags making up for the ceremony. Give us their number Jakey, I'll get in touch!'

We celebrate our success and try to persuade Bazza tactfully that the company will probably already have their own gift bag company with their logos on. He seems undeterred and excuses himself after a while, saying that he's off home to have a look for suppliers who can do him some samples. Helen comes back in to say goodbye to him.

'Did you get hold of Jen?' I say as Bazza disappears down the path.

'Yes,' she says, a bemused look on her face.

'How was she?' I ask, 'The training was a bit much and she was a bit down. Has work cheered her up, do you think?'

'She sounded pretty good,' Helen says, 'but just one thing, Kyle.'

'What's that?' I say.

'She says the social workers haven't said anything about having to approve all the things you buy for the children,' she smiles, 'so you could accept a gift basket from Bazza.'

'Oh really?' I say, 'well, isn't that good news!'

CHAPTER 37
– HELEN

Although I'm seven months pregnant and definitely look and feel it, it's still somehow rather surreal to be having a baby shower. It feels kind of 'showy' as well and even though it was Jen who suggested it to me, I still worry it's rubbing her face in it a bit. But she was undeterred and said it would also be a good way of receiving some slightly more appropriate gifts than the ones Bazza brought over the other week.

I'm happy to let Jen take over the organising – she seems keen to decorate the place ready with bunting and balloons. I had no idea what I was supposed to do, not really being into big displays. Some of the members of the theatre group are coming and they have already asked me what my 'theme' is. I just looked at them blankly. I mean, surely the 'theme' is 'having a baby', what further specification is needed? Jake's mum's friend Julie has baked her lovely cupcakes again and this time they have little chocolate teddy bears on top of the generous swirls of icing.

Tanya, who was one of the dancers in the panto was determined to help me pick a theme and offered to show me pictures of her baby's 'cake smash' on her Instagram.

'What's a cake smash?' I said as she rummaged through her handbag looking for her phone.

'You haven't heard of a cake smash?' she said, looking at me like I'd just announced that I didn't know what oxygen was. She proceeded to flick endlessly through photos of her one-year-old, Lucas, dressed like some kind of mini Chippendale in just a top hat, bow tie and nappy, covered from head to toe in cake and icing. His tiny fists were gleefully buried in the remains of a once beautiful, baked and iced creation, now obliterated beyond belief. And all of this was happening, by the looks of the spotlights and backdrop depicting the New York skyline, not at a birthday party playbarn, but a photography studio.

'Isn't it perfect!' gushed Tanya.

'Hmmm, yes, wonderful,' I replied.

'And I got it for under £200, because I booked it alongside Nikki's little Maisie's rabbit themed one.'

She flicks through her phone some more and shows me photos of a little girl, presumably the rabbit-themed Maisie, dressed in bunny ears and a nappy with a huge bobtail attached to it, sitting, beaming in the middle of an utterly destroyed three-tier cake covered in pink icing. What happens when these cake-smash kids go to someone else's actual birthday party, I wonder. Do they pop on a paper hat and watch happily as the birthday child blows out their candles? Or at the opening strains of 'happy birthday' do they strip off down to their nappies, pop on a headdress and hurl themselves maniacally onto grannie's homemade caterpillar cake?

Luckily my baby shower doesn't involve anyone diving into cakes, though I'm not certain about dad at one point when he knocks back a barcardi and coke without realising it contains bacardi. It's the same little crowd here as my hen night, along with Jake, Kyle, my dad and some of the blokes from work. Jenny has produced another game, this one involving baby name choosing. We don't know if we're having a girl or a boy so all names are possible. Jen enlisted the help of her youth group again and has made a large papier mache nappy, into which she's put lots of folded up bits of paper.

'So, everyone,' says Jenny, 'take two pieces of paper out of the nappy, answer the questions on them and that will give you your baby's first name and middle names.'

My mum dives up to take a turn. Jake watches as she digs about in the pieces of paper. 'Hmmm,' he says, 'I don't fancy sticking my hand in real nappies.'

'Don't worry, Jake,' says my mum, 'you won't mind when it's your own flesh and blood.'

I look at Jenny. She gives a big smile and shakes the nappy. 'Come on, Mary,' she says to my mum, 'let's be having you, or Helen will be going into labour before we've had the cakes!'

Mum seems oblivious to her faux-pas and unfolds her pieces of paper. 'They say,' she says grandly, as if presenting the scores on the Eurovision song contest, "name of your favourite singer" and "last thing you ate". Umm… Dolly Parton and a Bourbon biscuit.'

'Brilliant!' says Jenny, 'So your baby name suggestion for your grandchild, is Dolly Bourbon. What do you think of that one, Helen?'

'It's lovely,' I laugh, 'but let's try another one, just in case Dolly Bourbon turns out to be a boy.'

It's Jake's turn to choose now. 'Name of your true love,' he reads, 'and favourite snack food. Well, obviously our child will be called Beyonce salty popcorn.'

'Hey!' I say, 'do you want to have another think about that, darling?'

'Of course, my love,' says Jake, 'you're right. It's obviously Beyonce *sweet* popcorn.'

'Let me choose,' I say, 'we'll get no sense out of my husband!' I delve into the giant nappy and produce two pieces of folded paper. 'Name of your mother-in-law and…' I stop when I realise what I've said. I look at Jake. He comes and sits by me and takes my hand.

'It's okay,' he says, 'Christine was, *is* my mum's name.   What does the other piece of paper say?' I unfold it.

'Favourite band,' I say.

'So Christine Florence and the Machine?' says Jake.

'Perfect,' I say.

'Let's all take a break from the baby naming and have some of this lovely food Julie has made for us,' says Jenny. As everyone starts to gather at the buffet table, she comes over to me and Jake.   'Jake, I'm so sorry,' she says, 'the kids at the youth club helped me with the questions. I thought I'd checked them all in case of obscenities etc, but I must have missed that one. I hope I didn't upset you.'

'Of course not,' Jake says, 'it's absolutely fine. Now, let's get to the food before all that's left are old serviettes and carrot sticks.' He heads over to the table.

'Do you think he's really okay?' she asks me. 'I didn't mean to stick my foot in it.'

'He'll be fine, Jen,' I say, 'please don't worry.   It's great of you to go to all this trouble. The name game is a stroke of genius and I love the nappy!' Kyle comes over. He's been at the table with Jake and somehow already has a plate piled high with food.

'How's Jake?' says Jenny.   'I feel awful, putting him in that position, talking about his mum in front of everyone.'

'He's alright,' says Kyle, 'you know Jake, always a smile. Thank goodness we don't have to choose our kids' names, eh? Seems to be a minefield!'

'I'm not sure which is best,' says Jenny, 'Some of the names of children we've seen are interesting to say the least. I'm bracing myself to have to register little Beyonce Bourbon Williams at the local nursery.'

CHAPTER 38
– JAKE

Jenny's name game provides quite a few laughs, plus if we have quadruplets, we now know we could name them after the Beatles or the Teletubbies. Kyle and me manage to sit near the buffet table for a lot of the party and help ourselves to food and drink.

'How's the meetings with your social worker going?' I ask him.

'Alright, I think,' he says, 'hard to tell really if we're saying the right things. It's all a bit surreal. You sort of have to plan as if you're definitely having the kids, like kitting out the bedrooms, sorting out adoption leave from work, but all the while we don't know if we will be approved and even if we are, we have no idea how long it will take to be matched with kids, and how old they'll be.'

'Good point,' I say, 'At least me and Helen know we'll be having a baby who will be zero days old when we have them and roughly when that will happen. It must be strange trying to plan for all eventualities.'

'Yeah,' Kyle says, 'like the other day, we were thinking about going to the little music festival later this year. You know how you have to book months ahead or it sells out? Well, it's really family friendly and kids' tickets are free, so we booked ours and then ordered two kids' ones. We felt like frauds doing it, especially when we had to put their ages in. We just had to make something up.'

'That must be strange,' I say, 'but nice, in a way, to be making plans as a family, even if they're tentative plans at present?'

'I think it's good,' Kyle says, 'but I can tell it fries Jen's mind. She's been thinking about this for years longer than me, of course. I'm not sure what she'll do if we get turned down.'

'I can't see them saying no to you,' I say.

'I dunno,' says Kyle, shaking his head, 'I'm trying to be strong for Jen like I usually am, but I can't help getting the jitters every now and then. There's just so much to think about and so much that is unknown. And I think doing my knee in has made me realise I'm not infallible after all. I'm supposed to be convincing the panel that I'm so capable and we've got the CF thing covered and then I go and start the assessment on crutches.' He looks down at his feet and lowers his voice. 'And to top it all, I might be out of a job soon.'

'How do you mean?' I ask.

'Redundancies, lots of them,' Kyle says in a whisper, 'but keep it to yourself, I haven't worked out a good time to tell Jen yet and I don't want the social workers finding out.'

'They're going to have to know though, aren't they?' I say, 'Jen and the social workers, I mean?'

'I'm hoping I get one of the remaining jobs and then no one needs to worry about it,' Kyle says.

'Yeah, but *you're* worrying about it, mate,' I say, 'and surely a problem shared is a problem halved? You need to tell Jenny, she won't be happy if she finds out you've been keeping stuff from her.'

'She won't, but she's already trying so hard to hold it all together with the adoption assessment, I don't want to add to her stresses,' says Kyle, 'Don't want her to lose sleep and come down with a chest infection or something on top of everything else.'

'No, I suppose not,' I say, 'it's just I remember how I tried to keep my grieving about my mum to myself when I was first with Helen. She ended up thinking I was cheating on her. I should have been open with her about everything in the first place.'

'Sorry Jake,' Kyle says, 'going on about myself and bringing you down. How are you doing with impending fatherhood?'

'I'm good,' I say, 'wish I could contribute

a bit more effectively in the grandparent department, but Julie is going to make the best surrogate granny ever, I reckon.' We look over at Julie who is at the centre of a game which involves putting a nappy on a teddy bear whilst blindfolded and wearing oven gloves.

'Are you going to tell your dad about the baby?' Kyle asks.

I pause, grab a pork pie from the buffet table and take a bite from it. I'm not particularly hungry, but it gives me a chance to think whilst I chew. 'I dunno,' I say, 'I haven't told him I'm married yet. We're hardly ever in touch. He hasn't made any effort to be there for me since my early teens, so I'm not holding my breath for him to win any grandad of the year awards.'

Kyle lets out a big sigh and grabs us both a couple of beers. 'Sorry, mate, I didn't mean to put a downer on the baby party – what's it called again?'

'Baby shower,' I say

'Why's it called a shower?' Kyle frowns.

'Cos they shower you with gifts?' I ask.

'Of course,' says Kyle. 'Here's to the baby party – all your nearest and dearest showering you with presents and wishing you well. And hopefully a fair few of these folk will be visiting you when the baby comes and offering to baby sit.'

'We'll do the same for you and Jen,' I say.

'Yeah, thanks Jake, I know you will. But

you'll be a bit busy with your new arrival and anyway, they were telling us on adoption training the other week that we shouldn't introduce the children to too many people at once and that we need to choose our babysitters very carefully as not everyone will be able to deal with the behaviours and emotions that the kids are going to have. You'll both be great, but you're going to have your hands full already.'

We both take a bite of pork pie and chew in silence for a moment.

'Hey, you two! You look like you've dropped a pound and found a penny!' says Jenny appearing beside us. 'What you been talking about?'

We look at each other and back at Jenny.

'Our board game!' we say in unison.

CHAPTER 39
– KYLE

Mike is coming over again today to continue with our assessment and to give us some feedback from the social workers who run the training days. It feels like I'm back at my secondary school parents' evening and I'm about to have to sit there squirming whilst the art teacher tells my mum and dad that I talk too much in class.

Mike arrives on time as always and settles himself into what we've come to refer to as 'Mike's chair.' He smiles as I bring him a cup of tea and a digestive. Jenny perches on the end of the sofa next to me and looks at him eagerly.

'So, today we'll be discussing the reports from your training sessions,' he says. We nod.

'All good, I hope?' Jenny asks.

'No detentions or extra homework?' I add.

'Nothing to be unduly concerned about,' says Mike, opening his folder.

'Unduly?' Jenny says, 'That sounds ominous.'

'We'll cover everything in due course,'

says Mike.

'How do you mean though?' Jenny asks, 'If there's something to address, I'd rather start with that.'

'We usually go through the report in order,' says Mike, in a frustratingly calm voice. It's easy for him to be calm, his future doesn't rest on the opinion of others.

'Could you perhaps deviate from the norm, just this once though?' Jenny says, 'It would help me to know what we're up against, then I can relax a bit, hopefully and continue with the session.'

'Okay,' says Mike, flicking over the page of the report, 'It's only really that they said you asked a lot of questions, and…'

'Who said that?' Jenny says. I squeeze her hand gently.

'Don't worry Jen,' I say, 'Let's let Mike speak for a second. You have to admit, you are asking quite a lot of questions.' I can see her cheeks reddening, and from the look on her face I can tell it's partly with embarrassment, but also with anger. Jen has always said to me that asking questions is a good thing and she doesn't get why people get frustrated with her when she does this. She was very wound up after the last session, and I do see her point that you need to know the answers in complicated circumstances such as these. 'What do they want us to do,' she said when she was unable to sleep one night, 'just muddle through?'

'I'm on your side,' says Mike, 'everyone is. We all want to match parents with children and create new forever families. We just have to be sure we've ironed out as many creases as possible at the assessment stage so that we can minimise the bumps along the road once the children are placed with you.'

'But that's what I'm doing by asking the questions!' Jenny says indignantly. She takes a deep breath and I can see her making an effort to sound calm. 'Sorry, Mike, do go ahead.'

'So,' says Mike, 'the only concern is that they feel your amount of questioning could indicate that you have an anxious personality, and they were worried that if you came across in this way to your children, that would be an issue. Adoptive children need to feel safe and they will pick up on the anxieties of the adults who are caring for them. They need you to act calmly so that they feel you have everything under control. They have often been removed from chaotic birth families and they need to know their new life has boundaries, routines and adults they can rely on.'

'But that was precisely why I was asking the questions,' Jenny says, 'so that I would be prepared and calm and know what to do in all eventualities when the children come.'

'With the best will in the world,' says Mike, 'it's not possible to be prepared for *all* eventualities.'

'I know that,' she says, 'but it's all very well appearing calm at the training sessions if you get to the stage of having children and realise you don't have a clue what to do! Surely, it's best to ask as many questions as possible now, before the children are in the picture.'

'She does have a point,' I say. 'Jen does like to think through as many possibilities as she can – with everything, not just adoption, whilst I tend to assume it'll all be fine unless it's proved otherwise. Two quite different approaches, but I think it makes us the ideal team.'

'You could well be right there,' says Mike, 'and I would say that is the impression I certainly have of you both – that you make a good team, support each other, think similarly in important ways, but also that your differences actually ensure that you have each other's backs in areas where one of you needs more support than the other.'

'Thank you,' Jenny says, 'So you are still in support of us adopting?'

'I haven't come across anything in my assessment that has given me serious concerns,' says Mike, 'and neither have any of the other professionals. Part of my role is to give us time to unpick any issues as we go along, so we are prepared, for the panel and ultimately, for your children.'

I see tears well up in Jenny's eyes at the

words, 'your children.'

'So really,' I say, 'you agree that we're all asking lots of questions now, so that we're prepared when the children are placed?'

'Yes,' says Mike, smiling.

'And that's really, exactly what Jenny is doing when she asks her questions?' I continue.

'It is,' Mike nods. 'I think you'll agree, Jenny, that you like to be prepared, and possibly more so than the average person?'

'Well,' I say, 'when you have to carry out medical routines daily and look after yourself the way Jenny does...' Jenny gives me a look and my voice tails off – I hope I haven't said the wrong thing. We don't want Mike thinking that she won't be able to cope with the children without getting ill.

'Go on,' says Mike, 'don't be afraid to discuss your routines, it's a good thing that you have routines that help you both manage Jenny's health together. Lots of adoptive parents have things they have to do, whether it's health routines, job commitments or looking after existing birth children. You won't be parenting in a vacuum. My job is just to make sure that there is room in your new life for everything that you need to carry over from your current one. So, like you, I like to make sure that we have asked all the questions we need to and prioritised everything important.'

'Well, I'm certainly used to prioritising

things,' Jenny says, 'I have to prioritise so many things when I get up – physio, insulin, food, nebulisers. It's hard to prioritise everything at once. Things like make-up and hair styling don't really get a look in. But I manage, every day. And Kyle is a great help.'

'What would you do if Kyle was unwell and unable to help with the children in the morning?' Mike asks.

'Well, we have my parents nearby who are willing to help and our friends.' Jenny says, 'and Kyle is usually in excellent health anyway. When he ruptured his ligament, we managed. Also, at the moment, we're doing all this whilst working. But I'll be on adoption leave for at least a year and I may take further leave, depending on the age of the children.'

'And can you afford to do that, financially?' Mike asks.

'Yes,' I say, 'we've got some savings.'

'And you will be working full-time, Kyle?' Mike says.

'I will,' I say. I clear my throat.

'Something I've always been told with managing my CF,' Jenny says, 'is that prevention is better than cure. In other words, if for example I know I have a busy time coming up, I'll use some annual leave so that I don't get worn down and more susceptible to picking up infections. So, I think about things in advance, because then I'm less likely to be floored by them later, mentally or physically. Hence all my questions.'

'That makes sense,' says Mike, looking thoughtful, 'I'm making notes now so I can put all your points in my report. As you say, you've spent your life having to consider more things than the average person and have developed effective means for doing that by considering things in advance, to minimise problems further down the road. This is exactly, as you pointed out, what we are doing by carrying out a thorough adoption assessment. I will certainly feed that back and it should help to shed some light on things and ease these concerns.'

'Exactly,' I say, 'I've always found that about Jen. I have to say that sometimes I've just wanted her to go with the flow a bit more, but I have to admit, she's often right and her forethought has saved us on more than one occasion.'

'So, you could say, Jenny,' Mike says with a big smile, 'that preparation is your super-power?'

'Yes,' she says, smiling back at him, 'Yes, you could.'

Mike agrees to feedback that 'preparation is Jenny's super-power' to the social workers from the training day. Jen looks happier and brighter after this and the rest of the session goes well. We discuss the learning from the training, are able to clarify some of the topics we didn't have time to go into fully on the day and we make a plan for the remaining assessment meetings. Mike also delivers the good news that we now have a new panel date, a month after our previous one.

Once Mike has left, Jenny writes the panel date on the calendar. We both stare at the words there, on the square for the 12th August. Such small words for such a big, life defining event. A little way underneath it, two weeks later, Jenny has written 'Helen's due date.'

'Feels rather real, doesn't it?' I say, now it's less than two months away.'

'It does and it doesn't,' she says. 'I don't think I'll really believe it until we actually have two children sleeping upstairs in those empty bedrooms.'

I give her a hug.

'There's going to be a lot of change,' she says, 'September always feels like a new term, even though I'm no longer a student, but this September is certainly going to see some changes.'

'You're not wrong,' I say, 'Jake and Helen will be parents and we won't be far behind them.'

'Hopefully,' Jenny says quietly.

'Definitely,' I say.

'Thank goodness some things are staying the same, though,' Jenny says, 'with all this new stuff, it's good we've got our jobs as constants. My boss is really good about me taking a year or two off and yours is okay about you having parental leave too, isn't he?'

I nod as enthusiastically as I can, but Jenny sees through me. I don't know how I've managed to keep it from her this long. Maybe it's because there's been so much going on. But she's on to me now.

'What is it, Kyle?' she says, using my full name.

'Nothing,' I say, 'let's message Jake and Helen and go out for tea. Jake and me have a few things to discuss with the board game.'

'Not yet,' she says, 'there's something up, I can see it in your face. Aren't they going to let you have enough time off when the kids come? Do you want me to get Mike to write to them and explain how we need time to settle as a family?'

'No, no, it's not that,' I say.

'What is it, then?' she asks.

'Let's sit down,' I say, leading her gently to the sofa. I open the redundancy email on my phone and hand it to her. She reads it in silence.

'It'll be okay, Jen,' I say. 'I'll probably get one of the remaining positions and even if I don't, I'll find a new job.'

'But what if you don't?' she says, 'They're hardly going to give two kids to a couple with a disabled mother and an unemployed father!'

'Hey, Mike described you as having super-powers, and I've got a good work record. I'll find something.'

'How much time is there before you find out if you've got one of the jobs?' asks Jenny. She starts to read the email again. Her face darkens and she fixes me with a glare.

'Kyle,' she says.

'Jen?' I reply.

'This email was sent on Helen and Jake's wedding day. You've known about this for nearly three months and not said a word. I can't believe you lied to me.'

'I didn't lie,' I say, 'I just didn't tell you.'

'Same difference,' she says, 'When were you going to come clean? When I dropped the kids off at nursery and came back to find you in your pyjamas watching daytime TV?'

'No,' I say. I try to hug her but she pulls away. 'There's no point getting wound up about it, Jen, it won't help. I don't want you to get ill. You've got to calm down and just see how things go. You worry too much.'

'I worry too much!' Jen shouts, 'Don't you start telling me I'm too anxious as well! I've had enough of people saying I'm a nervous wreck who will traumatise our children just because I try to plan for things rather than coast along, hoping for the best!'

'Yes,' I say, 'but Mike said we work well together – it's good that I'm laid back.'

'Laid back?' Jenny continues to yell, 'Kyle, you're so laid back, you're bloody horizontal. Just like you were when you knackered your leg mucking about with Phil. We're trying to adopt two actual children, I can't bloody deal with you acting like a kid as well!'

And with that, she grabs her keys and phone and storms out of the house.

CHAPTER 40
– HELEN

Jenny's busy today and Jake is at work, so I decide to go into town on my own. I need to get a few bits and pieces ready for when I go in to have the baby. There's only just over two months to go until my due date now and I'm a swirling mix of excitement, nerves and good old hormones.

I glance in the mirror to see how I look. As I suspected, my fashion statement is 'stole a circus tent to wear as a dress'. My body feels like it belongs in a circus too, next to the elephants. I know I'm supposed to be blooming but I just feel fat and clumsy. Every time I go into a room, I knock something over because I've lost track of what size I am and where my bulk ends. I can't complain to Jenny, it would seem ridiculously ungrateful for this gift I've been given. Plus, she's been at work a lot, trying to plan ahead for someone to take over her projects as she prepares for adoption leave. She says this process is made all the harder by the fact she doesn't like to assume she actually will get to adopt so she feels silly asking people to cover her work. She told me she secretly worries they're laughing at her behind her back, although when I've met any of them when I'm out with Jen, they're all really supportive. I think she's just feeling uncertain because there are so many assessments to go through and so many people to convince that they're good enough. I feel so guilty that it just happened to me and Jake without us even planning it. We didn't have to prove anything to anyone and we'll be sent home from the hospital with a brand new little human life and everyone will just assume we know what to do.

Then there's the fact that unlike me, she has no idea how long it will be until she has children. She was really upset the other week after their social worker's visit and the fact that some of the assessors had said she was too anxious. They needn't worry about Jen, she's a force to be reckoned with once she sets her mind to things. I wish I could be more like her. I'm always second guessing myself and needing others to prop me up. Soon I'll have to be strong for the baby so I'm starting now and heading into town on my own, rather than waiting for someone else to come with me.

It's all going well at first. I have a lovely mooch around the baby department in Boots and buy some babygros and vests to take with me into hospital and some toiletries for me. I feel quite tired after this and head for a café. I've just managed to manoeuvre myself and my bags into a chair on a little table by the window when the door to the café tings to announce the arrival of more customers. I look up and to my horror see it's Will, my ex and his fiancée Katie. His fiancée Katie, who used to be my best mate Katie until she turned out to be Will's guilty secret and the reason he left me via a short but sour note.

I'm trying to hide behind the laminated menu when Katie spots me. For a split second, I can see that she's tempted to retreat back out the door, but she soon gathers her wits and gushes over to me.

'Helen!' she squeals, 'how wonderful to see you! Goodness, aren't you huge! I'd heard you were pregnant but I didn't realise you'd be so... big!'

'Thanks Katie,' I say, putting down the puddings menu and picking up the one with salads and sandwiches on it.

'Where's Jake? Should he have let you out alone this close to your due date?' asks Will.

'He's at work,' I say, 'and I'm allowed out on my own, thank you very much, I'm not due for ages. I'm nowhere near the 40 week mark as yet.'

'40 weeks?' says Katie, 'but that's ten months, not nine – are you having a baby elephant, Helen?'

'No,' I say, 'pregnancies are 40 weeks on average. Anyway, how are you both? Set a wedding date yet?'

'No, not yet,' Will cuts in. Katie remains uncharacteristically silent at this point, fiddling with her engagement ring. The ring that Will had waved under my nose in his drunken state of attempted reconciliation before I turned him down and he promptly turned his attentions back to Katie.

'Well, don't let me keep you,' I say, 'I must be getting on.'

'But you haven't eaten yet,' says Katie, 'we can't have you wasting away, Helen. You've got to embrace the eating for two whilst you can.'

'I've lost my appetite,' I say and somehow manage to squeeze my bags and my bulk past them and out of the door.

Luckily, Marks and Spencers is two shops away, so I install myself in their café and treat myself to a sandwich and a cake. I might as well eat what I want as I seem to be the size of a house anyway. The lady clearing the tables looks at me and smiles kindly.

'You alright, love?' she asks, 'You look like you've got the weight of the world on your shoulders. Baby will be here soon, don't worry. This bit is hard on the body isn't it?'

'It is a bit,' I say.

'Here,' she says, 'let me get you a pot of herbal tea, on the house,'

'Thank you,' I say, welling up at her kindness.

'Hey, what's up?' she asks, 'it can't be that bad.'

'No, it's okay, I've just bumped into my ex, that's all,' I say.

'Oh,' she says, 'is he the father of the baby?'

'Oh, no, thank goodness,' I reply, 'my husband is lovely.'

'There's no need to be sad then, sweetheart,' she continues, 'you don't still have feelings for your ex, do you?'

'No,' I say, 'not at all. At least, not unless you count bitterness, anger and extreme loathing.'

CHAPTER 41
– JAKE

Work is manic today. Everyone seems to have decided simultaneously that it's time to play board games, drink milkshakes and eat nachos. I'm run off my feet. I'd hoped to get away to meet Helen whilst she's in town. She messaged me earlier sounding a bit down but I couldn't get chance to call her.

I finally manage to leave the counter with a cloth and spray and start cleaning some of the tables. I feel a tug on the leg of my jeans and look down to see the little lad who I rescued from his milkshake disaster a while back. He's wearing a dinosaur T-shirt again, though I think it's a bigger one than last time. Bigger T-shirt, I mean, although possibly a bigger dinosaur as well. This one, according to the logo, is from Jurassic World Dominion.

'Hello matey,' I say, 'good to see you again.'

His dad appears, carrying a large bag and an even larger toy dinosaur.

'Hello again,' he smiles. 'Toby, leave the

nice man's leg alone!'

'I want a new T-shirt,' says Toby, 'please.'

'Not today, Tobes,' says his dad, 'maybe for your birthday.'

Toby's bottom lip threatens to wobble. I'm tempted to offer him some of our hard to shift stock again, but I'd best learn not to give in to every demand or I'll be a complete pushover of a dad and me and Helen will be bankrupt by the time our children start school.

'I know,' I say, 'why don't you see what new games we have to play in this section over here? I'm pretty sure I saw some dinosaur playing cards here yesterday.'

I dig out 'Happy Dino Families' and give it to Toby and his dad to play. 'Special offer today,' I say, 'no hire charge for the pre-school games section.'

'Brilliant, thanks so much,' says Toby's dad. Toby tips the pack of cards gleefully out of their brightly coloured box and starts to loudly announce the name of each of the dinosaur species. I leave them to it and finish cleaning the tables, smiling to myself as I hear Toby's dad trying to explain the rules to his son, with Toby interrupting him every few seconds to yell 'Dippy-docus' and 'Steggy-saw-us.' As I'm clearing the final table, I notice an older man come in to join Toby and his dad. Toby's eyes light up and he scatters cards over the floor as he runs to the man.

'Grandad!' he squeals, as the older man bends down and scoops him up into a hug.

'Hiya Dad,' says Toby's dad. 'Can I deal you into our poker game?'

Soon all three of them are engrossed in their card game, which Toby seems to be winning, from what I can tell, because he appears to be making up most of the rules as he goes along.

When I get back to the counter, it's calmed down a bit and I manage to go and sit in the break room for a few minutes and eat a sandwich. As I chew, I think about Toby and how happy he looked to see his grandad. I think about the relaxed way Toby's dad dealt him into the game and how they all laughed together. Three generations, bonding over some dinosaur playing cards. Before logic can get in the way of emotion, I pull out my phone and scroll through to my dad's number. 'Hi dad,' I tap out before I can think twice about it, 'just wanted to let you know I got married. To Helen. I told you about her at Christmas. And you're going to be a grandad in a couple of months. Hope you're all well, Jake.'

By the time I return from my break, Toby is leaving, dressed in a new t-shirt with our café logo on it. His grandad is paying at the till and carrying Toby's discarded dinosaur clothing. I wave goodbye to them all and return to my shift. The café is crowded and I don't get to stop and think for the rest of the working day. When I finally clock out, I look at my phone. My dad has seen my message. He read it not long after I sent it, according to the read receipt. But that was several hours ago now and there's no reply. Not so much as a thumbs-up emoji. I shouldn't be surprised and you'd think by now that I wouldn't be hurt or angry. But I am. And very, very tired.

When I get home, Helen is looking a bit down.

'Do you think I look like a fat elephant?' she says before I've even taken my coat off.

'No,' I manage to grin, 'you don't even look like a thin elephant. Shall I get us a takeaway from the chip shop, I'm too knackered to cook.'

'I don't want anything fattening,' she says.

'Oh come on, Hels, you're pregnant,' I say, 'you're supposed to put on weight. Unless this has all been a prolonged April fool's joke and you've actually got a black forest gateau under your jumper?'

'So, you do think I eat too much junk food?' she says.

'Don't be ridiculous,' I sigh, 'What's brought this on?'

'I saw Will and Katie in town,' she says, 'and they kept saying how big I was and how the baby must be due any day now. By the time it comes, I won't be able to fit through the door and I'll have to give birth in the hospital car park.'

'That would be terrible,' I grin, 'do you

know how much they charge for parking per hour?'

'Jake,' says Helen, 'I'm serious!'

'Helen, I don't know why you care for a second what that idiot pair say!' I say. 'Look, I'm off to get us some chips, then we can watch TV, I'm not really fit for anything else, it's been mad all day.'

There's a long queue at the chip shop and by the time I get back, I'm starving. There's still no reply from my dad. I know there's a time difference, but he must be awake as the app says he was last online twenty minutes ago. You'd think being told he has a new daughter-in-law and is soon to have a grandchild might have inspired him to send at least a quick message. Then again, having a son all these years doesn't seem to have prompted him to say or do much.

'Food's here,' I call to Helen. No reply. I go into the living room. She's not there. Wearily, I climb the stairs. She's curled up in bed.

'Come on, Hels,' I say, 'come and have some food, it'll get cold.'

'I'm not hungry,' she says.

'Well, I'm bloody starving,' I say. 'I'm going to eat mine. If you'd rather stay up here worrying about what your ex thinks than come eat with the father of your child, then I can't help you.'

'I just want a bit of comfort,' Helen says, 'it's alright for you, you don't have our child camping out in your body for 40 weeks!' She gets up off the bed and starts rummaging around in the wardrobe. She drags a holdall out and starts throwing clothes in it. 'I'm going to go to my mum and dad's.'

'Fine!' I say, 'at least you have a mum and dad to go to!'

Helen stops throwing clothes in the bag for a second and turns to me. 'I'm so sorry about your mum, and your dad, Jake, I really am, but I'm exhausted, I can't deal with this now. I'll go stay with my parents overnight and when I come back, we'll work out how to tell your dad about everything. I'm sure he'll want to be involved when he knows there's a baby coming. It could be a fresh start for you both.'

'He knows!' I say.

'How?' says Helen,

'I messaged him,' I say, 'but he can't even be bothered to reply.'

'But we said we were going to do it together,' Helen says, 'Why didn't you tell me? Jake, you can share things with me, I'm pregnant, I'm not made of porcelain. We can't keep things from each other, we're going to be parents. When did you message him?'

'On my break today,' I say, 'He's seen the message, look.'

Helen looks at my phone. Then she comes over and gives me a hug.

'Hey,' I say, 'stop kicking.'

'I'm not kicking you!' she giggles.

'Not you,' he says, kissing me on the nose, 'Baby Weston-Smith is practising his or her keepy-uppies by the look of it.'

'Come on,' says Helen, 'let's go and eat enough chips for the three of us. I'm sorry I was sulky.'

'You weren't sulky, you're just understandably tired,' I say, 'I'm sorry I didn't tell you about texting my dad. I saw this little lad in the café with his dad and grandad and it just felt like it might be worth a go and I wanted to do it before I overthought it. But I was obviously wrong – it wasn't worth it. I'll just forget about him again. I have all the family I need here. I love you, Mrs Weston-Smith.'

'I love you too, Mr Weston-Smith,' she replies.

CHAPTER 42
– JENNY

I've driven round for a couple of hours, following my row with Kyle. I can't believe he has known about the redundancies for this long and not told me. What on earth are we going to do if he loses his job? There's no way the adoption panel are going to say yes if we haven't got a steady income. I can't work full-time because of my health. I suppose I could go back to my part-time work after a minimal amount of parental leave, but then I'll be too worn out to enjoy having the children by the time I get home. And I haven't dreamt about and put so much into applying to adopt just to end up missing everything because I'm at work. I'll have already skipped the years of their lives before they came to us. I don't want to miss a second longer than I have to.

As much as I love my job, I don't want to spend all my energy and positivity on the kids in the youth club and have no patience left for our two. *Our two*. I feel a twinge every time I say things like that. I ordered two children's tickets the other week for a family-friendly music thing me and Kyle usually go to and I felt like the police were about to burst in and arrest me for planning a kidnap. The online ordering system wouldn't accept our order without us entering our phantom children's dates of birth, so I had to make something up. I fully expected a flashing red box to appear on the screen telling me that such children didn't exist and that I had been put on a database of people not allowed anywhere near festivals, music or children.

I really need to let off steam and talk to someone. I messaged Helen earlier but didn't get a reply. Maybe she's eating her tea. I decide to just turn up on her door. She won't mind. We're always there for each other and I can't face Kyle yet, I'm too wound up.

I knock on Helen's door and Jake answers.

'Hi Jenny, we weren't expecting you,' he says, 'everything okay? He pokes his head out of the door and looks up and down the street. 'Is Kyle parking the car?'

'No,' I say, 'he's probably sold it, for all I know. We might have to if he loses his job. Though that will make living in it difficult when we lose the house.'

'Oh, he's told you about the redundancies, then?' Jake asks. 'That's good, I told him you'd want to know.'

'Wait,' I say, feeling my temperature rising again. I take out my phone and scan my blood glucose monitor just in case I'm having a hypo. Nope, it's just anger making me hot. Jake is looking at me with concern. 'So,' I say, 'he told you about his job before he told me?'

Jake goes pale. 'Well, not long ago,' he says, 'I mean... er... why don't you come in and talk to Helen, she'll be happy to see you.'

I follow Jake into the living room. Helen is lying on the sofa, bundled up in her dressing gown. She doesn't look overly happy to see me. She looks half asleep. Jake's probably been giving her a foot rub or something. The remains of fish and chips lie on the coffee table and the television is paused on *Look Who's Talking.* John Travolta, Kirstie Alley and a smiling baby are frozen on the screen. Helen jumps up and reaches for the remote and quickly turns the television off.

'It's alright,' I say, aware that I'm still talking in a similar tone of voice to the one I last spoke to Kyle in, 'You don't have to protect me, I can handle seeing babies on the television. After all, I'm going to have to get used to seeing yours soon.'

'We were rather hoping people would want to see the baby, rather than have to get used to it,' says Helen, glancing at Jake and forcing a smile.

'You can say that again,' mutters Jake under his breath.

Helen puts her hand protectively across

her stomach. Whenever she does that, it looks to me like she's cuddling the baby. My insides lurch. Everyone is humouring me and talking as if I'm going to become a mum just like Helen, but my womb is as empty as our two spare bedrooms. And again, it's not that I see adoption as in any way inferior to giving birth. In many ways, I'm glad to forego the health hassles associated with pregnancy as I spend quite enough time with medical professionals examining me, thank you very much. It's just that there seem to be too many hurdles to leap to be approved and today it seems more out of reach than ever.

'You know I will love your baby, Helen,' I say stiffly.

'I know,' says Helen, 'sorry Jenny, I might be a little oversensitive, I've had a long day and Jake and me were just discussing some things that need sorting.'

'Oh,' I say, 'well I'd best not interrupt you then.'

'No, no, sit down,' says Helen, 'Jake, you said you were going in the shower after the film, if you go and do that now, I'll have a quick chat to Jenny.'

A quick chat, I think to myself. How many times have I dropped everything when Helen has been in a state over some bloke? The times I've talked to her whilst trying to do my physio and now I've actually come to her for help and all she can offer me is a 'quick chat.'

'No, don't worry, Jake,' I say, 'I'll be going. I don't want to disturb your baby planning.'

'No, sit down, Jen,' Jake says, 'I've got to go in the shower, I must stink from rushing around at work all day. Helen wanted to talk to you about Kyle's job.'

'So you all knew?' I say, still standing, 'and not one of you told me? Did you not think that knowing something that might completely derail our adoption plans was worth mentioning amongst the baby talk?'

Jake briefly squeezes my arm in what I assume is supposed to be a comforting manner and practically runs upstairs to have a shower. Helen looks enviously after him.

'We knew you'd worry,' says Helen, 'and you'd have questions which Kyle would be better answering than us.'

'I'm sick to the back teeth of people saying I worry too much and ask too many questions,' I say. I can feel my cheeks flaming red and I know I'm raising my voice. I feel resentment, hurt and guilt in quick succession as Helen instinctively strokes her stomach.

'Surely Kyle's job isn't a priority in the panel's decision?' says Helen, 'He's bound to get another one. The priority is them seeing what wonderful parents you'll both make.'

'That's the problem,' I say, angry tears threatening to run down my cheeks, 'everything is a bloody priority. We have to convince the world that we are ready for everything but according to Mike, me asking questions so that I can feel ready is convincing everyone that I'm a paranoid panic-merchant and unfit to parent.'

'That can't be true,' says Helen.

'What would you know about it?' I say, 'You're not there when they imply that as soon as I have to prepare some cocopops in the morning, I'll lose all track of my medical needs. That's the stress of it all, though. With CF and diabetes, everything is a priority in the morning. I need to eat, I need to do my chest physio, I need to take my nebulisers and my medicine. But the kids will need to eat and dress and go to school,' I flop down on an armchair. 'How am I going to fit it all in?'

'You will,' says Helen, 'you've done youth work residentials and managed all that whilst looking after a group of hormonal teenagers. And Kyle will be there to help, and your mum and dad are only a short drive away. You'll get used to it all, Jen.'

'It's easy for you to say,' I say, 'with your perfect family and perfect baby arriving at the perfect time. And the biggest kick in the teeth is that you didn't even have to *try*. It just happened, like a perfect surprise and everyone was happy for you.' Helen opens her mouth to speak but I can't bear to look at her. I fix my eyes on the floor and carry on, 'I was happy for you, Helen. I *am* happy for you. Like I've been happy for every other friend, relative and colleague whose babies I've welcomed and celebrated and bought gifts for and *cuddled*. The hours I've spent in baby departments, trying not to cry as I carefully choose baby clothes for others that I long to buy for my own.'

'Thank you for the lovely presents and the amazing baby shower,' says Helen, 'It was so kind of you. It must have been hard for you to do all of that.'

'You're welcome,' I say, angrily wiping away my tears with the back of my hand, 'You and Jake deserve a perfect baby, but no one has questioned your parenting abilities, no one is asking you to sit in front of a panel of people, judging you and asking you to explain how you will cope with every eventuality. No one is telling you scary stories of parenting children who are hurting through no fault of your own.' I've given up wiping the tears pouring down my face now. I know I'm upsetting my heavily pregnant best friend and I feel guilty as hell but now I've finally opened the flood gates, I can't stop.

'I was over the moon when I found out about your baby,' I say, 'but it broke my heart as well. I hate feeling jealous that it's happening for someone else again and not for me. If I just knew the panel would say yes, I would celebrate my children the same as I celebrate everyone else's. But how are they going to say yes to a mother who needs enough medication to run a small pharmacy and a father who hasn't got a job?'

'But the medication keeps you well,' says Helen, 'so that's not a problem.'

'But I need medication for eating and breathing, Helen,' I say, 'those are fairly basic functions.'

'And you function brilliantly,' she says, 'and your experiences of overcoming adversity make you the perfect parent for kids who need someone to teach them resilience. You're just having a low point, but it'll be okay.'

'It won't!' I cry, 'and I'm fed up of pretending it will. I'm fed up of being positive and strong and doing everything the social workers want us to do and trying to please everyone at work and trying to be strong for Kyle when he wobbles. I'm fed up of everything being so hard all of the time. I just wish it was easy like it is for you and Jake.'

I can hear the shower water turn off upstairs. 'Jake will be down in a minute,' I say, 'I won't disturb your cosy evening any further.' I turn to go.

'Don't be silly, Jenny,' says Helen.

'Don't call me silly!' I say, 'I'm fed up of being judged! I've always been strong for you and now you can't even spare me more than twenty minutes when I'm the one of us having the crisis,' - I finally look her in the eye - 'for a change.'

Helen stands up. 'Hang on a minute, Jenny,' she says, 'I've taken all your ranting but Jake and me have things to deal with as well.'

My heart sinks, 'There's nothing wrong with the baby, is there?' I say, the shock and thought of it finally softening my tone.

'No, nothing like that,' Helen says, 'but it's not easy being pregnant. But I feel so guilty all the time that I am and you're not that I have to keep smiling like someone out of a Mothercare advert even when morning sickness or exhaustion is flooring me. I can't tell you when I'm tired because I don't have to do physio and balance my blood sugars, I can't complain when my ankles swell because you're convinced Kyle's ruptured ligament has ruined your chances of adoption and I can't tell you when Will and Katie are horrible to me because, as you've made it perfectly clear, you've had enough of propping me up all the time.'

Just then, Jake comes down the stairs. He looks from one to the other of us.

'Sorry to interrupt, ladies,' he says.

There's a knock at the door. Jake goes to answer it. I hear Kyle's voice in the hall. He and Jake walk back into the living room and we all stare at each other in silence.

CHAPTER 43
– KYLE

'Is everyone alright?' I ask, looking from Jenny's flushed and tear-stained face to Helen's ashen one.

'I think I should leave,' Jenny says, 'Helen, I'm sorry I've upset you whilst you're pregnant, I really am, it's just…'

'I'm okay Jenny,' Helen says, 'I'm not that delicate.'

'Jake, you will look after her, won't you,' Jenny says, 'and let me know if she's okay.'

'I'm fine,' says Helen, 'really I am.'

'Don't worry, I'll take care of her,' says Jake. 'What happened when I was upstairs?'

Jenny takes her blood sugar readings and starts searching her bag. 'Damnit,' she says, 'I've run out of jelly babies,'

'Are your bloods low?' I ask, 'I've got your dextrose in the car.'

'Yeah, I didn't check my bag when I left,' Jenny says, 'I was in a bit of a hurry.'

'Come on,' I say, 'let's get you into my car,

you can have the dextrose and we'll go and get you some tea. Is it okay if we pick up Jen's car tomorrow folks?'

'Course it is,' says Helen, 'do you need any food here? We've got some orange juice too, that's fast sugar, isn't it?'

'Yeah, I can get you something to eat if you like?' says Jake.

'No, it's okay, thank you,' Jen says, 'I'll have the dextrose and we can pick up some takeaway down the road.'

'Come on then,' I say, 'See you soon, folks.'

Jen gets into the car, grabs the dextrose out of the glove compartment and starts shovelling them into her mouth.

'I'm sorry I didn't tell you about my job,' I say, 'I just couldn't see what point there was in adding to your worries. It wasn't going to help anyone.'

'But it might have helped you to share it with me,' she says, 'you don't have to protect me all the time, we're a team.'

'I know, and I'm sorry,' I say, 'I just want to look after you. I guess us thinking about having kids has changed everything.'

'Kyle, I can't discuss this calmly now,' Jenny says, 'my bloods are low and I've had a row with Helen, which is probably what made them drop.'

'And you're late having your tea,' I say, starting the engine, 'come on, let's get you some food and we'll go home and talk. How are your bloods now?'

Jenny scans her glucose monitor. 'Getting better,' she says, 'but I could murder a burger and fries.'

After we've inhaled a Mcdonalds, we drive home and sit together on the sofa.

'So,' Jenny says, 'You said the adoption thing has changed everything? How do you mean? You do want to have kids don't you?'

'Yes, of course I do,' I say, 'and before you ask, adoption is fine by me. Am I jealous sometimes that things seem simpler for Jake and Helen? Yes, but would I have it any other way? No. I want to have a family with you and doing it this way will give two kids the best mum and dad ever. We're a team.'

'A team who aren't going to keep things from each other any more?' Jenny says.

'No more secrets,' I say.

'So how do you mean it feels different then?' she says.

'Just that I've always wanted to be strong for you, even though you're the toughest person I know. It really shook me when I did my leg in. I'm used to being fit and healthy and all of a sudden you were having to sort the rooms out by yourself and drive me places and I was worried you'd get ill with all the extra stuff you had to take on whilst I was out of action.'

'But I didn't get ill, did I?' Jenny says, 'I

rested when I could, got someone to cover some of my clubs and we managed. As a team.'

'Yeah, you're right,' I say 'I suppose I just feel I have to be three times as strong once we've got two kids because I'll have three of you to protect then.'

'But I'm here too,' Jenny says, squeezing my hand, 'so rather than you being three times as strong, we can both be one and a half times as strong and we'll be fine!'

'I'm not sure that maths is right,' I laugh, 'if there's two of them, don't we both have to be twice as strong?'

'No,' giggles Jenny, 'children are only little.'

'So do you feel better now?' I ask.

'My bloods are fine,' she says, checking her readings again, 'but I feel awful for getting so cross with Helen. What if it effects the baby?'

'She'll be fine,' I say, 'Jake will look after her, but why don't you give her a call if you're worried.'

'Good idea,' says Jenny and grabs her phone.

CHAPTER 44
– HELEN

I feel terrible after my argument with Jenny. I've never seen her so worked up. I tell Jake all about it after they leave.

'I don't think she was really angry with you,' he says, 'it sounds like everything has got on top of her and it all just came to a head.'

'Yes,' I say, 'and I think she thought I couldn't be bothered to listen to her. It was just bad timing I guess but we've never actually fallen out before.'

'Are you feeling okay?' Jake asks, 'I don't want you getting stressed, it's not good for you or the baby.'

'I'm okay,' I say, 'I feel terrible that she thought I didn't care, but I just wanted to talk to you about your dad.'

'Oh, don't worry about that,' Jake says, 'he's not worth the time.'

'But you're worth the time,' I say.

'Honestly, put it out of your head,' Jake says, 'and let's see what a mess John Travolta will make of parenting.' He picks up the remote control.

'Jake, you're doing it again,' I say, 'protecting me. You're as bad as Kyle not telling Jenny about his job. We've all got to share things. Then we can help each other. I think that's what's been wrong with me and Jenny. So much came pouring out tonight that she's never said. I think that ever since we found out I was pregnant, me and her have both been trying to be strong for each other and have stopped sharing things like we used to. Jenny's been trying to act positive about the adoption so as not to stress me and I've tried my best not to talk about the baby to her for fear of seeming smug, or worse, ungrateful at having a baby.'

'So do you think you'll talk things over more openly now?' Jake says.

'I hope so,' I say, 'otherwise we're just going to grow apart precisely when we need to be closer than ever. But first, talking of hiding things, let's talk about your dad.'

Just as Jake is about to open his mouth, my phone rings. It's Jenny.

'I'm really sorry,' I say to Jake, 'I'd better get it.'

'Don't worry,' he says, 'there's really nothing to say about my dad. I told him about you and the baby, he's seen the message, he hasn't replied. What else is there to say?'

I give him a hug and answer the phone to

Jenny. Jake mimes that he's going to make a drink and goes into the kitchen.

'Are you feeling alright?' says Jenny, 'you know, with the baby? I'm so sorry I was so stressy with you, I feel terrible about it.'

'I'm fine,' I say, 'and how are you? I didn't mean to seem like I didn't want to talk to you, it's just,' I lower my voice to a whisper, 'Jake had messaged his dad today to tell him about us getting married and having a baby and although the message says he's read it, he hasn't replied. You know Jake, he hasn't talked about it, but I was hoping that after we watched the silly film, I might be able to coax something out of him.'

'Oh no,' says Jenny, 'and then I barged in.'

'Let's meet up soon and have a proper chat about everything,' I say, 'we've been keeping things inside, both trying to be brave and I think we'll feel better if we let it all out.'

'Good idea,' says Jenny, 'and in a much calmer way this time, I promise. Now you go and talk to your husband. I've just had a long chat with mine.'

'It seems to be the time for that all round, doesn't it?' I say, 'I suppose we'd best do all the talking we can now before all our kids come.'

'Yeah,' says Jenny, 'Dev says he hasn't finished a sentence since the twins were born.'

'You were so good with his twins, Jen, You're a natural mother. Everyone on the adoption panel will see that. And you manage your health conditions really well. You even sorted your blood sugars out during our mammoth showdown. Are they all okay again now?'

'All fine,' says Jenny, 'Are you sure you're feeling okay?'

'I'm sure,' I say. I say goodbye to Jenny and Jake appears with two mugs of hot chocolate with cream on top. We decide to take them up to bed and finish watching the film there. When it's finished, I turn to Jake, ready to casually bring up the subject of his dad, but he's fast asleep.

CHAPTER 45
– JAKE

I know Helen is trying to find a way to get me to talk about my dad but there's nothing to say. A week has gone by and he's still not replied to the message and I can see he's been online regularly. I've even checked his Facebook and he's been posting about some football game or another he's been betting on. Obviously, that's more important than his son and future grandchild.

I'm determined not to obsessively check my phone for a reply from him. On my day off, I'm relaxing at home with Helen and so put it on silent to stop myself jumping at every notification noise. We're about to start watching another film in the increasingly silly *Look Who's Talking* trilogy. The dogs are talking in this one so I don't think it's going to exactly help us to become parenting experts. I notice my phone vibrating so much that it's about to fall off the coffee table. I look at it and it's Bazza calling me.

'Jakey!' he booms.

'Bazza,' I say, winking at Helen, 'what can I

do for you?'

'Haven't you seen the email?' he says.

'What email?' I ask, scrolling through my cluttered inbox. I only ignored my phone for a short time and it seems every company in the world is desperate to sell me something.

'We've only gone and made it to the actual finals of the board game awards!' he says, 'We're not just semi-finalist invitees any more - we're now VIPs at the ceremony next week where they will no doubt announce us as the winners!'

'Really?' I say, finally finding the email and reading it. 'That's amazing!' I'd best tell Kyle. Just as I say this, there's a call waiting sound on the line. I look at my screen.

'Oh, speak of the devil, that's him calling now,' I say, 'Shall we all meet up this evening to celebrate getting this far? I'll ask him if he's free and drop you a message to confirm.'

'Certainly,' says Bazza, 'I'll look forward to it.'

I press to end the call to Bazza and Kyle comes on the line.

'We're in the finals!' he says, 'Isn't it brilliant!'

'Yeah, Bazza just called to tell me, I hadn't looked at my emails,' I say. 'Shall we meet up for a drink this evening? Do a bit of celebrating whilst we still don't need babysitters?'

'You're on!' he says.

The evening is just us blokes as Jenny is

working and Helen has gone out with some of the people from her work. Bazza's wife is at her meditation class. I can see why you'd need to meditate if you were married to Bazza. As warm hearted as he is, his exuberance for everything can get a bit overwhelming.

'Boys, we've done it!' he booms as we walk into the pub. He's wearing a satin bow tie and a maroon waistcoat and holding his arms out wide like a west end musical lead doing his big number. I half expect him to drop to one knee and start belting out something from *The Greatest Showman.* 'What do you think of my garb for the ceremony?' he asks.

'It's very striking,' I say, 'I must say, I was just going for a smart polo shirt and my black jeans. How about you, Kyle?'

'I might buy a new pair of trainers,' he says.

'You must all be your wonderful selves,' beams Bazza. 'I feel best in this clobber, but that doesn't mean you have to dress the same.'

'Cheers,' I say. 'Shall I get a round in?'

The evening is a blast. We discuss the game again and even have a go at writing our acceptance speeches, should we be lucky enough to win. I say 'have a go' but Bazza has already put some thought into his, if the three pieces of A4 he has in his pocket are anything to go by.

The week goes by quickly and it's soon the evening of the awards. I'm driving me, Helen,

Kyle and Jenny to the hotel it's being held in and Bazza and his wife, Alice are meeting us there. We arrive and the receptionist directs us to the ballroom.

'It's very grand here, isn't it?' says Helen.

'Yes,' agrees Jenny, 'but we deserve a bit of glamour.'

They link arms. Although it's been a couple of weeks since their argument, they haven't seen each other face to face until tonight. They've spoken on the phone a lot and things seem to be good between them again as far as I can tell, but Helen caught a cold from work and didn't want to give it to Jenny with her CF, so this is their first face to face meeting. Helen is cold-free now after spending a week on the sofa with her feet up, knitting away at the giant baby cardigan she started a while back.

We're shown to our table which has a mock-up of our board game in the centre of it and a helium balloon displaying our 'Halojen' logo floating above it, held down by a weight made to look like a giant pair of gold dice.

There are bottles of wine and mineral water on the table and goodie bags for each of us with our names on. Luckily, they didn't take Bazza up on his offer of providing the gifts, and he looks on scornfully as everyone looks delighted as they dive into theirs.

'Blimey, this is a bit good, isn't it?' I say to Kyle, 'Anyone would think we were official game designers!'

'I think we might be,' he says.

'We definitely are,' says Bazza, his smile returning, 'totally legit!'

The evening starts with entertainment from a stand-up comedian. Bazza laughs heartily at every joke and is in his element when the comedian picks him out and has a long conversation with him about his novelty gift company.

'So what's the best item in your stock?' asks the comedian.

'They're all magnificent pieces of merchandise,' says Bazza, 'but if I had to choose, I'd say the selection of welcome mats styled on famous Matts is a personal triumph of salesmanship.'

'Do elaborate,' says the comedian as the audience cranes their necks to get a better look at our business partner.

'Well, there's the "Welcome Matt Smith", which makes the TARDIS sound when you step on it, the "Welcome Matt Leblanc" which says "Hey, how you doin'?" and the "Welcome Matt Hancock" which says "I'm a celebrity, get me out of here!" People tend to enjoy wiping their muddy boots on that one.'

After the entertainment, we have some food and then the awards begin. There are quite a few minor categories before we get to the main one which will result in the winners having their game made and distributed by the company.

'Do you think it'll be long until your award?' whispers Helen, 'I need to go to the loo.'

'Should be a while, I think,' I say, looking at the programme. 'You alright finding your way?'

'Yeah, no problem, Jen's coming with me,' she says. And the two of them take off arm in arm together.

CHAPTER 46
– JENNY

It's so good to see Helen face to face again. Although we've spoken on the phone and video call, it's such a relief to hug her and see that she's really alright and that we're still best friends. We've talked things over a lot via video call. I think in a way it was easier as we could see each other's faces but talking via the screens also gave us the space we needed to be open about our worries. I told her about the stresses of the adoption meetings and she told me about how she feels physically and we talked about Jake and how he's hiding his hurt over his dad not responding to his message. She also told me about seeing her ex, Will and Katie and how rubbish it made her feel. Then she listened to me talking about how judged I felt when my need to be prepared had been misinterpreted as child-unsettling anxiety.

'Life just doesn't feel very fair, sometimes,' I'd said to her.

'It isn't,' she said, 'but you and Kyle know

that and know how to find ways to be happy in spite of it. So that makes you perfect parents for children who have also suffered injustice.'

When we come out of the toilets, we're just about to head back into the awards when I pull Helen to one side and gesture for her to sit next to me on a bench in the corridor.

'Everything alright?' she asks, sitting down and looking concerned.

'Fine,' I say, 'I just have something I want to give you.' I reach in my bag and pull out the little blue booties. 'I want you to have these, Helen,' I say, 'I bought them ages ago, way before we started the adoption process. I guess I just wanted to have something concrete to hold in my hand and say I would have children one day. We're not going to have a baby, and I'm okay with that, but you are and it couldn't happen to better people. I want you to have them.'

'Oh Jenny,' Helen says, welling up, 'are you sure?'

'I'm sure,' I say, 'it feels right.'

'Well,' Helen says, reaching into her bag and pulling out her knitting, 'I've been carrying this everywhere with me because I'm trying to knit a cardigan for the baby, but I've used such chunky wool that it's more like toddler size. I know you don't know how old your children will be, but I'd love to give you this when I've finished it, in the hope it fits one of them. And if it doesn't, I'll buy them a huge teddy bear that can wear it.'

'Helen,' I say, giving her a big hug, 'that's wonderful!'

We're both holding each other when the door from the main room opens and Bazza's wife Alice pokes her head round it.

'Quick!' she calls, 'they've only gone and won!'

We leap up, our differently sized knitwear clutched in our hands and follow Alice back into the room just in time to see Kyle, Jake and Bazza take to the stage to accept their award.

'So,' says the compere, 'Please welcome the winners, Jake, Kyle and Bazza of Halojen! What would you like to say, guys?'

'Thank you so much,' says Jake, he looks across to where me, Helen and Alice are cheering, 'I'd like to thank my wife Helen for putting up with me and to say now we can buy that buggy with all the accessories!'

'I'd like to thank my wife for putting up with me as well,' says Kyle, 'for all the time I spent pouring over the board game forms when I should have been filling in other paperwork!'

'And I'd like to say,' says Bazza, in a voice so loud that the microphone is rendered totally unnecessary, 'that Last Orders is going on sale soon so make sure you sign up to be amongst the first orders!'

CHAPTER 47
– KYLE

We're over the moon at winning the board game competition. I don't think it'll make us millionaires, but the prize money was generous and it won't hurt to have a bit of extra money coming in with all the extra mouths to feed.

I feel over the moon after the awards. But as the days go by, worries about my real job stamp all over the elation at my hobby job. It's my interview today for the remaining positions within my department.

'You look very smart,' says Jenny, straightening my tie and brushing some non-existent dust off the shoulders of my suit jacket. 'They're bound to give you the job.'

'I'm sure they will,' I say, pulling her close and kissing the top of her head.

The roads are clear and I arrive at the office in plenty of time. Plenty of time to fret, unfortunately. What makes it worse that I'm going up against colleagues of mine, all of whom I know need the work as much as I do. Redundancies are a horrible thing, not only because your livelihood is threatened, but because from the moment they're announced, you're in competition with friends and colleagues, knowing that your success relies partly on their failure.

By the time I'm called into the interview room, I daren't take off my suit jacket for fear that I've got two damp patches the size of paddling pools under my armpits.

'Welcome, Kyle, do have a seat,' smiles my manager as if she's just invited me round for drinks and nibbles rather than a series of questions which hold the fate of my present and future family in their grasp.

'Thank you,' I say, with what I hope is a smile.

'So, Kyle, let's not waste any time, I know you are applying to continue with your existing role. Can you tell me what you feel qualifies you to do this position?'

I don't feel that the obvious answer - that I've been doing the job perfectly well for several years now – is quite what they deem appropriate so I smile as broadly as I can and list as many qualities as possible that I hope they want to hear.

'And can you give us an example of when you went above and beyond for someone in the workplace?' my manager asks.

I think for a moment and recall when one

of Dev's twins had a really high temperature and his wife rang the office in tears. 'I don't know if this is what you're looking for,' I say, 'but this example is when I helped a colleague, rather than a customer. They were needed at home but didn't want to leave anyone in the lurch. I had a half-day's flexi leave booked but cancelled it so that I could step in to cover for them. They were able to help with a family situation and the standard of customer service didn't dip.'

'Excellent,' says my manager, 'Would you like to share who this colleague was that you needed to cover for?'

My heart sinks. The last thing I wanted to do was to throw Dev under the bus. He's been nothing but kind to me. No one should be penalised for putting the health of their family first.

'No,' I say, firmly but managing to muster up a smile, 'I don't feel that is relevant to the situation. You asked me when I had gone the extra mile for someone and I've given you an example. To name the person might seem like I was indicating that they were giving a substandard service, which I'm most certainly not. We should all help each other in the workplace and ensuring that someone can attend to family emergencies is part of being a good colleague. I know the person in question would do the same for me in a heartbeat.'

I can't tell how my response lands, but I

fret about it from the moment it's out of my mouth. I manage to finish the interview and I think I score quite highly in the practical test.

Jenny must have been watching at the window for me to return home as she's thrown open the front door before I've even parked the car. 'How was it?' she asks.

'Oh, okay, I think,' I say. I really hope I haven't jeopardised my job by refusing to add to the risk of Dev losing his. But what will we do if I have? There wouldn't be time to find another decent one before the adoption panel. Would they even consider us if we add 'unemployed' to our list of challenges? Jenny is amazing but will they see beyond the label of disability? Even the word is negative – '*dis*ability'. I certainly wouldn't describe Jen as someone who is unable to do things and in fact she's developed such a versatile way of dealing with challenges that I'd say she's more able than most to cope. Plus, she knows what it's like to feel different and to miss out on things that others take for granted. That has to be an advantage when it comes to adopting.

But I'm really not sure how to present my possible joblessness in such a positive light.

CHAPTER 48
– HELEN

Jake is working late tonight. At first, I think it'll be a good opportunity to get some peace and quiet and catch up on some of the TV programmes that he's not so keen on. But by about 7pm, I'm wishing he was here, even if that would mean sharing the remote control. I pick up my phone and think about who to message. Jen is at work. I hover over the names of some of the girls from my work but then scroll to favourites and call my mum.

'Hello?' says my dad. I can hear the television in the background and the voice of Alex Jones from the One Show which is on so loudly that you'd swear she was sat next to my parents on the sofa.

'Hi dad, it's me,' I say.

'Hello love,' he says, 'how are you doing? You're not calling to say I'm a grandad yet, are you?'

'No, not yet, dad,' I smile, 'baby's still not due for a few weeks!'

'Not long now, though love,' he says, reminding me of when I was a little girl and I'd keep asking when it was time to go on holiday or when it would be Christmas.

'No, just under a month,' I say, stroking my stomach.

'Do you want your mum?' he says. In a way, I can understand how things have got to the point they're at with Jake and his dad, Rick. Whilst it's obviously awful that Rick hasn't replied to his son telling him he's a husband and father to be, when you think about it, my dad is amazing, but he still hands the phone to my mum within a few minutes of me calling.

'Yes thanks, dad,' I say.

'How's everything in the land of my nearly-here grandchild?' asks my mum, breezing onto the line and drowning out Alex Jones.

'I'm alright, mum,' I say.

'You sure, love?' asks my mum, 'you don't sound it?'

For some reason I'm welling up and my bottom lip is quivering. I didn't think bottom lips really did quiver. I thought that was just something people wrote in over the top novels, but it seems it's actually a real thing.

'Is it your hormones?' asks my mum, not for the first time since I told her I was pregnant. Everything I've done or not done since we broke the news has been greeted by this question, whether it be refusing a third helping of pudding or getting annoyed by the painfully slow computer at work.

'Actually mum, this time I think it might be,' I confess.

'I'll be over in five minutes, you sit tight,' she says, 'talk to your father until I get there.'

And with that, she thrusts the phone back at my started father with instructions to keep me chatting until she arrives. Dad and me discuss the television schedule for the evening and are just moving onto comparing scores on the radio two music quiz when my front doorbell rings shrilly three times. I can see the outline of mum through the frosted glass panel.

'Is that your mother?' asks dad, trying to keep the relief from his voice.

'Yes, dad, but I'm okay, nothing to worry about, just a bit overtired, that's all,' I say.

'Yes, love, but that series I like is starting in a minute and if I don't watch it live, I'll never catch it,' he says. I smile to myself and say goodnight to him and open the front door to my mum. She's holding three pyrex dishes, four plastic takeaway tubs and a large bottle of Ribena.

'Hello mum,' I say, 'how did you manage to rustle all this up so quickly? You haven't stolen dad's tea for the week, have you?'

'Good grief no, love,' she says, sweeping past me into the hall and through to the kitchen, 'I've had these on standby in case you needed anything. Now, what can I throw away in this fridge to make room?'

'Er, I'd rather you didn't throw anything away, mum,' I say, watching as she unloads takeaway leftovers and bits of slightly sad-looking salad onto the counter tops.

'Are you sure you want this?' she asks, holding up half a lettuce that looks like it's been dipped in old tea and mauled by a dog.

'Well, maybe not that, actually,' I say, 'but best leave the leftover curry, I think Jake is going to have that when he gets in from work.'

Mum manages to squeeze all bar two of the plastic tubs into the fridge in a tetris-like fashion. I must remind Jake not to open the door too quickly in case he's buried under an avalanche of her home cooking. She turns to me with a beam.

'There!' she says, 'these two pieces of chocolate cake won't fit, so I suppose we'll just have to eat them now! Have you got any squirty cream?'

I somehow manage to find the can of cream wedged under two casseroles and a homemade soup. We cover our cakes generously in it and decamp to the sofa.

'So,' says mum, 'how are you doing?'

'Fine,' I say, 'just got a bit emotional all of a sudden. Jake's on a late shift and I had an image of me trying to get the baby to bed without him here and I realised I don't know any lullabies.

What kind of mum doesn't know any lullabies?'

Mum pops her cake onto the coffee table and wraps her arms around me.

'There, there,' she says, rocking me gently as if I'm still her baby, 'it doesn't matter whether you know any lullabies or not.'

'But you said you always sang me to sleep?' I say, 'I remember you singing to me.'

'I did,' she says, 'but they weren't lullabies.'

'How do you mean?' I ask, 'what were they then?'

'Jingles from adverts, themes from sitcoms, Monty Python songs, anything I could think of really,' says mum, 'you didn't mind as long as I didn't stop singing. We were both so tired it didn't matter what the words were. I used to alter any inappropriate ones, some of Monty Python wasn't quite right for a little one, but you just loved the tunes.'

Mum keeps rocking me and I start to feel a lot calmer. As my eyes begin to close, I'm sure I detect the opening lines from one of the big numbers in the Rocky Horror Picture Show.

CHAPTER 49
– JAKE

It's not too bad a shift tonight. It's the members' evening and everyone is fairly chilled and happy so there are no stresses to deal with. I even manage to take my break on time. I'm just enjoying a bowl of cheese and salsa covered nachos when my phone goes off. I grab it in case it's Helen, but I freeze mid chew when I see it's a message from my dad.

I put the nachos down and take a long gulp of my drink. I'd convinced myself he wasn't going to reply at all. I mean, if you can decamp to the other side of the world when your kid is a teenager, grandkids can't be on the top of your priority list. I tell myself not to expect anything, he's probably just finally decided to send a thumbs up emoji or something. Before I can overthink things, I press my thumb onto the screen and the message opens.

Congratulations son, it sounds like you're doing well. I'm not sure I'm ready for a flat cap and slippers yet, but I am really chuffed to be a grandad.

I stare at the screen. He's 'chuffed', is he? Well, that's more emotion than I've seen from him regarding his father status in a long while. But if it's taken him this long to reply to a message, I won't hold my breath that he'll be hopping on a plane any time soon. I don't know what to say in response. I type and delete a message several times, saying thanks and telling him the due date, but I cancel it each time without sending. Won't do him any harm to wait to hear from me. If he wants to know when the baby is due, then he'll need to make a bit more of an effort and actually ask.

I look at my half-eaten tea just as my phone goes again. I push the nachos away. It's impossible to digest a conversation with my dad and greasy food at the same time. But this time it's not him, it's Julie. Sometimes I really do think she's my guardian angel, the way she's looked out for me since my mum died. She's asking how Helen is and if we need anything for the baby. I take a screenshot of my dad's message and send it to her, saying 'The old man's finally got round to replying.'

My message has barely sent when my phone rings. For a second, I think it's my dad, but the old photo I've saved of Julie beaming with my mum appears on my screen. For a few seconds I gaze at it, imagining a world where my mum's voice is about to come on the line. She's smiling at the camera and her blue eyes are looking right at me. I hit the answer button.

'Hi Julie,' I say.

'Jake, how are you doing?' she says, 'are you at home with Helen?'

'No,' I reply, 'I'm at work for a couple more hours yet. But it's alright, the café is really quiet.'

'I'm out with some of the girls from my rock choir,' she says, 'we're in the pub, only a few doors down from you. Hang on, I'll pop and see you.'

Before I can say anything, she's hung up. I throw the remaining nachos in the bin and head back into the café. The door opens and there's Julie, dressed in her rock choir t-shirt. She comes over and gives me a big hug. My boss grins at us.

'Oy, oy, Jakey Boy,' he says, 'shall I tell your good lady wife that you've got another woman on the go?'

'Cheeky!' says Julie, 'I'm old enough to be his mother!'

'And you're made of solid gold, like she was,' I say.

She gives me a squeeze then looks at me with concern. 'So, what did you say to your dad then? Did you tell him he might still wear jeans that are far too tight for a man of his age, but that doesn't mean he isn't old enough to be a grandad!'

'I haven't replied,' I say, 'it took him so long to respond that I'm in no rush to get back to him.'

'I get that, I totally do,' Julie says, 'but he

seems happy about the baby. I bet he's really pleased that you've told him. Maybe this could be a bit of a fresh start for the pair of you, eh?'

I look down at my trainers. 'I dunno,' I say, 'If I let him back in, he'll probably just disappear again when he gets bored. I can't see him coming over here and offering to babysit. The nappy changing bag won't go with his leather jacket.'

'Well, he'll likely not do much, pet,' says Julie, 'but even he might be able to manage the odd video call to see his new grandchild. And you never know, he could surprise you.'

'What would mum say, though?' I whisper, 'I feel like I'm betraying her by letting him back in after he abandoned us.'

'Your mum would want you and your lovely little family to have all the relatives and love that you can muster,' Julie says, 'She would want her grandchild to be surrounded by family and friends.'

'But what if I introduce him to the baby and then he buggers off again?' I say.

'Then me, Helen, Helen's parents and your lovely friends will be here for you like we always have been. He might be a good grandad, he might not. But he can't do that much harm on the other side of the world. He might pop up to wet the baby's head and then go to ground again or this could be the thing that kicks him up the arse and prompts him to make up for lost time. But if you don't give it a go, you'll never know. And you wouldn't have told him if a little bit of you didn't think it was a good idea, would you?'

'I suppose not,' I say, 'Thanks Julie.'

'Anytime, pet,' she says, just as a group of women wearing identical t-shirts to hers conga into the café and sweep her away with them. I wave back at her as she blows me an exaggerated kiss and winks at my boss.

CHAPTER 50
– KYLE

Jen is due to take a street dance class exam this evening. She's amazing how she is into all these things with so much going on. She used to go to the class with Helen as it takes place at the drama studio she works at and they get a really good discount. It's good for her lungs and blood sugars and when the teacher suggested ages ago that some of them take the exam, she said it seemed like a laugh and something to tell people about. But obviously Helen hasn't been street dancing for a while now and we've got a bit more on our plate than when she signed up for it at the beginning of the year.

I'm dropping her off on my way to work. I don't normally work evenings, but they're having a meeting tonight to find out who has got the jobs and to provide support to the ones that haven't. Jen asked me if I wanted her to pull out of the dance exam, but I said it would be best if she was occupied rather than sitting worrying at home. We still haven't mentioned the job situation to the adoption people. Luckily, my employer reference was submitted before the redundancies were announced. I know we'll have to tell them if I don't get to keep one of the remaining jobs, but at the moment, we're hoping for the best.

So, here we are, trying our best to focuss on a dance exam. I've provided her with a massive 'snack pack' for afterwards and made sure she has the right things to eat before as she'll be using up a lot of energy and the last thing she wants is a hypo just as she's doing her best impression of an extra in *Step up two: The Streets*. The amount of times she walked in on me glued to that film on a Sunday afternoon makes me wonder if I should be doing the exam rather than her, although it might set back my thankfully speedy ligament recovery. There's a bunch of them from the class all taking part today and Jen's slot is at 8pm so it gives her time to have a decent tea with some slow-release carbs.

But first of all, we've got a new visitor coming to the house. Mike has finished his part of the assessment now, having carried out months' worth of visits, discussions and form filling with us. He's submitted his report ahead of the panel on 12th August. It's only a week away now. It's finally coming after all of this time. So today, a separate social worker has to visit us, have a look round our home and a bit of a chat to us, just to confirm that she agrees with Mike's assessment.

'Doesn't it seem a bit excessive to you, sending yet another person round to check us out?' Jenny says to me as we tidy up ready for Margaret, the social worker to arrive.

'Maybe they think that we've bribed Mike not to tell them about the drugs den we've set up in the conservatory or the alligator living in the bathroom,' I grin.

Margaret arrives at 3pm on the dot and is full of smiles. 'Jenny and Kyle?' she says, showing us her ID badge.

'That's us,' I say.

'That's a relief,' Margaret says with a twinkle in her eye, 'it would be a terrible mix up if I invited myself into the wrong couple's house and started poking about! Not that I intend to poke you!'

We laugh nervously and show Margaret round the house. She ticks things off on her list as we go. We've put a safety film over the glass panels in the living room door and installed safety catches on the kitchen cupboards and drawers. The only people who can get hurt in our kitchen now are me and Jen, every time we catch our fingers in the drawer when we go to pull it open and forget the safety catch is there.

As we go into the children's bedrooms she beams. 'Well, I would certainly love to sleep in one of these rooms,' she says, 'you've done yourselves proud. All the furniture looks safe and secure and I love the books and toys that you have put in here.'

'Do you think there's enough stuff in here for them?' Jenny asks, 'We wanted to leave plenty of space for any belongings they might bring. And we don't know what age they will be yet either. If, of course, the panel approve us.'

'Let's think positive, shall we,' says Margaret with a big smile, 'and with all the care that I can see you've obviously put into making your home safe and welcoming for your children-to-be, I feel we have every right to do that. And you have just the right amount of things in the rooms. They're coming to a family home, not a Disney store and we don't want to overwhelm them. You've got it spot on.'

'Thank you,' I say. Jenny beams with pride.

After we've finished showing Margaret around, she accepts our offer of tea and biscuits and tells us that she will be at the panel with us as well as Mike. It feels good to have two people there on our team.

'So, I won't take up any more of your time,' she says, getting up off the seat we usually give to Mike and brushing some crumbs off her top into the wastepaper bin. 'I will see you on 12th August when the four of us in Team Williams will wow the panel!'

'Thank you, Margaret,' I say, feeling a rush

of excitement and fear. For once, the excitement seems to have overtaken the fear.

'Absolute pleasure, my dears,' she says, 'it's always wonderful to be able to help create new families! Now, I must let you get on, have you got anything exciting planned for the rest of the day?'

'I have a street dance exam,' Jen says, 'just a silly thing I agreed to do ages ago.'

'But an excellent thing to tell the panel about when they ask about your fitness levels,' Margaret says.

'Yes, I said that to her,' I say, trying to smile as I feel the fear start to gain on the excitement once more.

'And you, Kyle, what are you doing this evening?' Margaret says.

'Oh, nothing much,' I say, as my fear storms past my excitement and blasts towards the finishing line.

***

As I drop Jen off at her dance exam later, she dives out of the car, still rattling off words of encouragement to me about what to do if I do or don't get the job.

'And remember if you don't get it, tell them that you are still available if someone offered it turns it down,' she gabbles as she grabs her dance shoes and a bag with her blood testing kit in and so many carb-laden snacks that it looks like she's about to set up a catering company rather than do a street dance exam.

'I will, don't worry,' I say. 'Are you sure you'll be alright here after your exam. Call me if you have any trouble with hypos and you need me to bring any extra food or anything. That's if we've left any in the supermarket.'

'I'll be fine,' she says, 'Carrie said she can give me a lift home if you're not out in time.'

'Good luck, I love you,' I say.

'Good luck, Ky, love you too,' she replies and scurries into the drama studio from which I can already hear the sound of thudding music.

I pull up at work and take a deep breath. As I'm locking the car, I see Dev.

'Alright mate,' he says.

'Hi Dev,' I reply, 'are we supposed to be on speaking terms, now they've pitted us against each other like gladiators?'

'It's alright,' Dev says, 'I've got some good news. I've found a new job. Closer to where I live too and a few grand a year more.'

'That's amazing,' I say, 'I'm really pleased for you.' I try to hide the fact I'm also a little bit jealous. Maybe I should have tried harder to find another job. We've had to spend so much time focussing on the adoption assessment that I haven't applied for as many jobs as I should have.

'I've already sorted out my voluntary redundancy package,' says Dev, 'I'm just here as a formality. But it's good news for you as well, Kyle - one less person to go up against.'

'Good point,' I say. Dev is right, that just leaves me and one other person, Nathan, ringfenced for my position.

We go into the office together. Soon, me, Dev and Nathan are called into see the PR manager. He's smiling broadly at us, as if we're here for a party, not to hear news that could devastate our plans to earn a living and support our families. Still, at least this is a bit more friendly and personal than the original notification of the cuts which amounted to little more than an email which went something along the lines of, *Please turn the lights off on your way out. In fact, we're cutting back on electricity so please work in the dark until we dismiss half of you.*

'Thank you for coming gentlemen,' says the PR manager, 'As you know, there is one position available at your level in your department and Dev has given me permission to tell you that he has decided to take voluntary redundancy. So, we would like to offer the remaining candidates, Kyle and Nathan, a job share. Now, we will give you some time to think about it and come back to us individually with your decision.'

My heart sinks. We can't afford to live off half my wages. Especially as Jenny wants to cut down her hours to have more time and energy to be with the kids. I look at Nathan.

'Thank you,' he says, 'but my wife has just been offered a promotion which means moving to Scotland. So, if it's not too late, I'd like to take voluntary redundancy as well.'

I am so relieved that I could hug them all. 'Does that mean I am the only candidate for the job, then?' I ask.

'It does, Kyle,' the PR manager says, looking relieved at the unexpected reduction in the amount of bad news he's having to deliver today, 'Congratulations, you are the successful candidate.'

'I'm not sure how much I deserve to be congratulated,' I say, 'seeing as I only got the job as neither of the other two wanted it, but I'll take it, thank you very much and congratulations and good luck to everyone.'

As soon as I get out of the office, I call Jenny, but it goes to voicemail. She must still be in the dance exam. I send her a text to tell her my job is safe and drive to the drama studio to pick her up.

As I sit in the car waiting for her, I start to sneeze. I must be allergic to one of the trees or something. By the time she comes running out, my head is pounding.

'Congratulations!' she says, diving into the car and going to kiss me.

'Hang on a minute, Jen,' I say, winding down the windows. 'Best not kiss me, I'm feeling a bit rough.'

She leans away from me as if I might give her an electric shock. 'Oh no,' she says, 'I can't catch anything just before the panel. If they see me with a cold or a cough, they'll think I'm always like that. They're never going to believe it's just a temporary thing. It'll confirm all the prejudices about CF and they'll write me off.' Her eyes fill with tears.

'Let's not panic,' I say, 'let's get home, I'll go to bed and I bet I'll feel better in the morning. It's probably just the stress of the day.'

'It's great you've got your job, though, isn't it?' Jenny says, managing a smile as she pours anti bac gel onto her hands and grabs a mask out of her rucksack.

'It is,' I say, 'and those children's rooms will come in handy. I'll sleep in one of those until I'm better, minimise the chance of you catching anything.'

We get home and I do a lateral flow test. It's negative. Must just be a cold or something, hopefully not the flu. I decamp into the spare room. It takes me ages to get to sleep, worrying about whether I've already made Jenny unwell before the panel and thinking about how I'm going to do the job of three men when Dev and Nathan leave. And, if all goes to plan and Jen and I don't end up attending the adoption panel sneezing and looking like zombies, I'll be an inexperienced dad to two children on top of my newly tripled workload.

I wake frequently in the night, each time wondering where I am, then remembering I'm trying to maximise our chances of becoming parents by sleeping away from my wife in the bedroom of one of the children we may never have.

CHAPTER 51
– HELEN

As soon as I wake, I know today is going to be special. It's the day of Jenny and Kyle's adoption panel. I message them good luck. Kyle has been sleeping in one of their spare rooms as he caught a cold and doesn't want to give it to Jenny as she needs to be as healthy as possible to give the best impression to the panel. Not that parents don't get colds. But Jen is worried that she gets this one chance to make the right impression, so Kyle has been a practical prisoner in there since he first started sneezing. He's taken covid tests each day and it's definitely not that, so they're still okay to attend the panel and Jenny became slightly reassured when his symptoms disappeared after a few days. He's feeling better but they're still keeping their distance to be on the safe side and she has luckily remained well.

At least they'll both be better by the time the baby's born in a couple of weeks. I'm enjoying my maternity leave, but I'm getting a bit bored just sitting around. I've packed my bag ready and checked it several times. I've read all the baby books we bought on honeymoon from cover to cover and we've got everything ready in the nursery. Me and Jenny have been talking about how strange it feels having the rooms ready before their little occupants have arrived. I've been going into the nursery and sitting on the white rocking chair we've put in there, cradling a toy rabbit I've had since I was little and trying to imagine what it'll be like to be a mum. But today, I can't go in there. I want to focus on sending good thoughts to Jenny and Kyle for the panel. Plus, the closer my due date gets, the less I am able to think about how my life is about to change. I keep picturing a computer screen flashing a warning that 'Motherhood is imminent' and it just all seems too huge to take in. Like when something is so loud you can't bear to listen to it or a light is so bright it's blinding rather than illuminating. And I don't know what I'll do if Jen and Kyle don't get approved today. I'll want to include them in everything with the baby and make them feel like the most important Aunt and Uncle in the world, but will that be the right thing to do or will it just rub it in and make them feel worse? But if I don't include them, will they feel I'm excluding them and treating them like some kind of childless freaks who I daren't let near my baby?

Then my mind starts to spiral and I worry that by feeling guilty about having a baby, fate will feel like I'm wishing it away. So, all in all, I'm trying to keep busy so I don't start to worry about something going wrong. I wish I could be with Jenny and Kyle and support them at their adoption panel, but you're not allowed to bring people with you and I'm supposed to be taking it easy. I'm going to be a mum in a fortnight after all.

Saying those words to myself makes my stomach twinge. I try to think of something else and start watching my *When Harry Met Sally* DVD. It's my favourite film and usually absorbs me and makes me feel calmer. But the twinges don't stop. In fact, they're getting worse. I pick up the phone and message Jake.

I think I'm nervous for Jenny and Kyle. I've got twinges in my stomach.

He's at work but replies straight away. *You're not going into labour, are you?*

He's put a laughing emoji at the end but just as I'm about to reply, telling him not to be silly, I get a much stronger twinge. In fact, to call it a twinge would be like describing an axe wound as a paper cut. I pick up my phone to call Jake but he's already ringing me.

'Are you okay?' he asks, 'I sent the text then thought I shouldn't be so flippant. The baby's only a fortnight off after all.'

'I think it might be a bit closer than that,' I say.

'I'll be home in ten minutes,' Jake says, and

I hear him shouting to his boss that he needs to leave right away, 'Are you alright? Do you need an ambulance?'

'No, I'm fine,' I say, 'see you in ten minutes and drive carefully!'

He must have rung my mum on the way to his car as she rings me almost as soon as he's hung up. She offers to come round but I tell her Jake's only a few minutes away and promise to call them if we need anything. When he rushes through our front door ten minutes later, I'm still on the phone to mum, clutching my hospital bag and my old toy rabbit. I put it on speakerphone.

'Thanks mum, Jake's just walked through the door. Well, ran through it would be a more accurate description,' I say, managing a little laugh.

'Right,' says mum, 'now, you call the midwife and see if they want you to go to the hospital yet. It might be a bit soon to go in but with it being a couple of weeks early, it's best to be on the safe side.'

'Oh mum, you don't think anything's wrong, do you?' I say, my eyes widening.

'Not at all,' says mum, 'my grandchild is just very impatient to meet us, that's all, now don't you worry, and call us if you need anything at all.'

We call the hospital and they ask us to come down there so Jake loads the bag into the car and tries to get me as comfortable as possible.

'Oh, god,' I say.

'What is it?' he asks.

'Jenny and Kyle's panel will be starting now!' I say, grabbing my phone.

'Are you going to tell them?' Jake says, starting up the engine.

'No, I don't want to distract them, they need to focus,' I say, 'I'm just going to send them a good luck message.'

'Good idea,' Jake says, 'Give them my love too. I'll message them again later when the panel's finished and we can update them on our situation too.'

'Do you think it's a *situation*, Jake?' I ask him, feeling myself getting hot.

'No, not at all,' he says, trying to use the calm, reassuring tone we practised at the anti-natal classes, 'Maybe the baby just wants to meet its lovely mum early, like your mum said, or maybe it's a false alarm.'

'I don't think it's a false alarm,' I say.

'Well, no,' he says, with a nervous laugh, 'You're definitely pregnant!'

'Yes,' I say, 'and my waters have just broken.'

CHAPTER 52
– JENNY

I'm so paranoid that we'll be late for the panel that we actually arrive forty-five minutes early. So as not to trigger another round of people thinking I'm overly anxious, we park at the back of the car park and then go to the café over the road. We sit down with our drinks and biscuits.

'Look, Kyle,' I say, pointing to a flyer on the table, emblazoned with a photo of a beaming spaghetti-covered child and the words 'Kids Eat Free!'

'It's okay,' he says, 'I've kept my job, we'll be able to afford to feed them! I think it might be frowned upon if we don't!'

'Shhh!' I say, 'Don't joke about not feeding them, the panel members might be in here for all we know.'

'Do you think the ketchup bottle is bugged?' he grins, teasing me.

'No, but it's just… no it seems silly,' I say.

'What does?' he asks, 'You can tell me.'

'Well, I've always looked at these kinds of

flyers and felt jealous that we couldn't use them,' I say.

'Big fan of smiley potato faces and dino burgers, are you?' he says.

'You know what I mean,' I say, giving him a gentle nudge.

'I do,' he says, 'and soon, we'll be able to join the Kids eat free brigade and the movies for juniors club and the soft-play, happy meal, peppa pig loving crew.' He looks at me and picks up the flyer, 'Shall we take one of the leaflets? We get a free clarence the clown lolly when we order extra vegetables!'

'No,' I whisper, shaking my head. 'I don't want to tempt fate.'

'Okay,' Kyle says, placing it back on the table.

We finish our biscuits and head over to the adoption agency. We're still quite early but I am worried that we'll somehow be delayed walking across the road and don't feel I can relax until we're in the building. Though now we're in the building, I feel even less relaxed than before. The receptionist smiles at us.

'Manage to find a good parking space?' she grins at Kyle.

'Perfect, thanks,' he says, 'I've left the engine running in case we mess up and have to make a quick getaway.'

We take a seat in reception as guided and glance at our watches. Still twenty minutes to go.

'Where's Mike and Margaret?' I whisper to Kyle, 'I thought they'd be here by now!'

'They'll be here, don't worry,' he says, 'let's message Jake and Helen to say we've arrived, take our minds off it.'

'I've already messaged them a few times,' I say, 'but they haven't replied. Hope everything's okay.'

'Bound to be,' he says, 'they'll just be making the most of the peace and quiet before the baby arrives.'

The door leading into one of the rooms bursts open and Mike walks over to us, a big smile on his face. 'We're on second!' he says as if we're about to perform in the Royal Variety Show and he's announcing great news about the running order.

'Is that good?' asks Kyle, 'I suppose they won't have had chance to get bored at that stage.'

'I don't think they'll get bored, Kyle' I hiss, 'it's a rather important job,'

'I know,' he says, 'I'm just trying to lighten the mood, you look as if you're about to go on trial for murder.'

'I feel like I am,' I mutter under my breath. Just then the main door opens and Margaret sweeps in.

'How are you both?' she asks, 'well, I hope?'

'I am,' I say, 'but Kyle caught a cold or

something a week ago. He's been sleeping in the spare room. I didn't want to catch anything and not look my best today.'

'Well, you seem to have achieved your aim, Jennifer,' says Margaret, 'You look a picture of health as do you, Kyle. Mike and I can sit in the middle of you both, if it makes you more relaxed, keep you safe from Kyle's cold germs.'

'Thank you,' says Kyle, 'though I've not had any symptoms for days now, but I understand Jen was just feeling extra cautious with today coming up. Either that, or she's trying to tell me something and she doesn't intend to let me back into the bedroom.' I give Jenny a wink. She smiles a nervous looking smile and glances at her watch.

The receptionist answers the phone, replaces the receiver and calls over to us, 'Mr and Mrs Williams?' she says, 'The panel are running a little early, so you can go in now, if you'd like to.'

'Where the people before us that bad they've been kicked out early?' says Kyle with a grin. Mike chuckles.

'Oh goodness,' I say, 'I don't know if I'm ready.'

'You were born ready, Jenny,' says Mike, 'Why don't we go in there and wow them with what wonderful parents you're going to make.'

'Okay,' I say. I stand up, despite my legs having decided that they really don't want to do their job. I just want to take Kyle's hand but we're still being careful, germ wise. I long to be held by him again. I always feel safe in his arms. I have one last look round at reception and all the posters of smiling new families adorning the walls, take a deep breath, smile at my husband and follow Mike and Margaret into the room.

CHAPTER 53
– KYLE

As promised, Mike and Margaret position themselves between me and Jenny, forming a human barrier. It's a good job they have because I hate to think of Jenny feeling so nervous and would struggle to stop myself hugging her the whole time if we weren't separated by our dynamic duo. The chair of the panel introduces himself and the panel members, who include, among other people, a social worker, an educational psychologist, an adopter and a grown-up adoptee. Everyone smiles and says hello. There's far more people here than I've ever experienced on any job interview panel, but then again, this is the most important job I've ever applied for.

'So,' says David, the Chair of the panel, 'we have all studied your application and the reports provided, and to put you at ease, we'd like to start by saying how impressed we are.'

'Thank you,' says Jenny.

'Much appreciated,' I say.

'Our job, as you know,' continues David, 'is to ensure we have covered all bases and asked all the questions needed to ensure that we make the right decisions regarding you becoming adoptive parents. I see,' he consults his notes, 'that you would like to adopt a sibling group of two. Could you explain your thinking on that for me?'

'Yes,' says Jenny, 'we have always wanted to have two children, and we understand that there are a lot of sibling groups needing homes where they can remain together and we would like to help that happen.'

'But you understand,' interjects the Educational Psychologist, 'that it is not always advisable for siblings to be placed together, for various reasons and that if you adopt two siblings, they could well be part of a larger sibling group that have needed to be placed separately?'

'Yes,' says Jenny, 'we learnt about that on our training and we've been doing some reading on how to have positive experiences of sibling contact.'

'Excellent,' says the Educational Psychologist, 'and would you be happy to meet up with your children's siblings if they are placed in a different adoptive or foster home?'

'Yes, absolutely,' I say, 'we're happy to do all that we can to help them maintain contact with their siblings.'

'And you are both only children yourselves?' asks Elaine, the adult adoptee. We nod. 'And do you feel that you are therefore ready to deal with sibling issues, not having had any brothers or sisters yourselves?'

'Yes, absolutely,' I say, 'our parents always made an effort for us to socialise with other children. We grew up making friends with people outside of the home and learnt about the importance of mixing with others. I think that will help us to help the children to settle in, after all, they will be moving away from all the people they know, their siblings in some cases,' I swallow hard, 'Our experiences as only children mean we are used to finding ways to get to know others and to fit in with people and having to make an effort to form new bonds.'

'Excellent,' says Elaine. The notetaker is typing away.

'And you, Jennifer?' she asks, 'How did you feel being an only child?'

'Similar to Kyle,' Jenny says, 'my parents always helped me to make new friends.'

'And how did having a health condition effect you, growing up?' asks the GP sitting on the panel.

'It was a challenge at times,' says Jenny, 'but my parents were always very supportive and looked after me well. I very rarely felt as if I was missing out on things as they would always find a way for me to be involved in pretty much everything my friends were.'

'And is it still a challenge now?' continues

Dr Stevens.

'I think life is a challenge for everyone in different ways, Dr Stevens,' says Jenny, sitting up straight. 'There isn't anyone on this earth who doesn't have to cope with something difficult at some point. It's just that with me, the thing I cope with has been with me since birth. But that gives me an advantage, you see, I already know what it's like to feel different, so I can empathise with the children when they feel different to their classmates. I know what it's like to stand out when you want to fit in and again, I can help them with that. I know what it's like to have to be resilient and versatile and adapt to change. I know what it's like to have to rise to life's challenges and I'm ready to help our children to do the same.'

Mike and Margaret give Jenny a reassuring smile.

'A comprehensive and very encouraging answer, Jenny,' says the Chair, 'we can see from your social worker's report that you are always very prepared. I admire the way that you have, as you say, risen to the challenges that life has thrown at you and agree that your experiences could come in very handy in helping you to understand the needs of adoptive children.'

'Could I ask?' interjects Michelle, the adopter on the panel, 'what happens if you become unwell once you are a mother?'

'I have a good support network,' Jenny

says, 'Not only Kyle, but my parents who live nearby, our friends who are also less than ten minutes away and friends from my work as a youth worker, who are very experienced in dealing with children and young people with behavioural and emotional difficulties, as of course am I, having been a youth worker for so many years.'

The questions continue, with the panel covering things such as how I will balance work and being a dad, how we would address difficult behaviour in the children and how we would support them if they had issues at school. We answer all these well, but I can tell by the look on her face that the wind has been taken out of Jenny's sails with the discussion about her health. When the questions are finally finished, the two of us are asked to wait in another room whilst the panel members discuss our responses. As soon as we are alone, Jenny's shoulders slump.

'It's no good, Kyle,' she says, a tear rolling down her cheek, 'they can't see past my health condition. They just see the label, not the person who's coping perfectly well and more prepared than most people are.'

'Hey,' I say, 'come on, they loved you. Can I come and hug you now it's done? My cold has gone.'

'Yes,' she says, 'and even if it wasn't, it's pointless now.'

We sit together, me holding Jenny in

my arms and Jenny smoothing out imaginary creases in her dress. After about ten minutes, the door opens. We look up. It's Mike and Margaret.

'Well folks,' says Mike, 'as you know, this is only the panel's recommendation. The information from today still has to go to the Decision Maker and we have to wait a number of days for the outcome to be official. It's highly unusual for the Decision Maker to disagree with the panel though.'

'They said no, didn't they?' Jenny says.

'Of course they didn't!' booms Mike, 'The panel all agreed you two would make wonderful adoptive parents!'

'What?' I say.

'Can you say that again please?' says Jenny who seems to be holding her breath.

'The panel are 100% recommending that you be approved to adopt two siblings aged between two and eight years old, says Margaret, 'Congratulations Mummy and Daddy to be!'

We all stand up and end up in a messy group hug. Jenny is the first to pull away.

'But what if the Decision Maker doesn't agree?' she says.

'Then I'll eat my hat,' says Mike, 'and the hats of everyone on the panel who were just in there enthusing about what brilliant parents you will be. Now, you two, there is something I need you to do, right away.'

'More forms?' I say.

'No,' says Mike, 'go home and celebrate!'

'There's something I need to fetch first,' says Jenny, grinning at me and gesturing towards the café over the road.

'Mike, Margaret,' I say, shaking their hands, 'we can't thank you enough, and now, there's a rather important flyer we need to collect.'

CHAPTER 54
– HELEN

'Oh my god!' I gasp.

'Shall I get the Midwife?' says Jake, 'are you alright?'

We're settled in a room in the hospital. I've been seen by the doctor and the midwife and everything is going to plan, albeit the plan has started a couple of weeks early.

'No, I'm fine,' I say, 'look at your whatsapp – Jen has messaged - the panel said yes!'

'Oh, that's bloody brilliant!' Jake says, 'shall we give them a ring?' I nod and Jake facetimes Kyle. His and Jenny's grinning faces fill the screen.

'Well done guys!' I say, 'you did it! We knew you would!'

'Well,' says Jenny, 'we have to wait for the official Decision Maker but Mike says they hardly ever disagree, especially when you have a unanimous panel decision like we did!'

'Oh, that's wonderf...' I say as another contraction hits and I nearly turn the f in 'wonderful' into another word entirely.

'Helen, are you okay?' says Jenny, 'hang on a minute, where are you?'

'We're in the hospital,' says Jake.

'Nothing's wrong, is it?' asks Kyle. Jenny looks stricken.

'No, everything is going smoothly,' I say, gripping Jake's hand so tightly that he starts to groan in pain as well, 'it's just I think the baby wanted to be part of your adoption celebrations and decided not to wait the full forty weeks.'

'But you're alright?' Jenny asks, 'Oh Helen, I'm so sorry I had my phone off in the panel.'

'No problem at all!' I say, 'I'm sure it'll be as easy as ABC.' Another contraction grips me and I reach for Jake's other hand. He digs in my bag and produces a squeezy toy carrot we packed.

'Here,' he says 'do your worst on this for a bit, I might need my hands to be in working order for nappy changing and stuff.'

'Is that a carrot?' asks Jenny.

'Yep,' says Jake, 'the anti-natal class suggested those stress toys might help.' There's a loud squeaking noise.

'What's that?' says Jenny, 'is it an alarm?'

'Nope,' I say, 'Jake, this isn't a stress carrot, it's a dog toy! I'm not a pregnant poodle!'

'Oops, sorry,' says Jake, tossing the carrot aside, gritting his teeth and giving me his hand again.

'Shall we let you go?' says Kyle, 'You seem

like you might be a bit busy!'

'Sorry guys,' I say, 'I wanted to celebrate with you, but I think young baby Weston-Smith wants my attention!'

'We'll come and see you as soon as we're allowed to,' Jenny says, 'Kyle's all clear of cold now. I think he's been okay for a couple of days, but I was just too anxious to take any risks.'

'And enjoying escaping Kyle's snoring?' grins Jake, rubbing his hand in between contractions.

'Something like that!' says Jenny, 'See you soon, lots of love! We'll be there to cuddle the baby soon as they'll let us in!'

Jake hangs up and puts the phone down on the side.

'Jake,' I say, squeezing his hand hard despite the fact I'm not currently having a contraction, 'we're all going to be parents.'

'I hope so,' he grins, 'otherwise I wasted £2.99 on that squeaky carrot.'

CHAPTER 55
– JAKE

I don't know how long Helen is in labour for. But I do know she's amazing. I don't have the words to describe it. All the films and television programmes that show people giving birth don't come close to explaining the surreal reality of it. Can reality be surreal? I'm not even sure I know what words mean any more. I just know that when we came into the hospital there was just the two of us and now we're a family of three. Baby Weston-Smith is perfect. I can only stop staring at her to gaze in awe at my amazing wife. I kiss them both gently on their foreheads.

'Thank you,' I whisper to Helen.

'You're welcome,' she says, 'but it's definitely your turn to empty the bins forever.'

'No problem,' I say, 'What shall we call her?'

'I've been thinking about that,' Helen says, 'How about Chrissy after your mum?'

'Oh Helen,' I say, feeling tears start to run down my cheeks, 'my mum would be so proud of you and she'd love you and Chrissy to bits.'

'Can you send the messages out to everyone to tell them we're all okay and that little Chrissy is looking forward to meeting them?' says Helen.

'Of course,' I say. I take a photo of the three of us and type out a message.

Within seconds the replies start coming in.

'Your mum and dad, Jenny and Kyle and Julie are already at the hospital,' I say, 'they've been waiting for our message. When you feel up to it, I'll let them know they can come in.

'Perfect,' says Helen.

We sit gazing at our daughter for a few moments more. There's a knock at the door. The nurse pokes her head in.

'Your dad is here,' she says, beaming at us all, 'is it okay for him to come in, he's been here almost as long as you both have.'

'Of course,' says Helen. The door opens a bit wider and a man appears.

'That's not my dad,' says Helen, 'it's…'

'Dad!' I say, 'I thought you were in Australia.'

'I was, son,' he says, 'but when you told me I was going to be a grandad, I thought I'd best get my butt over here and start building some bridges before you were knee deep in nappies and wouldn't want a bar of your lousy old man. My plane got in a couple of days ago. And I was glad that it did. I'd have hated to be on the other side of the world when your message arrived to say Helen had gone into labour early. As it was, I was staying in the Travelodge trying to work out what to say to you. When the message came, I decided actions speak louder than words and headed straight over here. I didn't want to interrupt, so I waited until the nurse said Helen and the baby were ready for visitors.' He looks over at Chrissy but doesn't move. 'Is it alright if I come in? I don't want to intrude and I'll understand if you tell me to get back on the next plane to Oz.'

Helen smiles at me. I smile back at her.

'No, come in, dad,' I say, 'come and meet baby Chrissy.'

My dad comes over and strokes my daughter's little hand. Then he turns to me, his eyes bright with tears and hugs me so hard, I stagger backwards and tread on the toy carrot.

At the sound of the squeak, the door opens again and Helen's parents appear, followed by Julie and Jenny and Kyle.

'Sorry to intrude!' says Julie, 'we heard a loud noise and thought we'd come check you were okay in here. Hello Rick, long time no see.'

'Let me see my granddaughter!' says Mary, rushing over to Helen and wrapping her arms around her and Chrissy. 'Oh she's perfect, a perfect little princess! Oh Helen, well done!'

'I told you you could do it, love,' says Len,

sitting quietly on a chair at the side of the room. 'How are you feeling?'

'I'm great, Dad,' she says.

'Hello fellow mummy and daddy!' says Jenny, standing near the door, keeping an eye out for any nurses about to come and evict them.

'Fellow mummy and...?' says Len, 'Have you adopted the children already, then?'

'No, not yet, Len,' grins Kyle, 'but we got approved by the panel and so it's only a matter of time, now!'

'Oh congratulations, all of you!' says Julie, 'You are all fantastic!'

'She's beautiful, Helen,' says Jenny, coming over to the bed. 'May I hold her hand?'

'Of course, you can, you can hold her completely!' says Helen. Jenny beckons Kyle over and cautiously, they sit on the chair by Helen's bed. Helen gently puts Chrissy in Jenny's arms.

'She's beautiful,' whispers Jenny.

'Well done, both of you,' says Kyle, his hand resting on Jenny's shoulder.

'Excuse me!' says the nurse, fighting her way through the crowd that has gathered in the room, 'I think we need to give the new family a little bit of a rest, come on, let's get you all some tea and you can come back in a few minutes, two at a time!' Everyone starts filing out of the room, chatting excitedly to each other and calling to me and Helen that they'll be back soon.

'Could you make an exception for me?'

asks Mary.

'Because you're a new Grandma?' asks the nurse, smiling kindly.

'Yes,' says Mary, her voice breaking, 'but also because I'm a mum, and my little girl has just had a little girl.'

'Of course,' says the nurse.

'Well, Daddy,' the nurse says, seeing me well up. It takes a moment to realise she's talking to me, 'would you like to come and choose some of the best biscuits from my trolley for you and your marvellous wife here?'

'I'll help you, son,' comes a voice from the doorway and me and my dad go to fetch biscuits for the mother of my child.

CHAPTER 56
– JENNY – 3
MONTHS LATER

Even when Mike rang us a few days after the panel to say the Decision Maker had agreed with their approval, I made him say it three times and then send it to me in an email. It's good to have things in writing. The last three months have been full of phone calls and emails about various sibling groups that we might be matched with but so far, it's come to nothing. We had to go back to our jobs the day after the panel which felt all wrong, like going to work on Boxing day. It was hard to concentrate on anything when there was so much to celebrate. Baby Chrissy and our children-to-be.

'They're already out there,' I say to Kyle one evening, 'our children, being tucked into bed by their foster parents.'

'I wonder when we'll be matched,' Kyle says.

'When it's right,' I say. Strangely, since the

panel approved us, I feel calmer than I have done in ages. I know our children are coming so the fact that we don't know when, or how old they will be or what they will be like, doesn't matter. They are coming and that is all I need to know.

I'm at work today, in the office. Doing some reports on the youth clubs. I like to keep all my paperwork up to date, now more so than ever, in case I get the call. Once we have a potential match, things will move quite quickly. We will be visited by the children's social workers, and if they agree we are the right parents for them, things will go to a matching panel and then we will finally meet our children. There will be a carefully planned schedule of us spending time with them over the course of a week or two, and then we will bring them home with us, for good.

My phone rings. It's Margaret. Mike has already been assigned to do the assessment for some new prospective adopters and so we have been handed over to Margaret, who is part of the team looking to match parents with children.

'Jenny?' she says.

'Hi Margaret,' I say. I work in an open plan office so in order to discuss the necessary confidential information, I've taken calls from Margaret in the toilets, the staff room, the car park and a stationery cupboard.

'Where are you today?' she says. I can tell by her voice that she's smiling.

'I'm perched on the edge of a dusty table

by the fire exit,' I say.

'Well,' she says, 'you might want to photograph that dusty table for your scrapbook. I think we've found your children.'

The End

ACKNOWLEDGEMENTS

Thank you so much to everyone who has ever told me stories or poems or been invested in mine. I really appreciate you all so much.

It all started with my dad reading and making up bedtime stories for me and my sister and my mum discussing the meanings of films and TV programmes with us. Fast forward to quite some years later and my sister's love of Jane Austen led to us both accidentally becoming mature students on the best English Degree ever.

Thank you to my husband for everything, not to mention the true romance of the cold, hard, slog!

I'd love to name everyone individually, but I have been so lucky to have so many supportive and wonderful friends and family members and met so many giving professionals in the creative industries that I'm worried I'll leave someone out.

You know who you are, you're the absolute bee's knees and the cat's pyjamas.

Hazel xxxx

ABOUT THE AUTHOR

Hazel Meredith-Lloyd

Hazel Meredith-Lloyd has wanted to be a writer as far back as she can remember, but it took her accidentally enrolling on an amazing English Degree to realise that she should just get on and write.

To her surprise, people seemed to enjoy reading it, so she is going to keep on writing and performing her poetry, prose and carefully highlighted to-do lists until her pen runs out. Then she'll buy another pen and write some more.

Hazel has been shortlisted by the Primadonna Prize and Poetry on Loan and longlisted twice by Penguin Michael Joseph. She has been highly commended by The Literary Consultancy. Her husband also thinks her writing is okay, but he doesn't like to go on about it.

Twitter/X, Insta and Threads: @novelcharacters

If you've enjoyed this book, please do check out my Amazon author page for my other books and if you'd like to leave a review, that would be much appreciated. If you haven't enjoyed it, I'm sorry to hear that and I hope you enjoy the next book you read. Perhaps get straight on with reading that one, rather than stopping to write a review...

Printed in Great Britain
by Amazon